the very wo[...]
noble cause[...]
and deadly betrayals. Now you can return to
Camelot in all its glory in such stirring and
imaginative tales as:

"The Raven's Quest"—Transformed from
bird to human, he followed the road to Camelot on a quest that might have no solution. . . .

"The Queen's Broidery Woman"—Hers was
a magic that would not be denied—even
when she wished to undo it!

"The Feasting of the Hungry Man"—Must a
king's pledge be honored, even if Camelot itself might fall to an invader whose hunger
could not be denied?

CAMELOT FANTASTIC

More Spellbinding Anthologies
Brought to You by DAW:

TAROT FANTASTIC *Edited by Martin H. Greenberg and Lawrence Schimel.* Writers from Charles de Lint to Tanya Huff, Rosemary Edghill, Nancy Springer, Kate Elliott, Teresa Edgerton, and Michelle Sagara West cast fortunes for the unsuspecting in such unforgettable tales as: A woman searching for her missing brother turns to a street tarot reader as a last hope, and gets far more than she bargained for. . . . Tarot cards come to life, and a skeptic is forced to face her destiny whether or not she believes in it. . . . An imprisoned woman receives a magical tarot deck from a mysterious stranger. Will it prove her salvation or her ruin?

THE FORTUNE TELLER *Edited by Lawrence Schimel and Martin H. Greenberg.* Seventeen mesmerizing stories by such forecasters as Billie Sue Mosiman, Peter Crowther, Ed Gorman, Nancy Springer, Tanya Huff, Rosemary Edghill, Brian Stableford, and Michelle Sagara West. From the tale of a man caught between two worlds . . . to a ganbler cursed with the ability to see possible futures . . . to a brand new Vicki Nelson adventure . . . here are tales of those who cannot or will not avoid their futures and those whose lives may well be transformed by the fortune teller.

CASTLE FANTASTIC *Edited by John DeChancie and Martin H. Greenberg.* From the final tale set in Roger Zelazny's *Amber,* to a floating castle in search of a kingdom, to the legendary citadel of King Arthur, here's your chance to explore truly unique castle keeps—from the deepest dungeons to the highest watchtowers. So join such master architects of enchantment as Roger Zelazny, George Zebrowski, Jane Yolen, David Bischoff, and Nancy Springer on a series of castle adventures that will have fantasy lovers and D&D players begging for the keys to the next keep on the tour.

CAMELOT
FANTASTIC

EDITED BY

Lawrence Schimel

AND

Martin H. Greenberg

DAW BOOKS, INC.
DONALD A. WOLLHEIM, FOUNDER
375 Hudson Street, New York, NY 10014

ELIZABETH R. WOLLHEIM
SHEILA E. GILBERT
PUBLISHERS

First Printing, July 1998
1 2 3 4 5 6 7 8 9

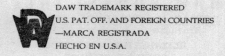

For Tony Kushner,
one of my heroes.
—L.S.

CONTENTS

THE COURT WITH A THOUSAND SCRIBES

by Lawrence Schimel

The myth of Camelot is one of hyperbole: home to the bravest knights and the fairest maidens, the place where the most courteous of manners hold sway and the most sumptuous of feasts are given. Camelot, home of King Arthur, one of the greatest of heroes ever to capture the human heart and imagination—not to mention rule Britain and defend her from all enemies.

Information about the historical Arthur is scant, and what little there is lies shrouded in the mists of time; scholars and historians (as well as storytellers) can do no more than peer into the hazy records and conjecture. And speculate they have, for more than eight hundred years, since Geoffrey of Monmouth wrote the first full history of Arthur in the twelfth century, in his *History of the Kings of Britain.* Writers have retold and nuanced the stories of Arthur's exploits and the adventures of the Knights of his Round Table countless times, as well as adding their own characters and adventures to the mythos, to fill in the gaps in the tale. This cast of characters have been treated with hard-biting realism and fanciful satire, idolization and more than a touch of magic and the supernatural. This accumulation of prose, drama, and verse over the years, multilayered and embellished, offers the reader conflicting stories, a dizzying wealth of variation.

But there are some constants, and these have become the Truths of King Arthur, irregardless of their occurrence in our actual historical past. Honor, chivalry, justice, true love, courage—ideals which often seem to be nothing more than myths in the real world in which we live, and are sometimes much more magical than any fantasy powers might be— are the virtues which dominate the world of Camelot; even when characters betray these codes or one another, or are tested for their purity of heart and body, or otherwise stray from the path, these characteristics are the standard by which they are measured.

Camelot is a world that is black and white; there is a clear separation between good and evil, and everyone knows the difference between the two. Many of the stories in this volume, however, explore or create gray areas in these tales, welcoming a sort of moral ambiguity as they examine different relationship between the familiar characters, plumb the darker sides of the human character, and portray a grittier side of life in the court. What happens when doing the right thing will hurt people and help no one? What to do when overlapping loyalties require conflicting actions? How much can one rebel against Fate?

Herein you will find adventure and quests, romance and betrayal. You won't find any battles, though swords will flash (and clash). Magic runs through them all, and often mystery (and one of the tales, even, is a magical whodunit). You'll find characters you know—or think you know—and stories you'll recognize, though you won't know where they're going now.

But always you'll find heroes, likely or unexpected, familiar or new, faced with a dilemma of one sort or another, and confronting it with a nobility of soul if not actually of birthright. And this is one of the Truths of Camelot, the egalitarian social justice of the Round Table, where are all equal. Just as we are all equal—readers, writers, historians—before the myth of this fantastical place, Camelot. Be welcomed within its walls in these pages.

THE RAVEN'S QUEST

by Fiona Patton

Fiona Patton is the author of two heroic fantasy novels for DAW, *The Stone Prince* and *The Painter Knight,* and is working on a third set in the same mythos, *The Granite Shield.* She was born in Calgary, Alberta, and grew up in the United States. She currently lives in rural Ontario with her partner, a small dog, and rather too many large cats.

In "The Raven's Quest" she asks the reader a question—for is not any questing also a questioning?—about the nature of Truth as much as her character asks his question of the people he meets.

In a cluttered tower room on Bardsey Island, a large, black raven perched on the edge of an iron cauldron and pulled the guts from a dead mouse. Snapping up the grisly meal, it swallowed, then allowed the carcass to fall. The mouse struck the inside of the cauldron with a hollow ping and was reborn. With a brisk, businesslike flap of its wings, the raven stabbed downward, catching the rodent up in its beak. It swiftly disemboweled it again, chuckling at its own cleverness around a mouthful of entrails.

In the center of the room an old man sat hunched over a desk, scrolls of vellum and parchment strewn

about him. Without turning his head, he made a disgusted noise in the back of his throat.

"I hardly think Bran's cauldron was meant for
such a gruesome purpose, Corvus," he noted.

The raven turned its glossy head sideways, fixing
the old man with one black eye. "Did I not serve him
well for over two decades?" it demanded, splattering
blood across a nearby chessboard. The silver pieces
continued to play themselves, oblivious to the gory
shower.

"That gives you the right to use the cauldron of
rebirth to eat mice?"

With a disdainful toss of its head, the raven flung
the empty carcass into a nearby hamper. One hundred mice instantly emerged to scatter over the floor.
The bird watched them with interest before taking
wing across the room to land on the old man's shoulder. "Was I not the greatest of all Bran's ravens?"
it asked.

"Were you not merely *one* of Bran's ravens?" the
old man retorted.

"Did he not love me above all the rest? Did he not
give me the power of intelligence and speech that he
might more clearly commune with me his purpose
in protecting the Realm of Logres?"

"I'll bet he regretted that part."

"What part?" Snapped out of its singsong cadence
by the sudden statement, the raven swiveled its head
so that one eye regarded the old man's ear.

"The speech part."

Digging through its breast feathers, the bird removed a mite and devoured it before deigning to

reply. "Am I not the only one who remembers that he was king and protector over Logres?"

"Logres has a new protector now," the old man answered testily. "Arthur, who was prophesied to be the greatest king of all time."

"Prophesied by who?" the raven sniffed.

"Prophesied by me, Merlin, the most powerful mage of this or any era!" the old man shouted, pushing the raven off his shoulder. With an awkward flapping of wings, the bird landed on the desk, scattering its contents.

"Did Arthur not put the Realm in danger by desecrating Bran's remains at the White Tower so that he might become the only palladium against invasion?" it persisted.

The old man snatched at a falling scroll. "Insufferable creature!" he muttered, ignoring the question. "Move your great, bloody head!" Smacking the scroll down on the desk, he shot the bird a fierce glance from under his eyebrows. "I will not get involved in a pointless debate with you about Bran and Arthur. I've told you that before."

"But am I not Bran's only raven left alive in Logres? Should I not be told if the Realm was in danger?"

Composing himself, the old man returned to his writing, dipping his quill into a large crystal inkwell before answering. "I'll grant you that Rhian and Calas have joined Bran in death at least," he replied, glaring at the inkwell until the sudden riot of colors returned to their natural state. "But Leanan and Cradel are still alive."

"Have they not gone wild in the Perilous Forest

and so lost any chance they might have had to protect the Realm?"

"I suppose."

"And was Nemain not killed by one of Arthur's own archers when she tried to prevent him from disinterring Bran's head at the White Tower?"

"Corvus . . ." The old man's tone held a distinct warning, and the raven hopped back a step.

"Was not Deirdren killed by Lancelot and taken to Avalon in human form?" it asked instead.

"That is what they say."

Eyeing the cauldron of rebirth for a moment, the raven hopped onto the old man's book, smearing the ink. "Will I take human form when I die, Merlin?" it asked.

"No, you are too irritating. You will take the form of a swamp-midge."

"Truly?"

The raven's voice was so melancholy that the old man threw down his quill in disgust. "No, Corvus, not truly, but I will not tell you your future. We've been over this before. Now go away, I have things to do."

He shoved the bird with his elbow, and it rose gracefully into the air to return to its perch.

"And don't put that revolting thing back into Bran's cauldron," the mage shot after him. "I'm tired of having my workshop spattered with entrails."

"Is it not a revolting thing?" the raven answered reproachfully. "Did I not throw it into the hamper of Gwyddno Garanhir to make it a hundred little live things?"

With an impatient gesture, the old man spoke a

word and the hamper closed with a snap. The raven hunkered down into its feathers in a sulk. The old man ignored it, and after a moment it straightened.

"What sort of things do you have to do, Merlin?" It asked in a mollifying tone.

The scratch, scratch of the old man's quill was its only answer.

"Merlin?"

"Writing things," the mage replied tersely.

"What things?"

"Words."

"What words?"

With an exaggerated sigh, the old man set his quill down again. "I'm writing about the future," he answered. "Not that it's truly any of your business."

Recognizing the forgiveness in the tone, the bird returned to its place on his shoulder. It leaned forward to regard the book quizzically. "Why?"

"Why what?"

"Why are you writing about the future?"

"So I don't forget it."

"What will the future be?"

"Whose future?"

"Whose future do you write about?"

"The future of Logres and of Camelot."

"Why?"

"So I don't forget it. Go away."

"Am I in it?"

"Go away, or I'll turn you into a swamp-midge here and now!" The old man threw his quill at the bird who took flight and returned to the lip of the cauldron.

"And why must you sit there? It blocks the light."

The raven obediently hopped down onto the window seat and looked through the rainy mist to the courtyard below. "Is there someone coming, Merlin?" it asked.

"I don't know, is there?" Picking up his quill the old man hunched over his book again.

The air grew warm.

"Is there . . . ? Merlin . . . ?" The raven's eyes grew wide as the faint image of a woman, hair and eyes as black as the bird's own feathers, began to form in the center of the room. The old man seemed not to notice.

"Merlin? Do you not see . . . ?"

The woman reached pale arms toward the old man, and when she spoke, her voice had the soft sibilance of a serpent.

"Merlin."

He turned, unsurprised. "Nimue."

"You have been long absent from my side."

"I . . . have been busy."

The raven returned silently to the lip of the cauldron, watching as the mage rose as if in a dream.

"Merlin?" it asked softly. "What are you doing?"

The old man ignored him and the woman smiled.

"Come to me, my love," she whispered.

He moved forward.

"Merlin!" Corvus cried. "Do you not sense danger here?"

The mage swayed and half-turned. Nimue snarled. Throwing her arms wide, she sent a dozen bands of light whipping forward to ensnare him.

"Merlin?"

She turned then, her dark red lips drawn up in a

cruel smile. "He cannot hear you, little carrion-eater," she said. "Keep silent."

Snapping her wrist forward, she sent a ball of fire flying across the room to smack the bird from its perch. With an audible crack, it hit the wall and crumpled to the floor in a jumble of feathers.

Nimue returned her attention to the mage, continuing to wrap him in bands of light until he was securely cocooned. Then, weaving her hands in the air, she spun the bands in an intricate design. A huge hawthorn began to take form about him. From seedling to sapling to full grown tree it grew in the space of a few heartbeats, encasing the old man in a prison of wood. The raven, its one wing flattened against the floor at an awkward angle, its beak smeared with its own blood, watched through a haze of pain, unable to rise or speak.

Nimue leaned forward to kiss the old man's lips. "Sleep, my love," she whispered. "Sleep in the woods of Broceliande until Logres has dire need of you again." She gestured, and the mage and his arboreal prison slowly faded away.

Standing quietly, she watched until the last flicker of his presence faded, then turned to eye the tower's collection of magical and historical items with disdain.

Beside Bran's cauldron the raven grew very still. The pain lacing through its wing made it want to squirm, but it was afraid to draw attention to itself.

Too late. Nimue came forward, her eyes frighteningly luminescent.

"And what shall I do with you, little meddler?" she asked almost to herself.

Its vision swimming, the raven tried to answer, but only a whistle of pain made its way past its cracked beak.

She leaned down and ran one pale finger along its wing.

The raven shuddered.

"Broken," she murmured. "Such a pity. Time to die, little blackbird."

She straightened, bringing her foot forward to crush his skull.

Desperation found the raven its voice again.

"Why . . . why would you kill me?" it gasped.

"Why should I not?" she replied, her voice honestly curious. "You are a troublesome detail, more easily removed then allowed to remain."

The pain threatening to make it faint, the raven struggled to find an answer that would deflect her intention.

"Would my life not speak more eloquently of your greatness than my death?" it tried.

"I have no need for others to speak of my greatness, eloquently or not."

"Would you not always feel in your heart that you killed me because you were not powerful enough to stave off my death?"

"No." Her eyes narrowed. "Must you always speak in questions? It's very annoying."

The raven shuddered as her foot touched its breast.

"Am I not one of the sacred birds of Logres? Is my speech not drawn from the magic of Sovereignty?"

"Is it?" Her voice was cold now. "What do you know of Sovereignty? Do you think that by flapping

about Owain and Bran you gained some small scrap
of their bond with the land?"

"Do . . ." A trickle of blood ran past its beak and
the raven swallowed. "Do my kind not also accompany Morrighan, Badh, and Nemainn to the battlefield?" it asked.

She gave a barking laugh. "So now you share in
the divine? You are a fool and your questions are
the prattling of a child."

Stung by her words, the raven struggled to meet
her eyes. "Do I not know all of the greatest questions
of the ages?" it asked recklessly.

"Do you?" She paused. "Well then, perhaps I will
spare your life after all if you can find a question
that amuses me. Ask."

Dizzy with sudden hope, the raven searched its
memory. The pain in its wing and beak was a constant distraction, and it finally blurted out the first
question that came to mind.

"Who can remember the coldest winter night?"

"Arawn, Lord of the Underworld, whom you are
perilously close to meeting. Try again."

"What . . . what is it that women desire most?"

"You would bring up Sovereignty again? Don't
test my patience." Her foot came down to rest
against its broken wing and the raven cried out in
pain. It could feel the shock of its injuries beginning
to cloud its thoughts and it tried desperately to keep
hold of the clarity necessary to save its life.

"What . . . what walks on two legs in the
morning . . . ?"

"Enough. That is a riddle, not a question. I grow

bored with you, little philosopher. Time to join Bran in his endless sleep.''

The raven cried out again, unable to think past its fear of her. ''Will you not hear pleas for mercy?'' it choked out. ''Is not mercy the greatest human virtue?''

Nimue paused. Bending, she lifted the trembling bird up and cradled it in her hands. The pressure against its wing almost caused it to black out, but it just managed to hold on to consciousness as she walked to the window.

''You are a foolish creature,'' she murmured. ''Mercy? What is mercy? For that matter, what is virtue? You tell me, Corvus, Bran's little lover, what do you think is the greatest human virtue?''

The raven tried to hold onto her words, but the pain was throbbing up into its temples and it could not concentrate. It felt the weakness of death creep over its limbs, and its head lolled back against her fingers.

''Does not . . . a human . . . know this better than . . . a raven?'' it managed finally.

She gave it a withering smile. ''You don't know, do you?'' she said, not unkindly. ''Questioner with no answers. I think I shall give you the chance to find out, shall I?'' She held the raven over the windowsill and it felt the cold rain against its face. It was suddenly reminded of the day, long ago, when it had stood unsteadily on the edge of its first nest and knew it was meant to fly.

''*I set you this task*,'' she intoned and the raven felt a sharp tingling all over its body. ''*Go forth into the world and ask this question of all you meet: What is the greatest human virtue?"*

She dropped it.

The wind rushed through its feathers and the raven tried to raise its wings, to let the updraft take it away from this frightening woman and the pain she inflicted, but its wings would not catch the wind and it plummeted down to land upon the cobbled courtyard below. The world grew very dark.

He awoke to a blue light flitting past his closed eyelids. The tingling had become an itch. Far away, he heard her voice and knew he was, somehow, still alive.

"Your death is averted for now, little philosopher. When you know the answer to your question, I will come to you again. Now, awake!"

His eyes snapped open, and Merlin's stone tower loomed above him.

He was alone.

Shivering, he tried to rise. His limbs ached frightfully, and he was so cold. Struggling to sit, he pushed his hands forward to catch his suddenly unfamiliar weight and started.

His hands.

Hands.

His gaze traveled down, to arms and chest and naked manhood to legs and finally to feet. Human feet.

He might have sat there forever, staring down at his sudden transformation, but the cold of the cobblestones finally drove him to make an attempt to rise.

Untangling his limbs, he managed to get to his feet, took one step forward, and fell.

After catching his breath, he stared down at his knees, and cautiously flexed the muscles. They bent the wrong way. Slowly his muddled senses began to function again. He'd seen many humans walk and run, but he'd never stopped to study them, and Merlin had always worn a robe. Finally, he called up an ancient memory of Bran the Blessed standing naked on the banks of the Irish Sea as he prepared to swim out to rescue his sister Branwen from King Matholwch. Corvus scrutinized the image and then slowly stood.

It took him several hours to make his way down to the shore where Merlin kept a small fishing craft. By this time he was shaking with cold, but in the bottom of the boat, he found an old, black robe. Wrapping it gratefully about himself, he then studied the oars, turning his head sideways as he was used to doing. He'd often sat on Merlin's shoulder while the old man had rowed out to deep water to fish. He thought he remembered how the mage had done it. Glancing wistfully up at the sky, he climbed cautiously into the boat.

Fortunately the water was calm, and so, with some struggling, he managed to get the craft across to the opposite bank. With no particular plan in mind, he set out walking.

He met no one. At nightfall he curled up in a bed of leaves and slept, his dreams filled with images of Nimue and Merlin.

In the morning he was ravenously hungry. Pacing

back and forth across the road, he searched for mice in the long grassy bank, but his skills as a bird had deserted him, and he found himself unsure of how humans provided for themselves. Their mouths were soft, their hands no good for catching or rending, their eyesight poor. They needed weapons, but he had none. Finally he set out walking again, hugging himself to calm the rumbling of his stomach.

At length he smelled a familiar odor and, looking to one side, saw the carcass of a drowned hare lying in a stream. He didn't question his luck, merely plunged into the water to retrieve it.

Tearing at the bloated body with his hands and teeth, he ripped off hunks of meat and fur, swallowing them without regard to their state. It wasn't until he was almost sated that he heard a noise behind him. He whirled about, dropping the body into the water and came face-to-face with a golden-haired young woman. He stared.

She returned his look frankly, her own gaze traveling from his ragged robe to his blood-covered face. Suddenly aware of how he must look, he wiped his mouth with the corner of his sleeve.

"You shouldn't eat carrion anymore, Corvus," she admonished, her voice low-pitched and musical. "You never know how long it's been there."

Shocked that she knew his name, he made to answer and felt a sudden oddness in his mouth and throat.

"What is the greatest human virtue?"

She folded her arms over her breasts, her eyes narrowing. "From the sight of you, I'd guess I'd have to answer charity," she replied. "When was the last time you had a decent meal; one that didn't involve . . ." She shuddered.

Thinking back to his mice on Bardsey Island, he shook his head. "A long time," he answered and stopped in shock. All his life he'd spoken in questions; the only way he'd known to communicate. He'd always thought that his tie to Sovereignty and the triple Goddess had precluded any other form of speech. But now . . .

"I think I ate yesterday," he tried. "I'm very hungry." He paused, unsure of what to say next.

She gave him an appraising stare then nodded. "My name is Linet. You're to come with me." Without waiting for a reply, she turned and made her way back to the road. Corvus splashed water over his face, then followed, his mind in turmoil.

When he'd scrambled back up the bank, he hurried to catch up with her determined stride. "Why am I to come with you?" he asked when he finally reached her side.

"The Lady of the Fountain requires it. She saw you in a vision and sent me to fetch you to her."

"She saw me?"

Lifting her skirts, Linet stepped lightly over a break in the path before answering. "The Lady had a dream last night that one of Rhiannon's children was in need. She saw the place and sent me there to wait for you."

"But how did you know it was me?"

She shot him an amused look. "Only one who was new to human form would find such a meal as you were eating palatable."

"Oh."

They walked in silence for a time. Finally he glanced sideways at her. "You're very beautiful," he noted. "Are you a queen?"

She laughed. "I am the Lady of the Fountain's servant and guardian, but my grandfather is King Lot of Orkney and my father is Sir Gaheris, a knight of the Round Table."

"So you're a Princess, then."

She favored him with a wry smile. "I suppose. Come, my dwelling is this way."

She led him through a copse of yew trees to a clearing filled with wildflowers where a small cottage stood beside a large, three-tiered fountain. The water sparkled so invitingly as it splashed against the bowls that Corvus found himself desperately thirsty. Linet indicated that he should drink, and when he was finished, he looked up to see a beautiful, unearthly woman standing before him. Suddenly shy, he dropped his gaze, but the woman reached out one slender hand and lifted his chin so that he met her eyes.

"Don't you have something to ask me, follower of Bran?" she asked, her voice the sound of the wind dancing over the water.

He nodded. "What is the greatest human virtue . . . My Lady?"

She tilted her head to one side in so birdlike a gesture that he smiled, free from all fear of her.

"It is different for each person," she answered, "depending on your destiny. For myself it is patience, but for another, who can say."

"Linet says that it's charity."

The Lady smiled in the direction of her handmaid.
"And so for Linet it is. What is it for you?"

"I don't know."

"Then you must discover it."

"That's what *she* said. Nim . . ."

The Lady touched a finger to his lips. "Do not
speak her name, Corvus. I can see whose geas lies
upon you." She straightened. "Go to Camelot. There
you will find your answer. Linet will go with you.
The children of Rhiannon are innocents, and often
come to some harm on their own."

"Will I see you again?" Corvus asked shyly.

She gave him a mysterious smile. "Perhaps." Bending down, she kissed him on the forehead. She
smelled of lavender and roses, and Corvus closed his
eyes to more fully drink in the scent of her. When
he opened them, she was gone. He blinked.

Linet took his hand with a wry smile. "Come, we'll
eat first, and then we'll go to Camelot to find your
answer."

It took them three days of walking to reach their
destination. In that time they talked of many things;
his life as companion to first Bran and then Merlin;
her childhood on Orkney surrounded by uncles and
cousins. She spoke at length of the world of humans,
explaining their ways and customs and patiently answering all his questions. By the third day they were
walking, arm in arm, like old friends.

But nothing she'd told him had prepared him for
his first sight of the greatest city in Logres. As they
crested the hill that overlooked the capital, Corvus
stopped, awestruck, staring down at the mass of spi-

rals, bell towers, and slate gables that made up the roofs of Camelot. Birds of every description made their homes in its nooks and crannies. The air was filled with their song, and the longing to be among them was so strong that he nearly choked on a sob. Linet squeezed his hand reassuringly and led him down the hill.

Once through the huge south gate, the streets became crowded with people. Corvus gawked at every passing merchant or tradesman, overwhelmed by the riot of sounds and scents all about him. Taking him by the elbow, Linet guided him expertly down cobblestone streets. But when a herd of sheep heading for market collided with a company of soldiers, they found themselves flattened against a wall, unable to go any farther.

She was just about to suggest that they turn back and try another street when a tall, golden-haired knight, the five-pointed star of the Goddess prominent upon his surcoat, urged his mount between them and the crowd.

"Linet?" he asked, looking down with a quizzical smile. "I thought it was you. What are you doing in the middle of this chaos?"

She returned his greeting with a tired smile of her own.

"I've come on the Lady's business, Uncle Gawain," she answered wearily. "I'm to bring this stranger to Camelot. He's on a quest. His name is Corvus."

Sir Gawain glanced down at him with an open, friendly expression. "Well met, Corvus."

Corvus opened his mouth to reply and felt the now familiar tingle.

"What is the greatest human virtue?"

He clamped his mouth shut, horrified at his lack of manners, but Sir Gawain did not seem offended.

"Is that your quest?" he asked. "It's a worthy question. Valor would be my answer, although some would likely say love." He turned to Linet. "Did the Lady give you any instructions other than to bring him to Camelot?"

"No, Uncle."

"Does she require that you return immediately?"

Again she answered in the negative.

"Well, Gaheris has gone to Gorre on the King's business so you must rely on me for hospitality. As for Corvus," he smiled down at him again. "His Majesty is always interested in quests and noble deeds. He holds an open court tomorrow where any might come who have such a tale. How be it if I bring him before His Majesty? Perhaps my fellow knights might be able to aid him in his quest."

Corvus felt his jaw drop. "Go before the King?" he asked weakly. "*The* King? King Arthur?"

"The very same."

"I . . . I couldn't . . . I . . ."

He turned to Linet for help, but she was nodding sagely. "That would be most kind of you, Uncle," she answered.

Gawain now glanced over the street from his higher vantage point.

"This crowd will not slacken off for several hours," he said. "It's market day. Linet, you come up before me in the saddle. Corvus, you take hold of my stirrup, and we'll see if I can get us clear of it."

His heart pounding, Corvus did as he was told

and Sir Gawain urged his mount slowly forward. The crowds gave way before him and soon they were past the worst of it and heading for a quiet street. Gawain reined up before a respectable looking hostel.

"I keep rooms here," Linet explained to Corvus' confused expression. "They're quiet and clean. I find that after the peace of the Lady's fountain I'm unused to the bustle of the capital."

Gawain helped her down from the saddle and then turned to Corvus. "I'll send for you tomorrow," he promised. "Don't be nervous. The Court of King Arthur is not so formidable as you might have heard."

He waved at his niece and then turned his mount and clattered away up the street. Corvus watched him go.

"Not so formidable as I might have heard?" he muttered. "Easy for you to say."

Later that night, after dining with Linet, Corvus leaned his arms against the windowsill of his room and looked out across the slate roofs of Camelot. The moon had risen, casting a luminescent glow across the city. A sudden urge to be out in its tangled streets came over him and he gave in to it at once, clambering over the sill and making his cautious way down a drainpipe. Once his feet touched the cobbles, he made off in the direction they'd come from that afternoon.

It wasn't long before he was hopelessly lost, but he paid that no mind as each step took him deeper into the city's fascinating depths. He passed stone houses and timber houses; statues and monuments and obelisks, tiny cemeteries surrounded by stout stone walls, and even tinier gardens with rows of carrots and beets lined up like soldiers. He passed shops and taverns and warehouses, their multicolored signs turned fantastical in the moonlit night. At the door to a particularly well-lit establishment, he asked his question of a woman leaning against the doorjamb who laughed and led him inside.

It was crowded in the main room, men and women lounging about a long, wooden ledge or sitting around small tables. The fireplace to one side belched smoke into the room and Corvus began to cough. The woman beside him said something he could not hear, and then she was gone and another woman was looking down at him, her expression amused. Her hair was thick and black and her pale features and luminescent eyes so reminiscent of Nimue that Corvus paled and began to tremble. She smiled then, the same cruel smile, and drew him to a quiet corner. Once there, she regarded him as one might regard breakfast after a long night.

"I knew I felt my sister's magic," she mused. "I thought it might be she herself, but I see now that it's merely one of her minions." Her eyes roved boldly over his body and he found himself blushing. "No, not a minion," she amended, "but one who's fallen afoul of her, I think. Pretty enough. Too young a man for Nimue's taste, but . . ." she licked her lips, "quite old enough for mine. I am called Morgana." When he started, she smiled again. "Don't believe everything you hear. And do you not have a name? Speak."

Corvus wet lips were suddenly dry.

"What is the greatest human virtue?"

She laughed. "What a stupid question." Dark eyes bright, she ran a hand along his cheek. "Lust."

He took an involuntary step backward. "Lust? Isn't that a vice?" he asked weakly.

"That depends on whose lust you're discussing. Mine is truly a virtue. Now, your name?"

"Uh, Corvus, My Lady."

She regarded him thoughtfully and he felt a power so subtle that he might have imagined it, probing his mind.

"A follower of Rhiannon?" she asked.

"Of Bran."

"Bran is dead."

"Of Merlin, then."

"Merlin has left this world." She placed her fingers on his lips as he made to speak, and her touch made him shiver. "It is of no matter." Giving him a predatory look that caused his heart to skip a beat, she caught his hand and pressed it to her breast. "Have you ever lain with a woman, Corvus?"

His breath ragged, he thought of the various mates he'd had over the years and answered truthfully.

"No."

"How nice."

Tucking his arm in hers so that their bodies pressed against each other, she whispered her intent, then led him, unresisting, down a narrow hallway and into a small chamber.

The morning found him back in his own room, unsure of what to say in response to Linet's innocently asked question of his night's sleep. He found himself unable to meet her eyes, and merely mumbled something incoherent, but before she could press him, the landlady appeared with breakfast and a young man in tow. He introduced himself as Gingalin, Sir Gawain's son and squire, and answered, "love," to Corvus' question. He was here to summon them to the King's court, he explained, but he could join them for breakfast first. He helped himself to a piece of bread, ignoring his cousin Linet's frown.

An hour later, Corvus clasped her hand nervously as they followed Gingalin down some of the same streets he'd explored the night before.

"Linet?" he began, and then fell silent.

"Yes?"

"I'm not sure this is a good idea."

She smiled at him. "You mustn't be afraid of the King, Corvus. He's not at all fierce. He's really very kind and just."

Corvus made a face. "Perhaps to you, but my late master and he didn't exactly see eye to eye on several important matters."

"Bran?"

"Yes."

"Don't worry. The King wouldn't hold their struggle against you. Besides you were in bird form then. How would he recognize you?"

He gave that serious thought. "You're right," he answered finally.

"Of course I am. Just don't mention Bran, and all should be well. If you have to speak of masters, speak of Merlin. That should distract the King, for he was the mage's student for some years."

"I know," Corvus answered testily. "Merlin spoke of him *far* too often."

Linet gave him her wry smile. "You're jealous of the King?"

"No! It's just . . . he was Bran's rival and he dug up his head and . . ." He frowned. "I am not jealous of King Arthur."

"Of course you're not." She squeezed his hand to show she was teasing and he gave her a sour smile. "Anyway, don't worry," she continued. "The Lady of the Fountain would not have sent you into danger, and once you meet the King, you will love him and honor him as we all do."

"Don't bet on it," he muttered.

"Hm?"

"Nothing."

Around them, Camelot was awake and beginning the day's trade. They passed through streets of fishmongers, tin smiths, weavers, coopers, chandlers, sign painters, and bread makers. Corvus' head was spinning by the time their path began to rise. Soon they stood above the city and the forest of roofs and towers became evident again. The early morning sun cast a golden hue over the buildings, and Gingalin paused a moment to allow Corvus to stand, gaping once more, in awe of its beauty.

"Have you ever seen the like?" the squire asked, amused.

Corvus shook his head. "Never."

"Camelot is first among all cities. London, even Rome, is not so lovely. But come, it wouldn't do to be late." He turned away as the many bells of the city began to toll, filling the air with music.

At the top of the rise, the palace came into view and Corvus stumbled.

If the city itself was lovely, Camelot's Royal Palace was beautiful beyond words. Its delicate, spiral turrets stretched toward the clouds, ending in tiny points of gold. Its towers were made of shimmering marble; its windows of stained glass so perfect that the sun, reflecting off their surface, cast a rainbow of colors across the walls. Within its gates, vast gardens encircled the keep, hosting more flowers and birds than Corvus had ever seen.

He found his eyes filling with tears. "Oh, Merlin," he whispered. "What a thing you have wrought here."

Gangalin led them through the cobbled inner courtyard, past the main doors to a small side portal guarded by two sentinels in the livery of Orkney. He spoke with them and they stood aside as he led them into the palace and down a narrow passageway. At the end was a small door, which he opened and ushered them inside.

They found themselves in a small, richly paneled chamber. Benches stretched along one wall, an intricate latticework screen covered the other. Peering through it, Corvus saw Arthur's Great Hall in all its splendor. More than a dozen knights and ladies took their ease on chairs or leaned against the hall's huge, stone fireplace, which was cold this morning. Above in a gallery he saw a group of musicians, but realized suddenly that he could not hear the music they played, nor the words of those gathered. Linet explained that it was another of Merlin's masterpieces. Gangalin nodded.

"I shall leave you now. Sir Gawain wishes to escort you to the King himself and shall be along presently." He bowed and withdrew.

Corvus peered through the lattice again and shifted uneasily.

Linet gripped his hand. "Don't be afraid," she said. "I shall make you acquainted with all here before you meet them. You see that man there, the one with the white hair?"

Corvus' gaze followed her finger and he nodded.

"That is Sir Bedivere. He's the King's most trusted councillor. The man he's talking to is Sir Kay, the King's foster brother, and behind him are Sir Dinadan and Sir Dragonet. They have a terrible predilection for practical jokes, so be on your guard if you meet them together." She smiled at the two men fondly. "There is my uncle, Sir Agravaine, by the window. Isn't he handsome? And beside him is my cousin Aleine and my aunt Clarrisant."

"They look very much like you," Corvus noted.

"All our family share certain characteristics," she agreed. "Standing by the garden doorway is Sir Lionel, Anna, the King's sister, Sir Sagramore, and Alice, cousin to Sir Lancelot."

"Is he here?" Corvus peered through the lattice anxiously.

"No. He's gone to visit Sir Baudwin at his lands in Brittany. Do you have difficulty with Sir Lancelot as well?" She had her wry smile on again, and Corvus shook his head.

"Not personally. It's just that such men make me nervous. They have a habit of throwing stones. They all do," he added nervously.

Linet frowned, returning her attention to the hall.

"Well, there's a man who would not throw stones," she said, pointing. "That is Sir Galahad."

Corvus stared curiously at the man she indicated, half expecting to see a halo of light shining about him. What he saw instead was a brown-haired youth with an open, pleasant face and the faraway look of a mystic.

"He seems very young to be so renowned," he noted.

"He is young, but they say his purity of heart gives him the strength to overcome all adversity."

"You're right. He doesn't look as if he'd throw stones."

"Nor, I should think, do Sir Tristan or Sir Perceval."

Corvus ducked his head. "I've offended you."

She paused and then gave him a rueful smile. "Perhaps just a little. I've known many of the King's knights since I was a child. I love them all though, yes I must admit that some of them are reckless and sometimes even a bit cruel. But here comes Uncle Gawain. You must admit that he would never throw stones."

Stepping through the door, Sir Gawain favored them both with his open smile. "You're here, then," he said in a pleased voice. "Are you ready to come before the King?"

Corvus swallowed but allowed himself to be ushered from the chamber by both the knight and the maiden.

The Hall was much noisier than he'd expected, and he flinched, stilling the urge to flap wings no longer there. Linet squeezed his hand, and Sir Gawain gave him an encouraging smile as they led him through the crowd. Silence followed in their wake as the assembled nobility turned and watched curiously. Corvus was suddenly aware of his dusty, ragged appearance and would have run if Linet hadn't kept a tight grip on his hand. Finally, two knights parted, and they stood before a simple, wooden throne. A tall, black-haired man, whose eyes and face held a nobility that Corvus had never encountered before was seated upon it, speaking with a young woman. As they approached, King Arthur looked up and smiled, his blue eyes twinkling.

"Well met, Nephew," he said to Sir Gawain, his voice even and warm. "You also, Linet, but who is this man with you?"

Gawain bowed. "He is called Corvus, My Liege. He is come to Camelot by instruction of the Lady of the Fountain in the hopes we might aid him in a most difficult quest."

The King turned his warm regard on Corvus who found himself smiling shyly in return.

"A quest!" The King said loudly and the gathered turned all their attention toward the throne. "That is always of the greatest interest to us. What is this quest, my friend, and how might we help you with it?"

Gawain gave Corvus a friendly nudge in the back which pushed him a step forward.

"What . . . what is the greatest human virtue, Majesty?" he whispered.

Twirling a ring on his finger, the King considered

it gravely. "What do you think it is?" he asked after a time.

"I don't know, Sire."

"That is no doubt why he has been sent, Majesty," Gawain offered and Arthur nodded.

"For myself, my answer would have to be duty, I think," he answered, "the duty of the crown. What do you have a duty to, Corvus?"

The King looked at him with such kindness that Corvus almost blurted out Bran's name for if he had a duty to any it would be to him, but instead he said, "The protection of Logres, Majesty."

Arthur smiled as the assembled murmured their approval of such a word. "A fine answer. The Realm needs many such if it is to remain strong and free."

Again Corvus clamped his teeth shut on an involuntary response. Arthur did not notice.

"But that can't be the answer you seek, for it came right readily to your lips. Come then, you will ask your question of all my noble knights present, and we shall see if any may find the answer that touches your heart."

And so he bade Corvus go to each knight and ask his question. Most gave its personal meaning due thought, and each answered according to his nature. Sir Dinadan replied humor after a dour Sir Belliese said fidelity, and both Sir Perceval and Sir Bors said honor. Sir Galahad chose faith and Sir Bedivere loyalty, and both Sir Tristan and Lionel chose love as did most of the others. True to his Orkney heritage, Sir Agravaine replied valor as had his brother Gawain.

When Corvus had asked each knight in turn, he found himself before King Arthur again.

"A dizzying array," the King noted.

"Yes, Your Majesty. It seems, if I may make so bold, that it's different for every person."

"That is the fabric of our lives, Corvus. We all have a destiny, and what we value is colored by that destiny."

"But our destinies are hidden in the mists of time, unassailable by all but the most powerful of Seers," Corvus replied, his inquisitive nature drawing him into debate despite his wariness before the King. "How can we then know what we value?"

"Perhaps each person's values influence their destiny," Arthur answered.

Corvus shook his head vehemently. "That cannot be, because then you're trapped in a circle with neither a beginning nor an end."

"What came first, the chicken or the egg?" the King shot back, obviously enjoying himself.

"The chicken."

"Ah, but where did the chicken come from?"

"The Gods."

"And the Gods come from where?" The King's eyes sparkled with mischief and Corvus frowned.

"I don't know," he snapped.

"And what is the greatest human virtue?"

"I . . . I don't know that either." Corvus deflated, but the King gave him another kindly smile.

"Then abide in Camelot a while. I give you free access to any part of our fair city, only you must come before me again should you find your answer."

Corvus gave him a grudging nod. "I will, Your Majesty."

And so Corvus left King Arthur's presence feeling more confused that before he'd arrived.

He remained in Camelot all that summer. Linet and Gawain guided him through the city, stopping noble, merchant, and beggar alike so he might ask them his question. He got so many answers that he lingered through the autumn and winter to spring and back to summer again. Soon he became a familiar sight, many of the citizens taking it upon themselves to bring strangers to him to hear their answers. Linet and he grew closer, until he could no longer remember a time when he did not love her. They lived happily together when her duties at the Lady's fountain permitted, and at other times he stayed at the home of Sir Dinadan, whose temperament suited him very well.

On most days he could be found seated in the palace gardens debating the question with Sir Bedivere or perched in the Palace Hall's upper gallery. Back pressed against a marble pillar, he became the silent witness to all of Camelot's greatest events, and so the years passed swiftly.

He was there when Sir Bertilak, the green knight, challenged Arthur's court to the beheading game, and there when, to his joy and relief, Sir Gawain returned from his meeting with that strange man to remark sourly that humility might perhaps be his answer now.

He was there to watch each newly made knight swear his vows before the King, and there to see which lady caught their attention and which held it. He witnessed the struggle between the Druidic and Christian religions and watched as one by one, each knight chose the way of the cross; all save Gawain who remained the Knight of the Goddess to the end.

He was there when a light so bright that it caused his eyes to fill with tears and spots to dance before his vision marked the appearance of the Holy Grail, and there as each knight of the Round Table spoke of his adventures seeking it. And he was there to grieve with the King when Sir Perceval and Sir Bors came home, bearing Sir Galahad's body and a tale of the completion of the Grail quest.

It seemed to him that something in Camelot dimmed that day, although outwardly it was still as beautiful as ever. Often he dreamed of flying over its slate roofs and common pastures and wondered if his spirit returned to the raven form that, in his waking life, he had all but forgotten.

And so the years passed.

He was still there, although the glossy black of his hair was beginning to gray, as was the King's, when Arthur learned of the love of his wife and the Realm's greatest living knight and with it of the deaths of Sir Colgrevave, Sir Tor, Sir Gareth, and Linet's father, Sir Gaheris.

He watched as, mad with grief, Sir Gawain swore on his honor to seek out Sir Lancelot and make him pay for his brothers' deaths; and he wept as Gawain's body was returned to Camelot to be laid at the King's feet.

He watched with an ever heavier heart as Arthur, his bright eyes and quick smile dimmed, led his few loyal followers to Joyous Gard in France, leaving Sir Mordred to almost destroy the Realm. But when Arthur returned to give him battle, Corvus left his perch and followed the King's army to Camlan.

Linet went with him. Together they helped carry the wounded from the field and bury the dead. As each battle dwindled their numbers, Corvus grew more fearful for the King's safety, until finally, standing on a rise overlooking the fields of Camlan, as the last of Camelot's shattered Round Table fought a terrible battle against itself, they saw King Arthur fall.

A pain worse than any he had ever felt struck Corvus in the breast, and he cried out as the Palladium of Logres fell. Heedless of the danger, Corvus turned and plunged down the hill.

Running between the few remaining combatants, his eyes streaming with tears, Corvus stumbled and fell to his knees before the dying King. Sir Lucan and Sir Bedivere were already there, openly weeping and they did not protest as Corvus clutched the King's hand.

Arthur's eyes were glassy, but he looked up at him with a pained smiled.

"Have you found your answer yet?" he asked weakly.

Corvus could only shake his head, splattering tears across the King's face.

"I fear I can no longer help you. You'll have to find it on your own now, follower of Bran."

Corvus started. "How did you know?"

The ghost of his old smile came to Arthur's lips. "The king and the land are one," he managed, "and all things are made clear to him." He grimaced in pain. "I am glad . . . that Bran and I could be reconciled through you." Spent, he let his head loll against Sir Bedivere's breast. The two knights lifted him up and slowly bore him from the field.

Corvus remained, his mind in shock. Already his fellow ravens were flocking to their feast and a terrible longing to be among them, with no care save filling an empty belly, came over him. He raised his head and keened for all he had lost in both bird form and man form.

He never saw the arrows which flew toward him. One grazed him across the jaw, the other took him through the arm and pierced his side. He fell.

It was some time before he regained his senses. He found himself lying on a grassy knoll, his head cradled in Linet's lap, her arms about him. She was weeping, and he raised his good hand to catch her tears.

"Lin . . ." He coughed and pain laced through his mouth, making him want to squirm.

"Don't talk," she choked out. "You're going to be all right."

A sharp tingling began to move throughout his body. "But I never . . ." he strained to speak as his mouth filled with blood. "But I never found the answer," he whispered.

"Be still." Linet passed her hands frantically over his face and he reached forward to catch and hold them still.

"Dying," he said simply.

"No. You can't be. We'll get you to a physician."

"Too late. I did . . . so want to stay with you."

"We all want what we cannot have, little philosopher," a voice said above them.

They looked up to see the Lady Nimue standing over them. No longer the terrible presence she'd been in Merlin's tower, she seemed tired and careworn, as if the battle had drained as much life from her as Corvus' wounds had from him. There were fine lines about her mouth and her dark eyes were cloudy. She looked down at him with weary sympathy.

"Have you found your answer yet, Corvus?" she asked.

He tried to shake his head, but it hurt too much to move. "No," he whispered.

"You're almost out of time."

"I know."

Linet looked up. "My Lady, please help him."

Nimue shook her head sadly. "I cannot. Soon I must join my sisters to carry Arthur to Avalon."

Corvus stirred. "Is he . . . is he dead?"

She gave him a faint smile. "King Arthur will never truly die," she said. "He will sleep, the greatest of his knights beside him, until Logres has need of him again." She crouched down. "I cannot save you, little blackbird, but I can bear you to Avalon to lie beside the King."

He managed a weak smile. "Merlin said I would not go to Avalon."

"To the Blessed Realm then, to join with Bran in his endless sleep."

Corvus coughed, and a thin trickle of blood ran down between his lips to spatter onto Linet's sleeve. His heart began to beat laboriously. To be with Bran again. To never be in doubt again. He closed his eyes and several tears squeezed their way between his lids. To never see Linet again. To never fly over the fields of Logres again.

He opened his eyes, and Nimue's face swam in and out of focus.

"Who will protect the Realm," he managed, "if we are all gone?"

"Who, indeed?" She tilted her head to one side. "Would you stay, Corvus, and protect the Realm if you could?"

His answer was easy enough. "Yes?"

"Even if it meant returning to your raven form and losing the power of speech. Could you give up all your questions and all their answers?"

"Yes."

"Even if it meant losing all the memories of those who went before you; of Bran and Merlin and of Arthur?"

"Yes."

"Even if it meant losing Linet?"

He paused and she raised her head angrily. "He won't lose me!" she spat out. "Who are you to say he'll lose me?"

"I am a vessel of Sovereignty."

Corvus felt the tears come as he finally recognized her for what she was. He felt like a fool for not seeing it before, but Linet gripped his hand and faced Nimue fearlessly. "I won't leave him," she growled.

"He will not know you."

"I don't care. I will know him."

"Is that your choice then, follower of Bran?" Nimue asked, turning back to Corvus."

He nodded weakly.

"And you will stay with him and aid him?" she asked Linet.

"Yes!"

"Then stay, both of you; stay and protect the Realm; for Bran, for Arthur, and for me, until it has need of us again."

She stood, and between the space of one heartbeat and the next, she was gone.

Corvus lay, feeling the tingling in his limbs and the pain in his mouth and arm growing.

"Linet?"

"I'm here, Corvus."

"I'm so cold."

She gathered him up in her arms as he began to shake. The shock of his injuries made his thinking fuzzy and he struggled to concentrate.

"What is the greatest human virtue?" he asked aloud. His mind moving sluggishly as he thought of Bran, of Arthur, of Gawain and Galahad, and finally he knew.

"Sacrifice," he whispered.

Linet glanced down at him. "What?"

"Sacrifice," he repeated. "Because it's motivated by all the rest; duty, honor, love, valor."

She sighed. "Truly."

"Linet?"

"Yes, Corvus."

"You must . . ." His mouth twisted and found it impossible to form the words. "Will you . . . find Leanan and Cradel in the Perilous Forest?" he croaked out. "Take them . . . Will you take them, take us, to the White Tower?"

"The White Tower?"

He nodded. "As long . . ." he struggled against the encroaching change, fighting to speak this one last sentence as a statement and managed to gasp out . . . "as long as we remain . . . the Realm will be safe."

He fell back, the last of his strength used up in the attempt. The tingling was now all over his body, and he felt himself shrink and his hands grow numb as his arms returned to wings once more.

"Will I . . . will I know you?" he managed through his broken beak.

Linet bowed her head, tears dripping down onto the glossy black of his feathers. "Yes," she answered defiantly. "We will fly together in our dreams, Corvus."

"Will . . . that be enough?"

"Yes."

"Am I not . . . the greatest of Bran's ravens?"

She favored him with her wry smile through her tears. "You are the first of Bran's ravens," she agreed.

"And . . . you will stay with me?"

"I said I would. I will be the Keeper of the Ravens of the White Tower."

The love in her face his last conscious sight, Corvus closed his eyes and slept.

And in the days following the battle of Camlan, a fair, golden-haired woman could be seen traveling toward London, a great raven cradled in her arms. She made her home in the White Tower and called the others of his kind to dwell with them so that England might always be safe against invasion.

And there they still remain.

THE QUEEN'S BROIDERY WOMAN

by Nancy Springer

Nancy Springer's more than thirty books include *Fair Peril, The White Hart, The Book Of Suns, The Sable Moon, The Silver Sun, The Black Beast, Larque on the Wing, Metal Angel, Toughing It, The Boy on a Black Horse, A Horse to Love, Looking for Jamie Bridger, Colt, Wings of Flame, Chains of Gold,* and *The Hex Witch of Seldom,* among others. Her stories have appeared in many magazines and anthologies, and she has won the Tiptree Award and is a two-time recipient of the Edgar Award. She lives in Pennsylvania with her family.

"The Queen's Broidery Woman" examines the nature of fate and its inexorable force, even on those who help create it.

S how me how to make French knots, Norrie."
Looking up from the green samite baldric she was embroidering with thread of gold, Norrie saw the queen sitting down beside her with a length of fine lawn in her fair young hands.

"It's for me to wear in my bosom and give to Sir Lancelot at the tournament," Guinevere declared, glowing and girlish as always, "in an offhand sort of just-so fashion, as my favor for him to flaunt on his helm."

She reminds me of—of her. Norrie would not complete the thought with the name, because she wanted to believe that she had forgotten, because she did not care to entertain dangerous memories of what had befallen her long, long ago, and what did it matter that Queen Guinevere resembled the big-eyed, skinny, by-the-way wench who had stolen her young husband from her? If it had not happened, Norrie considered, then she, Norrie, would likely be long since dead in childbed, as was the common lot of married women. Or if she lived, it would be in a serf's hut, worn down with children and grandchildren and cares. But as it was, she spent her days in a cushioned chair by the sunlit window of a Camelot tower; she was to be envied. As the queen's broidery woman, she had the finest fabrics, the finest threads— gold, silver, Phoenician crimson, Indy blue—to work with. She had a soft bed, good food, and new clothing, including shoes, twice a year. She was indeed greatly to be envied.

"I want to put pansies on it, and roses. And my device." Guinevere was struggling to stretch the bleached lawn in an embroidery hoop. Trying not to show her dismay, Norrie contemplated the mess Guinevere was going to make of the fine linen. The queen was no needlewoman.

"And I want to do it all in French knots," Guinevere prattled on, "for Sir Lancelot, because he's from France."

She's young, Norrie reminded herself as her harsh old fingers tightened on the green samite in her lap. *She doesn't know any better.* But how the girl loved to play these dangerous games. It was all just fun to

Guinevere, as it had been all just fun to that long-ago so-called maiden who . . . no. *It's not your place to think such things.* Norrie made herself think instead of French knots, with the result being the same fated feeling. Her voice straw-dry and scratchy, as always, Norrie spoke. "Knots mean trouble to come."

"They do?" Like a butterfly poised between flights, Guinevere stopped fidgeting with the linen for a moment and stared at Norrie.

"Surely." Norrie glanced down at the baldric she was decorating for Guinevere, which she was bordering with sunspoke stitch for happiness and wheat ear stitch for fertility; did the queen think she chose her designs at random? Why did the young chit think embroidery went on hems and the edges of sleeves? It was to keep the bad out. "All stitches are like wishes." Stitches had meanings; didn't Guinevere know that? The queen understood well enough the meanings of devices and flowers. Pansies and roses, forsooth.

"But then—but then why put French knots on anything?"

"A few in the centers of the flowers, they're only natural. A few troubles must come to everyone."

"I don't want *any* troubles." But then Guinevere tossed her golden head and smiled. "No, that's not true. Life would be boring without troubles. All right, Norrie, show me, and I'll make just a *few* French knots."

Norrie laid aside the baldric and got to her feet, her aches slowing her movements. A lifetime of broidery had shaped her body to the task; standing, she formed a curve, a cup like the curve of her sere hand shaped to the coaxing of the needle as she bent over Guinevere and showed the girl how to make French knots. Around the needle two, three, four, even five times, went the scarlet thread—colors had meanings, too, as Norrie, saying nothing, guessed the queen knew. Then, securing the knot, the needle plunged in—like a knife to the heart. Trying not to think how nearly the thread was the color of heart's blood, Norrie guided the young queen's hands, hands as soft as satin and nearly as white as the linen, baby-tender beneath the hook of Norrie's callused forefinger with its thick, ridged nail. When Norrie took her hand away, Guinevere stitched on, clumsily. Her knots wobbled. "Let me do it for you," Norrie offered, or begged.

"But it will mean more if I can say I made it myself."

Norrie sat down and took up the green samite baldric again, saying nothing more. The end would be the same no matter what she said.

Within a short time, as Norrie had known she must, Queen Guinevere tired of French knots, stem stitch, rose stitch, and all the rest of it. She jumped up, dropped her stitchery on the chair, looked at what Norrie was doing with the baldric and declared, "That is just beautiful, Norrie. There's nobody else who can embroider like you do. Your stitches are so true." She flitted away.

Norrie could not help smiling—not at the compliment, which was merest justice, but at Guinevere. As if watching a bird fly, Norrie watched her cross the solarium to the spiral stairway, this comely girl, the queen of Camelot forsooth, lilting off in her lapis-

blue gown bordered with a wide featherstitch pattern
in gold, her darker blue overgown bordered in lapis
scrollwork couched with gold. Golden stitches true
from Norrie's hand and as fair as the queen, as fair
of portent as a summer's day. Norrie herself wore an
old-fashioned narrow bliaut with an overtunic to
keep her aging bones warm, both bliaut and overtunic
well made of the finest wool, but their color plain
dull black, their hems stark, not a stitch of color on
either of them. Plain clothing was a commoner's lot.

Setting aside the baldric and reaching for the
queen's stitchery, Norrie lost her smile. For a moment she sat quite still with the needlework taut between her chalky hands. In clumsy running stitch,
she saw, Guinevere had sketched out Lancelot's es-
cutcheon, white with three ribbons of blood red. The
queen had added the Lodegreaunce device, the coat-
of-arms of her father's house, as if she were still a
maid. And twining around and joining the two
shields, she had stitched a knotty scarlet rose.

She wants it to happen.

She knows. She knows well enough what she's doing.

She reminds me . . .

Norrie shook her head to shake away the thought,
then laid the stitchery in her lap. For a moment more
she studied it, feeling trouble settle in her like a
stone, not so much in her heart as in her slack old
belly, in her spleen, a trouble too deep for frowning.

Then from her deep tunic pocket she drew her
most prized possession: tiny, bright steel scissors
cunningly wrought in the shape of a raven's head.
The raven's bill was the scissor blades, curved like a
reaper's scythe, and with them she snipped the

queen's wavering stitches. As she labored, she grew aware of the steel-gray hair atop her bent head, old hair coiled heavy like a crown on her, pressing down with a sense that she must do something—although she was not yet sure what.

She pulled out Guinevere's stitches, sighing at the spots where the queen had stretched holes in the delicate linen. She restitched the botched work and continued it, including a number of French knots.

"Eleanor," said King Arthur to Norrie, "how are you?"

Norrie's name was not Eleanor—why would King Arthur think a commoner woman like her would bear such a fine name?—but she smiled anyway, feeling the furrows of her face deepening with the effort. Arthur could call her what he wanted, even were he not king. Such a fine lance of a man he was, a sweet, handsome man, his broad shoulders set off by a purple mantle fastened at his throat by a coil of gold. It was kind of him to speak to her, to notice her sitting in the great hall, supping with the others. She told him, "I'm well, thank you, Sire," and wished that she could soften her sere voice.

"Good. May you remain well to continue adorning my beautiful wife." King Arthur turned doting eyes to where Guinevere sat laughing on the dais. She would have looked beautiful to him in sackcloth, Norrie could tell, yet there he stood, speaking with an old broidery woman. "Your skill bedecks her as a queen of queens."

Both of them watched as Queen Guinevere tilted her comely head and whispered to the knight next to her on the dais, flirting. It was not Lancelot, but it did not matter; Guinevere practiced her skills at will or at whim, and Arthur smiled on, besotted; how were some women able to befool men so? The skinny wenches with big fluttering soft-lidded eyes, had they bartered their souls for the power to enchant? Why did they choose to—to captivate, to enslave. . . .

In that moment Norrie knew—not yet what to do, but that she must begin without knowing. Now. It was a moment fate had put before her.

Norrie opened her dry mouth. She said to King Arthur, "Sire. My sister—"

He turned to her in smiling surprise. "You have a sister, Norrie?" As if it had never occurred to him that an old woman could have something to her: youth that once was, dreams and reachings, common thread with others, sisters, a history. As if he looked at an old woman and saw only an old woman, as separate as a stick. But in that he was typical of most men.

"I have two sisters."

"*Two* of them!" As if this were utterly amazing.

"Yes. But the one of whom I spoke, my sister—" She had to say it quickly, seize the moment fate had dropped in her lap. "My sister dyes thread of the richest colors ever seen, brighter and deeper than any threads of Indy." This was much for Norrie to say, yet she spoke on. "Reds redder than a true love's heart. Greens greener than jealousy. Blues bluer—"

Half laughing, King Arthur interrupted. "Truly?"

"Yes."

"Why, then, we must have some of these wonderful colors for Guinevere!" The king spoke with the joy of a boy. "Where does your sister live?"

"A day's journey from here. Near the sea."

"I shall send . . ." He peered at her and smiled. "Would you like to visit your sister, Norrie?" He saw at once, for she let him see, that she would. "I shall send *you*, Eleanor. With a Knight of the Round Table for escort."

She smiled back at him, her old face crinkling like crepe, her old heart young with a downy lamb's-wool feeling she had thought never to know again. She would never be so foolish as to embroider a token, but she could not help the warmth in her heart; she was fond of King Arthur. Very fond. He reminded her all too much of a sweet and comely young man she had once known.

As her own.

For all too short a while.

Dear husband. Dear and besotted. Besotted with her, until that wench had flirted him away from her.

For her escort, Norrie requested, and received, Sir Lancelot.

She chose him partly out of spite, to keep him away from Guinevere for a few days, but also out of compunction, to see whether he was perhaps worth saving.

Traveling to visit her sister on a fair June day, she rode behind him on a pillion, her black-clad arms around his mailed waist, soon weary, her old bones jounced by the gait to which he kept his steed. All day, weary and jolted, and all day he spoke nary a word to her unless she spoke to him first. He seemed

to feel that the matter was beneath his dignity, that
he was being made a jest of, escorting an old broidery woman—as indeed, perhaps he was. Perhaps
King Arthur was not too besotted to find some
amusement in giving this task to his wife's admirer.
Perhaps King Arthur was smiling.

"You would rather be riding with a fair young
damsel at your back, Sir Lancelot," Norrie said to his
hard shoulder, "would you not?"

"Not at all," he replied with briefest courtesy.

"Then you would rather be back in Camelot, is it
not so?"

"Not at all, um . . ." He could not remember her
name. An old woman, she was not worth naming or
talking to.

He was a massive broadsword of a man, this
Lancelot, a weighty weapon of a man shining in the
sun, steely-edged. Norrie found nothing more to him.
Without further compunction, she gave up considera-
tions of him.

At her sister's house, Sir Lancelot stayed outside,
with his horse for company, refusing hospitality on
the basis of some sort of knightly vigil he had decided he must keep.

"Is he going to sleep on the ground?" Norrie's sister asked. The sister's name was also Norrie. This
did not seem odd to Norrie the queen's broidery
woman. Their other sister, who lived far to the west
among rugged tors, was also named Norrie.

Sir Lancelot did not know these things, because Sir
Lancelot had not come into the house. If he had
asked their names, they would have told him. But
they were old women; he had not asked.

"He'll sleep on the ground and in his armor, most likely," Norrie said dryly. Sir Lancelot would do this as a self-imposed penance. Or perhaps more of a martyrdom. And certainly, Norrie thought, as a knightly way to avoid the boring conversation of two old women.

"How sad."

"Not at all. He has chosen."

Norrie's sister wore a plain narrow bliaut and overtunic much like Norrie's, but not black, for she was not a widow; she wore a brown weave of the undyed wool. Her dying was all for others, not for herself. On the table in her cottage by the sea lay the threads redder than heart's blood, greener than jealousy, bluer than truth. And many other colors also: silver, gold, shining black, bride white, and midnight indigo and daylily pink and cuckold yellow and all the myriad bright, dark deep-dyed colors of life in silk threads and spun linen and cotton flosses. The Norries sat at the table in their stark dark gowns and fingered the colors, all of them, as they talked.

"Did he choose," asked Norrie-by-the-sea, "or is he somehow fated, even now?"

Such riddling annoyed Norrie of Camelot. "What does it matter?"

"It makes me wonder, that is all."

"Bah. Why should we wonder? We're merest commoners; we have no fates. We have the ordinary lot, or occasionally we have luck, good or bad, that is all. Good luck or ill."

"So the great folks have fates, destinies, but we have merest luck?"

"That's right."

Her sister smiled. "Was it luck that made you who you are?" For the Norries had borne other names as maidens, although they no longer remembered them.

"It must have been," said Norrie, the words scorched dark and deckle-edged. "It must have been merest luck. After all, Merlin did not speak of me."

"Bah. That old fraud." Norrie-by-the-sea lost her smile. "He did nothing, he only prophesied, and they called him a wizard."

Norrie said nothing, for she was struggling with the riddle she did not like, that of fate versus choice. Supposing Merlin had known many things; had he chosen what to prophesy? Might there have been matters, great and fated matters, regarding which he had kept silent?

Nonsense. It did not matter. Merlin had spoken of King Arthur's death at the hands of a mystery named Mordred, but blessedly, Merlin had said nothing of Guinevere's fate, or of Sir Lancelot's.

"The old fraud," muttered the other Norrie again, shifting in her wooden chair, trying to find some comfort for her stony old bones. "But confound him, he knew the power of good thread." Merlin had worn wizard's gowns deeply bordered with warding stitchery, thickly broidered with mystic sigils. The sisters knew; Norrie of the western tors had spun the thread, and Norrie-by-the-sea had dyed it, and Norrie of Camelot had stitched the designs. And after a while Merlin had gone away never to return. But that was long ago.

Norrie of Camelot fingered a skein of deepest red. "It is well dyed."

"All the better for the dying thereby." It was their

dry joke, timeworn so thin that it no longer made
them smile. "What, may I ask, are you going to do
with it?"

"That," said Norrie, the paradox of fate and choice
enfolded in her desiccated voice, "is entirely up to
Guinevere."

Within the week after Norrie returned to Camelot,
Guinevere chose to consummate her fate, with
Lancelot. In bright afternoon light, no less, for all to
see, even an old broidery woman. Norrie looked up
from the couvrechef she was edging and saw Sir
Lancelot stride through the solarium on his way to
the queen's chamber; he wore a crimson tunic under
a tabard bordered with real gold, but Norrie considered that all the gold broidery in the world would
not help him once he took the things off. A moment
later, Guinevere sent her maidens-in-waiting out of
her chamber. Norrie saw them pass through the solarium with their silky young faces closed into knowing looks.

Norrie bowed her head, for she knew more than
they did.

Her bent hands, as rough and gray as the woolens
she had worn as a child, grew still upon the dainty
white head linen she was bordering with tiny daisies
for the queen.

There it lay in her rusty black lap. She gazed at it.

A moment later, quiet and true, her hands moved
again, picking out the daisy stitches. When the light
of the solarium was going dim, when Sir Lancelot
left the queen's chamber, Norrie was still sitting in
her chair by the west window, edging the queen's

couvrechef with delicate flowers in a stitch she had not used for years. Spider stitch, folk called it.

When the queen saw the completed couvrechef, days later, she was well pleased. "It looks different," said Guinevere.

"Yes," Norrie agreed, "it is different."

"I like it. It's elegant. Very modish."

Few others noticed any change except to think that the queen looked lovelier year by year.

It often takes years for things to work out, Norrie knew. For matters like these, it needed to take years; fate takes time. And it took years, also, for innocent clothing to grow old and be discarded, for new silks and linens to take on elegant adornment from Norrie's hands. Even had she wanted to, Norrie could not restitch Guinevere's entire wardrobe in a day.

It was all right. She felt sure she would not die before she was done.

Few others noticed. It made no difference to King Arthur, for instance, whether his wife's gowns were bordered in daisy stitch or in French knots and lashwork. It all looked beautiful to him. "You make her more beautiful season by season, Eleanor," he said to Norrie. There was something in King Arthur too honey golden to let him be a jealous cuckold; he knew that he was betrayed, and the whole world knew that he knew, but the more Guinevere dallied, the more Arthur grew in gallantry—to Norrie's mind, at least—and the more sweet became his devotion, all the more noble for being saddened.

One day a page came and summoned Norrie to King Arthur—for the king himself came seldom anymore to the queen's quarters; he knew. Wondering,

Norrie waited her turn in the audience chamber, her hook-shaped hands wandering like small animals on her lap, feeling empty and adrift, autumn leaves in the wind, without their stitchery. The king greeted her with a smile as she bobbed before him; his gentle glance helped calm her hands.

"Will you do a job of broidery for me, Norrie?" King Arthur couched his command as a request, drollery at the corners of his handsome mouth, for the king had his own stewards and tailors and broidery women, all of whom would be insulted when they found out what he had done. "I have a new mantle of the finest Indy velvet I have ever seen. Will you edge it for me?"

Much honored, she bordered it deeply in thread of gold, in chevron stitches and Grecian stitches and all the sword-straight noble stitches worthy of a king, for she wished only good to King Arthur. Anything bad that might happen to Guinevere could mean only good for him, was it not so? It would be good riddance if he were relieved of his deceitful wife. Merlin was nothing but an old humbug, foretelling an ill fate for King Arthur.

It took her nearly a season's turning to embroider the mantle to her satisfaction, for she had Guinevere's gowns and girdles and frocks and kerchiefs and other fripperies to tend to as well. But she had put them all aside and was finishing the last few inches of the mantle one sunny winter afternoon when a young man walked into the solarium and sat down beside her.

She liked him at once, deep in her heart she liked him, and this seldom happened in Norrie, this warm blooming of her sere heart, and she could not tell why it did. He was an ordinary-looking youth—Sir Lancelot's latest squire, perhaps? Just a slim youth with lank hair and quiet brown eyes the color of marten fur. Perhaps it was the way his soft brown glance rested on her as he entered, the way he *saw* her, that made her like him. The way he crossed the room to sit with her.

"Exquisite," he said, studying the mantle with wide-open eyes.

"It's lovely velvet," she agreed.

"No, I mean the design you've wrought. Every line as straight and true as a lance."

"Thank you." Her hands stilled in their labor as she looked at him, almost staring, for rare was the man who gave good stitchery its due. Even King Arthur acknowledged of Norrie's embroidery only that it was beautiful, seeing only the shine, the colors, not the design.

"Very different than these," the youth said, fingering the projects she had set aside, the ribbons and other bits of folderol that she was decorating for Guinevere. "These are sly, are they not? Like vines taking over a garden. Yet they are just as exquisite, in quite a different way. What do you call these long knotted stitches?"

Gawking, she found it hard to catch her breath, to answer him. "Bullion stitch."

"Gold with a twist, is it?" He pointed again, laying his quiet finger gently on the cloth. "And these, that look like roses but are not?"

"Whipped spider stitch."

"Most elegant."

Norrie blurted, "That's what the queen says." This young stranger had put her utterly off balance, yet her heart opened warm wings to him.

"Yes. That is what Queen Guinevere would say." The youth regarded her quietly. "You love King Arthur," he said for no reason and every reason, all the unspoken reasons that lay between them because he saw her truly and he saw her stitchery in like wise. It was not necessary for him to say more, to say that she could have loved Guinevere like a daughter but now she hated her as the play-between-the-sheets wench she had become. She knew that he knew.

"I am a loyal subject," Norrie told him, her voice like parchment.

"Quite. I can see that." He meant it; no quirk of sarcasm marred his tone.

She stared at him frankly now. With more of softness in her voice than there had been in years, she asked him, "Who are you?"

"I am nobody."

"Surely not. What is your name?"

He told her, "I am Mordred."

From the moment she met Mordred, Norrie began to understand what "doom" meant. Doom was fate without a sense of any choice in it.

King Arthur's doom.

And her own.

On the face of it, she had choices. She could have chosen to go away. She could have left Camelot and lived out her days with her sister by the sea or her other sister, she of the western tors. Or, if that would not do, Norrie could have chosen to stay but to make a different choice of stitchery. She could have started bordering Guinevere's cloaks with warding stitches again, and putting the daisies and sun rays back on her frocks. Perhaps it would have made a difference.

Or perhaps not.

Norrie did neither of those things, for she could not. From the moment in which her heart opened warm wings to Mordred, she had no choice anymore.

Almost every day he came to sit by her, if only for a few minutes. Almost every day his quiet eyes regarded the cape or kerchief or necklet she was embroidering and knew just what she was doing. Almost every day his quiet eyes regarded her and knew just who she was.

And just for that, because he looked upon her and saw her truly, she could not choose otherwise but to stay as she was and do as she did.

It was not so much that she loved him—although she did. She adored him as much as she adored that King never to be called his father, Arthur—or perhaps even more, because Arthur had not looked upon her to see her truly. This youth never to be called a prince, this Mordred, knew better than to call her Eleanor.

He did not call her anything at all. He never asked her name. He did not need to.

He faithfully came to see her, season after season, whenever he was in Camelot, and study the design of her stitchery, the whip stitch and spider stitches and the knotwork. And sometimes he gave her a quiet smile. He knew. He knew just what she was doing. And it was his knowing that brought roses to bloom in her dry old heart. And because of the way he knew, she went on doing it.

And through all those passing seasons, Guinevere went on knowing Lancelot.

And the one knowledge became as fated as the other.

Doom. Norrie knew what it meant now.

She knew Mordred. She knew who he was.

She knew what he was doing.

With her. To her.

And even knowing, she could not stop.

And then it became far too late.

As the sun set in the jagged west on the day of the final battle, Norrie Spinster came walking down from the tors, slow but strong on her ancient legs, in her coarse brown gown, and Norrie of Camelot hobbled to her and embraced her. "Sister," she whispered like the voice of wind in parched grass. They had not seen each other in years and years.

"Why are you weeping?" asked her sister.

"I did not want this." Norrie of Camelot gestured toward the battlefield, the tears welting her arid face like seeping burns. "I stitched the bane for her, not for him. Not for King Arthur."

"Bah," grumbled the third sister, Norrie far from her cottage by the sea, standing in a hazel copse with the others, a skein of red looped in her hands as she looked out upon Glastonbury Plain. In the ruddy sunset light it lay like a red clay field plowed up into heaps of dead and dying, mounds of dead yeomen, dead knights, dead horses, a russet waste in which only three men remained standing—among them the one for whom Norrie wept. "Bah!" grumbled her sister. "King Arthur, forsooth? He'll be a king not much longer. What is he that you should wish to spare him?"

"He is—he is—" Norrie of Camelot could barely speak, and when she did speak, she blurted a name she should have forgotten years ago. "He is just like my own dear Hugh."

"Oh. He's a fool?" said Norrie of the tors, her spindle standing like a candle in her hand, her voice as cuttingly dry as the thread.

"No! I mean—Hugh was misled, but King Arthur—he is faithful—"

"He's a fool," said the Norrie-of-the-dying with decision. "Just like Hugh, indeed; Norrie, don't you remember how we settled Hugh's fate? How you stitched the runes on a winding sheet for him before he knew he needed it?"

Norrie remembered. But she shook her head, flung it from side to side so vehemently that her bun of steely hair loosened and coiled down like gray snakes. "No," she cried, a wail, a moan like the moans of the men dying not far from her feet. "No, I cannot do it. How did I come to be Norn? I did not want this. I cannot be fated to be fate."

But the other two Norries were barely listening to her. They were watching a fourth knight, a tall knight, slouch onto the battlefield, his armor reddened, his shoulders hunched with pain or weariness.

"I cannot bear it," Norrie said, her voice breaking like a heart. "Mordred." Her dear Mordred.

The three sisters watched as Sir Mordred drew his

sword, letting out a wordless snarl, a lion grunt, and as King Arthur turned to meet the challenge.

"It is time," one of the Norries said. Norrie of Camelot could no longer tell their voices from each other, or from her own. Dusty voices, they were, all three, like the croaking of the ravens that flew over Glastonbury and swooped down now and then to peck an eye out of a corpse. Dark-robed the sisters stood, three in a row, like three ravens in a gray tree.

"I shall die," Norrie said.

Her sisters looked at her and nodded, for they knew she spoke truly, always. "There'll be another, then," said Norrie-by-the-sea thoughtfully, wondering who it might be.

"Maybe that Guinevere. Maybe in the convent she'll learn proper stitchery at last." Norrie's own words surprised her, for in their bitterness she heard a wry, dark acceptance; how could that be, when all her stitchery had gone wrong? Guinevere should have gone down to doom. Guinevere should have burned at the stake. Guinevere should have died, not—

"Come, sisters, quickly." As Mordred tottered into a charge, hurtling toward Arthur with sword brandished high, Norrie-of-the-tors pulled thread from her spindle. Two threads, intertwined. Norrie-by-the-sea seized them, and as the threads passed through her hands, they turned red, the deepest of noble reds, redder than sunset, redder than a sword-riven heart. "Your little scissors, Norrie," she told her sister. "Now."

Norrie reached into her deep tunic pocket. And as King Arthur caught Mordred with the fell tip of his lance, and as Mordred ran up the lance and smote a deep wound to King Arthur's head, Norrie of Camelot raised her raven's-head broidery scissors to one last twist of thread.

As Guinevere knelt weeping and praying in her chilly stone chamber, a flittering shadow crossed her, darkness cutting through the ruddy sundown light. Guinevere looked up. In the high stark rectangle of her single small window perched a raven, folding its rusty black wings.

It clacked its steely bill, downcurved like a grim reaper's scythe. In a voice as dry as straw it spoke.

"Do not fate yourself, Guinevere, child," it said. That sere voice; where had Guinevere heard it before? She could not remember; she could not think. In her sorrow she could barely comprehend the words. "Do not begrudge, do not be fated, do not become a black thing flying down on the dead, pecking away their eyes. Forgive,' the raven told her, its scratchy voice wafting low, a whisper in the wind. "Forgive yourself, Guinevere, and forgive the dead. Live."

And the raven flew away toward the sinking sun.

THE ARCHITECT OF WORLDS

by Brian Stableford

Brian Stableford is an author, editor, and critic who has published over fifty books, including *The Werewolves of London*, *The Empire of Fear*, *Angel of Pain*, and *The Hunger and Ecstasy of Vampires*. His stories have appeared in numerous magazines and anthologies, including *Omni*, *Asimov's Science Fiction*, *Interzone*, and *The Chronicles of the Holy Grail*. He lives in Reading, England.

In "The Architect of Worlds," Stableford constructs a web of overlapping—and conflicting—loyalties, which provide the foundation for much intrigue and betrayal, and build the possibility for some new relationships.

There was great consternation in Camelot on the day the dying rider appeared at the gate, clinging as hard as a desperate man can to a fine white horse that had all but galloped itself to death. The castle was already restless, its inhabitants hungry for portents to settle their unease. The rider, alas, only served to increase their anxiety.

Camelot had a deep moat around it, and it was upon the drawbridge crossing the moat that the messenger finally collapsed, amid a crowd of farmers and husbandmen bringing provisions to the overcrowded fortress. Sir Kay, the steward of the castle, was working within the shadow of the gate, doling out coin to the carriers and sending servants scurrying hither and yon with the produce he bought. He was the only nobleman who ran to the stricken man's side, but there were thirty commoners who heard the last words which the unlucky fellow contrived to pronounce as clearly as the knight.

"I bear a message for the king," whispered the dying man, "on which the fate of Britain might hang."

Then he died.

Sir Kay, as the surviving rumors of his nature clearly attest, was not a good-humored man, but that was not his fault. The stewardship of Camelot would have turned the most amiable man alive into a curmudgeon even at the best of times, and those were not the best of times. Camelot had five towers, one central and four peripheral, and three of the outer four currently housed visitors. The western tower was host to a company of emissaries from the Druidic Order, led by the bard Taliesin himself. The eastern tower accommodated the Abbot of Glastonbury and two dozen of his monks. The northern tower was occupied by a number of Saxon lordlings who were not entirely clear in their own minds as to whether they were prisoners, hostages, or human pigeons intended to fly home with offers of peace and amity. Every one of these parties required feeding, according to the principles of hospitality—and if that were not enough to make a steward's job difficult, every one of them also required a continual supply of flattery and reassurance, for they were all equally

fearful that any bargain King Arthur might make
with one party might work severely to the disadvan-
tage of the rest.

Given all this, it is not entirely surprising that Sir
Kay's response to the messenger's inconvenient silence was to pluck him from the ground where he
lay and to shake him like a rat, cursing him for his
impoliteness in falling dead after offering such a tan-
talizing explanation of his presence.

Half a minute had passed before Kay realized the
absurdity of his action and looked around for someone else to take the brunt of his anger. When his eye
lighted on me, he found his target. "Don't just stand
there, stupid boy!" he howled. "Fetch your master
Merlin, and tell him to bring the most powerful magics he has, for this dumb oaf is well beyond the assistance of mere medicine!"

It would have made no difference had there still
been a little life in the man before Sir Kay snatched
him up; it would certainly have been extinguished
before I brought my master to the scene. Old though
he was, Merlin still insisted on occupying the highest
attic in the central tower, a full nine dozen steps from
ground level. Had he consented to move to a more
convenient apartment he might not have needed me
at all, for I was not his apprentice in magic, much as
I would like to have been; I was only the servant
commissioned to help him in his peregrinations. On
the other hand, even a great magician requires *someone* to fetch and carry for him, and it is a great convenience to have a servant who can carry information
as easily as bread and slop.

"What is it, Amory?" Merlin said, when I arrived at his open door.

"A messenger, Master," I told him dutifully. "Shot in the back by an arrow, laid out on the drawbridge." I knew better than to opine that the man was beyond all possible help, even of the kind an abbot or a necromancer might offer. Nor did I take much comfort from the fact that our subsequent passage down the winding stair was relatively easy, for I knew that the real test of my fortitude would come when I had to help my limping master climb them all again.

By the time we reached the drawbridge, the crowd had swelled to a full hundred. Men-at-arms were holding back the peasants and petty merchants with horizontal half-pikes, while Sir Gawain and Sir Lancelot were examining the corpse. The two knights were nodding earnestly at one another, as handsome men often do in the false belief that it makes them seem more serious, sensible, and sagacious than they actually are.

"Elf-shot," said Sir Gawain, indicating the arrow which had lodged in the messenger's back, to the left of his spine.

"Definitely elf-shot," Sir Lancelot confirmed, as if the observation required confirmation by a man of his fine stature before it could be reckoned true.

I looked at the only man of authentic sagacity who was present.

"It *looks* like elf-shot," Merlin said, carefully qualifying his agreement. He bent over the body and gently pulled the arrow out so that he could examine its head as well as its fletchings. "Not iron, certainly," he said. "Black glass, of a kind usually found in Faerie, more commonly used in scrying."

The faery folk abhor iron, and always prefer to shape their arrowheads from jet or flint, or even silver. There were some men who would have reckoned it a lucky privilege to be shot by a well-born elf, so long as the silver did not penetrate the heart, but one of that kind would have been sorely disappointed to find that he had only acquired a sliver of glass for his pains.

"I *said* it was elf-shot," said Sir Lancelot, drawing himself up to his full and extraordinarily impressive height, as if his intellectual prowess had now been demonstrated for once and for all.

"What did he say before he died?" Merlin asked, although I had already told him, word for word. Everyone in the crowd knew by now, but rumor had begun to inflate the portent.

"He said that the kingdom is in terrible danger," Gawain told my master, with a perfectly straight face, "but the elf-shot did not give him the chance to say precisely what the danger is."

Merlin looked at me, and I looked back, insisting with stubborn implacability that I had given the more accurate account.

"Did anyone see from which direction the rider came?" Merlin asked, raising his voice so that the entire crowd could hear him.

"From the south!" cried a man burdened by a basket of apples.

"From the southwest!" called a man with a pig in a poke.

"Nay, 'twas from the east of south," opined a jug-and-bottle man.

"From Avalon! From Avalon!" cried a chorus whose members had leaped to a conclusion of which they could not possibly be sure, given that Avalon lay so many leagues beyond the horizon, when its queen condescended that it should show itself at all. No communication had come from Avalon during my lifetime, and such reports as I had heard of elves hunting on earthly soil might well have been exaggerated.

"Not from the north, at any rate," I muttered in my master's ear.

By this time, the unsummoned abbot had come of his own accord, with two of his black-clad crow-men in tow, and I saw Taliesin come striding through the gate with two of *his* harper-apprentices scuttling behind.

"What evil has come here now?" demanded the abbot, looking back at Taliesin so that everyone would know what supposed evil he had found already here.

"What manner of man was he?" Taliesin asked, quietly. "What kind of harness has his horse?"

Sir Kay had been inspecting the horse, presumably to weigh the value of its tack and the quality of the meat it might provide if it were irredeemably broken down. "None but the Romans had horses as fine as this," he announced—although the last *real* Romans had left Britain before his grandfather was born. "The stirrup is iron, the saddle exceptionally good. A knight's horse, or a petty king's—but there is no coat-of-arms to be seen, nor any other identifiable livery."

"The man has no colors either," Sir Gawain observed. "The hair upon his head is fair and untonsured—but that does not necessarily make him a Saxon, and it leaves open the possibility that he might be the servant of a priest." Unlike Lancelot, Gawain did have an adequate measure of common sense.

"The servant of a priest?" said the abbot immediately. "Let me see his face!" After a moment's pause, however, he said: "Not from Glastonbury, that's for sure—but he has the look of a good Christian about him in spite of his fair hair."

For myself, I thought the dead man looked a great deal better than the cowled and hawk-faced individuals who formed the abbot's bodyguard, but I knew better than to say so, even as a whisper in my un-Christian master's ear.

"No horseman could be so anonymous without design," said Merlin. "If he wears no colors, it is because he did not want his colors recognized by those who saw him on the road. If it was a wise precaution, it was not precaution enough."

"No man can hide from magic," Sir Lancelot opined—more accurately than he knew, as matters eventually transpired.

"The only thing about him which declares its origin," Merlin murmured, "is the thing which killed him—though any man might make an arrow in the elvish style, and fire it from any kind of bow." He did not mean the speech for my ears alone, but I doubt that it reached any other, for the crowd at the far end of the drawbridge was becoming excited and clamorous again. Its outermost members had turned around and were pointing at the signal tower on the southern horizon.

Signal towers are a fine thing, more eloquent by far than beacon fires, but they lack the privacy assured by carrier pigeons. Common men are not supposed to be able to read the code of the signaling flags any more than they are supposed to be able to read the Druid script, but common men have to be clever to survive, and their actual accomplishments are often far advanced beyond those of armor-bearing knights. Sir Lancelot and Sir Gawain could not read the message that the signal tower was transmitting, nor could the Latin-literate abbot, but I could read it and even the man with the pig in the poke could read enough to deduce its meaning. He it was, I think, who first let loose the cry "The Queen of Avalon is coming to Camelot!"—but no sooner was it first let loose than it was everywhere, both within and without the castle walls.

"Morgan le Fay! Morgan le Fay! The messenger was shot by an elf-bolt, and the Queen of Avalon is coming in his wake!" It was an unprecedented event, although everyone in the crowd must have known that Arthur had once claimed the mistress of Avalon for his half sister, in the days when he was not yet King of All Britain.

No doubt I would have had more opportunity for sober contemplation of the import of this news had I not been standing so close to Sir Kay, who was growing purple with rage. "Not *more* guests!" he protested, raising his eyes to heaven. "Where shall I put them? How shall I feed them? How shall I seat them at this evening's dinner? Where shall I find another cloth and forty spoons? And how shall I keep them all *apart?*"

I sympathized with his predicament. The southern tower was full to bursting with liegemen and ladies dispossessed of their usual apartments by guests already arrived, but their redistribution would only be the beginning of the steward's problems. It was bad enough that the Druids feared the Churchmen, that the Saxons hated the Druids, and that the Churchmen hated *and* feared the Saxons, without the faery folk being added to the stew. *Everybody* feared the faery folk, and Morgan le Fay most of all. Even Merlin— who was reckoned by some to be a renegade elf himself—had cause enough to fear the faery folk *now.*

All that Merlin muttered, however, while he listened to the steward's ranting, was: "Why could she not stay away? Why could she not content herself with the company of elves for just a little longer, or turn to another citadel than this?"

I was quite certain even then that I was the only person who heard *those* words spoken, and that they were not intended even for my sharp ears. Old men—even old magicians—are sometimes wont to say too much when they believe they are speaking only to themselves.

As legend now insists, the apartments of Camelot were the richest in Britain. Every wall of every apartment was hung with carpets, tapestries, and embroideries of extraordinary beauty and complexity.

Guests placed in such well-decorated rooms were

invariably delighted by the gaiety of the hangings and their remarkable capacity for quelling drafts. They might have been a little less pleased had they known that the carpets and tapestries had more functions than the obvious, but only a handful of trusted men knew that—and none of them were knights. Only those who *needed* to know it knew that the hangings were so contrived as to conceal narrow coverts in the walls, and to mask numerous holes through which inquisitive eyes might peer and inquisitive ears catch whispers.

Because Merlin was its architect, the walls of Camelot had been built for the convenience of spies—Arthur's spies, ostensibly, but actually Merlin's own. Even I did not know *every* hidden nook and cranny, but I knew more than any other man save for the wizard himself; as the power of Merlin's own eyes and ears had declined, the burden of their work had been transferred to me. Merlin trusted me, precisely because of the fact that I was not his apprentice in magic.

I knew, while Sir Kay was still installing Morgan le Fay and her retinue in the southern tower, that I was in for a busy night. The only thing I did not know was where my master would send me to hide in the expectation that I might hear something to his advantage. Even he took time to decide, casting the knucklebones in search of sound advice.

"Arthur will want me to raise the shade of the messenger," he muttered, "and he'll want us tightly sealed away while I do it. The mice are sure to play, but which will play together first? Morgan will not wait for anyone to come to her; if Arthur will not receive her—and he shall not while I can contrive to keep them apart—she'll go to Taliesin. That will clear the way for the abbot to make mischief with the Saxons, but they have no common cause but hatred of others, and I doubt that they have secrets still in store. You must go west, Amory, and soon—while the bards are still at table. The harpers will play afterward, but Taliesin will excuse himself. You must be waiting for him."

When shall I have a chance to eat? I wanted to know. *And how shall I avoid the eyes of Taliesin's watchful servants?* I knew better than to ask; those were problems for my own ingenuity. "Yes, master," I said—and set about my work with customary cleverness. Suffice it to say that my stomach was by no means empty, nor my bladder overfull, when I positioned myself to hear whatever passed between the faery and the bard. I could see them, too, albeit from behind a blur of needle-pricked canvas.

Taliesin must have been handsome in his youth, but he was past his prime when I knew him. He had a skin the color of monks' parchment and wrinkles like the surface of a tree stump whose softer wood has rotted in the rain—but his dark eyes were not without a certain gleam, and he still had his wits about him. Morgan's skin, on the other hand, had the porcelain quality of the Unchanging. Although her hair was as raven-dark as the bard's had been before the gray set in, her complexion was far whiter. Her lips were redder than a human's, and her teeth untouchable by decay—which gave her mouth an uncanny beauty—but when I first looked at her, I thought that her eyes seemed unexpectedly soft. It was not until later that I discovered how disconcerting a woman's eyes can be when their color changes with her moods, from gold to green and then to purple—and even, at the extreme, to blazing crimson.

"Someone knew you were coming," Taliesin told her, "else they'd not have taken the trouble to fake that elf-bolt—assuming that it *was* a fake."

"It was no man of mine who fired it," she told him. "Did *you* not know that I would come, Taliesin? They say you have a little of the sight, inherited from some pixie ancestor."

"I assure you that I did not expect you, my lady," the bard replied.

"*My lady!*" she echoed, although she did not seem to be taking undue offense "I am *Your Majesty* now, it seems. Ever since Arthur claimed me for his kin, I have had to be reckoned a queen by his loyal subjects—but he will not condescend to see me, even so."

"Kingship and empire are human notions," Taliesin replied. "Nor are they universal even among men. My people reckon wise men more significant than kings and wisewomen more significant than queens. You know that I mean no insult."

"The Romans called your wise men priests," Morgan observed, speculatively. "I dare say this *abbot* of whom I have heard rumor would agree with your estimation of the insignificance of kings."

"The Romans never understood Druidic lore," Taliesin countered. "In any case, what the Romans meant by the word *priest* is not what this new breed means, even though its bishops reckon themselves heirs of Rome and renewers of the Imperial quest. Have you come to me merely to debate fine shades of meaning, or have you something else to say?"

"I came to ask your advice," she said. "I did not know that there would be Saxons here, or Druids either. I came because I heard that this new Church had set its heart on Arthur's capture, in spite of the fact that he once pledged himself to another faith. I dare say that you came for much the same reasons, although I am merely curious, while you must feel endangered."

"*Are* you merely curious?" Taliesin asked. "Your folk and mine have had our differences in the past, but we have a common enemy now, and perhaps two. I hoped that you had called upon me to ask me what progress our common enemies have made, and to confer with me as to how we might put a stop to that progress."

Taliesin did not have the air of a man who would readily trust an unhuman being like Morgan, but he did seem sincere in his hope.

"Tell me, then," the faery said, without confirming or denying that she thought of the Church and the Saxons as enemies.

"I daresay that you have your own means of measuring the situation," said the bard, "but for what it is worth, the Church seems to be making far more progress than I would have ever thought possible. Five years ago I would never have believed that Arthur might be ripe for conversion—but I daresay that the aristocrats of Rome thought the same about Constantine. The abbot offers Arthur the same seduction that his counterpart must have offered the Emperor of Rome: the chance to bind a crumbling community with chains of faith and a set of virtuous ideals. In fact, the abbot offers Arthur more than that, for Constantine's converters could not offer his reunited empire safety from the barbarians, while the Abbot of Glastonbury is claiming that if Arthur embraces Christ, the Saxons will very likely follow, and Britain will be saved from devastation—assuming, that is, that *Britain* can be redefined to exclude the true Britons."

"I am content to let that judgment pass unchallenged," Morgan replied, meaning his judgment that the Welsh alone could be reckoned the *true* Britons, amid the wreckage of stranded immigrants that Rome had left behind. I wondered whether her reckoning might be that there were no true Britons at all among *human* folk.

"Will you tell me your understanding, in exchange for mine?" Taliesin asked.

"Your judgment is likely to be better than mine," the fay acknowledged negligently, "but for what it may be worth, it seems to me that Arthur has always held fast to the belief that *he* is Britain, and the Round Table its one and only symbol. Were he to convert, then *Britain* would be Christian in the eyes of all believers in Camelot—and everything un-Christian would become un-British by definition. Arthur is a king of kings and a maker of peace; perhaps he would be perfectly ready to forget that he *became* a high king and peacemaker by honoring very different symbols and professing very different beliefs. The question which intrigues me is: Why would Merlin allow it?"

"With all due respect, my lady,' Taliesin said, "the *real* question is: Could Merlin prevent it if he would? You might have taught him well, but I fear that he is no longer able to apply his learning. I think the faery folk sometimes forget that men grow old, and underestimate the changes that age brings."

Morgan made a show of taking due note of the criticism—but what she said was not really an answer. "I think men grown old sometimes underestimate one another," she opined. "If Merlin seems feeble, he may have his reasons for so seeming. I can hardly believe that Arthur would do anything that Merlin does not allow, and I can hardly believe that Merlin would allow the Church to extend its empire to the British isles. But why, then, is the abbot here? Why is my arrival preceded by a rider seemingly killed by elf-shot, crying danger? Why does it seem to me that Merlin, child of my Art, is bent on my betrayal?"

"Mine, too," said Taliesin soberly. "I played my own part in the making of Camelot; if Merlin really is responsible for throwing Arthur into the waiting arms of the Church, his treason is against Druidic lore as well as faery magic. If there is a why, I certainly cannot fathom it; I have to believe that Merlin has grown feeble, or that Arthur has become too vain to take advice. Arthur was a better man when he had fewer knights, and when those he had were far less eager to increase their reflected glory by feeding his grandiosity. Lancelot has not been good for Camelot, no matter what the ladies of the court may think."

"I see," said Morgan thoughtfully. "A man might

listen to his half sister, if his other advisers had grown feeble—but not if he himself has grown deaf."

"No one truly believes that you and Arthur had the same father," Taliesin told her bluntly. "In fact, no one believes any longer that it matters a jot who Arthur's true father was. Before he was the king, legitimacy might have been an important issue, so Merlin told a tale which appointed Uther Pendragon his progenitor. The fact had to be established somehow, no matter how ridiculous the story by which it was claimed and supposedly proved. Now that he has been king for as long as common men care to remember, such tales can be recognized as the convenient myths they were and dismissed with a shrug—and the fancy which made Uther Pendragon *your* father was even more ridiculous. You have no effective claim on Arthur, my lady, no matter what lies he was once prepared to tell or courtesies to offer in order to bind you to his cause. He might well continue to deny you an audience, if it suits him to do so."

That was when I saw her eyes change color for the first time, from gold to vivid green. I had no idea then how much alteration they still had in reserve.

"Does he think it suits him?" she murmured. "Well, I suppose it is the nature of a man to think only of his future, and to forget his past—but I am not human, and I see things differently. And I have a claim on Merlin, have I not?"

I watched Taliesin then, to see how he would respond to this. The faery had come to him as a potential ally, but *he* was not unhuman; no matter how powerfully he might hate the Church, he was as human as the abbot, as human as Arthur, as merely human as my poor eavesdropping self . . . and Morgan had no claim on *him.*

"I know how differently you see things, my lady," the bard said. "I, too, have spent a *little* time in Faerie, though not with you."

"So I have heard," she answered softly, although it was not really an answer at all. "Like Merlin, however, you have only seen the borderlands of Faerie—never its golden heartland."

"I know that too, my lady," he said. Although I was looking directly at his dark and faded eyes, I could not judge the depth of his bitterness. I wondered what gifts he had been privileged to bring into the world, and how he had used them after his return.

I escaped the bard's chamber as cleverly as I had entered it, and ran light-footed down one secret stair and up another. As I had been trained to do—without, alas, the aid of any magic—I repeated to my master word for word what had passed between Morgan and the bard. I knew that he would not be pleased by what he heard, but I risked his ire anyway by asking how his business with the king had gone.

He cuffed me about the head. "Why?" He demanded. "Do you also think that I am feeble? Do you think me so poor a necromancer that I could not summon the spirit of the messenger to complete his task?"

An excellent memory for recitation does not necessarily extend to thought and feeling. I know now that Merlin's necromancy was all pretense, and that it was his own artifice and cunning that supplied the voices which possessed him with whatever wisdom they displayed. I *think* I knew it then, but I am not certain. I was certainly in awe of his authentic abilities, but I had no better understanding than Taliesin of why a man like him would be prepared to countenance a union between Arthur and a Church whose dogmas reckoned *all* magicians and Druids to be instruments of evil, ripe for extirpation.

"I do not doubt you for a moment," I assured him. "I only thought that I would be better placed to spy on Morgan and Taliesin if I knew which one of them—or which third party—was responsible for the danger of which the messenger came to warn us, and which of them hoped to prevent the message reaching the king."

"None of your business," Merlin snapped. "You've work to do before you go to your bed—get on with it."

Would I have thought better of him, I wonder, if he had told me the truth? Might I have remained loyal, if he had confided in me? I think not.

I left the room carelessly, never thinking that someone might be lying in wait in one of my own little coverts—no less lying in wait *for me*. Even had I been on my guard, though, I probably would not have seen him as I passed him by, nor would I have heard his footfalls as he followed me. He had advantages I had never had.

My pursuer had the good sense to wait until I had discharged my load at the cesspit before making his move—it is always unwise to attack a man who might wield a bucket of shit against you, no matter how accomplished you are in the martial arts. He came up behind me silently and clamped a cloth over my mouth. I did not even know enough to hold my breath, let alone how to defend myself with only a pair of empty pails for arms and armor.

As things were, I gasped in alarm, and promptly felt my nostrils flooded with something sickly-sweet. I tumbled on the instant into a whirling dizziness that led to oblivion.

When I awoke, I was on the less familiar side of a sumptuous array of tapestries and silks—and could not help but wonder whether someone else might be behind them, looking in.

Morgan le Fay was seated on a stool, looking down at me. Her eyes were golden, and seemed amused. I managed to sit up, but could not immediately stand; I moved instead to a kneeling position, and bowed my head as a commoner was obliged to do in the presence of a queen—even a queen appointed by incredible rumor.

"What is your name, little spy?" she said, reassuring me that even though her magic had more honest power than Merlin's, she still did not know *everything* without having to ask.

"Amory, Your Majesty," I told her, not bothering to deny that I was a little spy. I was sure that she had not caught sight of me in Taliesin's room, but I knew that any natural or supernatural means she might have employed to spy on Merlin would have told her clearly enough what I had done when I had reported my findings to him.

"Don't call me '*Your Majesty*,' " She instructed me sharply. "I never was a queen, and should never have consented to Merlin's trick."

"Yes, my lady," I said, already wondering how a faery could be misled by a mere mortal's trick—and how, if it could be done, I might do it myself.

"As far as anyone knows," she said, "you have disappeared. No one saw you taken, or carried here, and no one is hiding behind those tapestries you eyed with such suspicion a moment ago. If you are never seen again, no one will be any the wiser. I could kill you now, or take you to Avalon and send you back a fortnight older to find that a hundred years had passed. No one here would know, and *no one here would care.* Merlin might guess, but even he could never be certain that you had not been waylaid by the Druids or the Saxons, or had not simply thrown his stinking buckets into the pit and fled his unkind care. Do you understand me?"

"Yes, my lady," I repeated.

"Do you further understand," she said, "that I have a vial of serum close at hand which could compel you to speak the truth, once for every drop I cared to place upon your tongue? Do you understand that if I thought it too precious to waste on a cur like you I could take your newly-fallen balls in my own delicate hand and make you scream in agony until you begged me to let you tell me everything you know—and that I would not hesitate to do it, if I thought it might amuse me?"

"Yes, my lady," I said yet again, wishing that it were a lie.

"Good. Taliesin is a better man than any I know—although I was foolish enough once to think Merlin better still—but Taliesin does not know what is happening here, or why. Absurd as it may seem, little spy, you may be a better judge than he. Unlike Taliesin, I am not frightened by what is happening here, because I have nothing to fear—*but I want to know.* I have been moving in one direction, and it may now be desirable for me to move in another. In truth, it makes very little difference to me whether I go this way or that, but I will not consent to be seduced by promises one minute and set aside the next. I will not take insult lightly, whether the insult is aimed by Merlin or Arthur or any other man. Has Merlin tried to teach you magic, Amory?"

"No, my lady. I am his servant, not his apprentice."

"Are you glad of that, or resentful?"

That question surprised more than anything else she had said, and I actually looked up to meet her golden gaze. "How could I be glad, my lady?" I asked, revealing more than a more straightforward answer would have done.

"Most humans fear magic," Morgan told me, "and because they fear it, they learn to hate it. Of those who have a glimmer of the sight, six out of seven begin by counting it a gift but six out of seven end by counting it a curse. When Merlin was in Faerie, I gave him more than a glimmer. Taliesin, it is said, had sight enough before his own sojourn there to know that he ought not to ask for more. Has Merlin told you that he would be doing you a terrible wrong were he to teach you any magic?"

"Yes, my lady," I said again.

"But you do not believe it?"

"No, my lady."

She leaned forward then, commanding me with the

gesture to look up at her again, and to measure the intensity of her yellowing eyes.

"The real question, Amory, is: Does *he* believe it?"

Her eyes were measuring my cleverness, not my honesty. She wanted to know whether I understood the implications of the question; if I had not, the truthfulness of my answer would have been worthless. Fortunately, I did understand. She wanted to know whether Merlin had grown feeble because he had begun to regret and resent his own gifts. She wanted to know whether Merlin might be looking to the Abbot of Glastonbury to relieve him of an imagined curse.

"No, my lady," I said with perfect honesty. "He does not."

Her eyes were emerald now, and I had begun to comprehend what their changing meant. If Merlin were not intent on getting rid of his magic powers, his seeming feebleness had to be a stratagem, and Arthur's refusal to see her might still be Merlin's stubbornness rather than his own. She probably did not know at that moment that Merlin had put about the rumor that she had learned her magic from him rather than the other way around, nor that the majority of Arthur's subjects were more than ready to believe it. She had not yet begun to realize the true extent of Merlin's ambition. Nor had I—but as I knelt before her, quailing beneath the wonderful fury of those magnificent eyes, I knew how absurd it was to think that Merlin had been the master and she the pupil.

She reached out to me with her delicate hand—the

hand with which she had threatened to torture me—
and touched me gently on the shoulder.

"What is happening here, Amory?" she asked.
"How much of what Taliesin told me is true?"

It did not occur to me to lie, but not because of
the threat of torture. It did not even occur to me to
plead ignorance, although that would have been
more honest than claiming authoritative knowledge
of the gleanings of my eavesdropping. I wanted to
impress her. I wanted her to think me wise. I wanted
her to take me to Faerie with her, even though she
might return me after a matter of hours to a world
far older than the one I knew.

"Taliesin is right, my lady," I told her, trying with
all my might to speak as a grown man might speak,
with all the wisdom innate in all the words I had
learned as Merlin's eavesdropper. "Times have certainly changed, although I am not old enough to remember any others. Whatever pact Merlin made with
the Druids and the faery folk in order to secure Arthur as King of All Britain has served its purpose.
His knights are supposed to be invincible, but they
cannot defend the isles against the Saxon host.

"The Saxon invaders believe that they need not
fight the whole of Britain all at once—that its internal
stresses make Arthur's kingdom of kingdoms very
fragile. They think that they have only to be patient,
while the seeds of dissent which have festered since
Arthur took the throne grow into terrible quarrels.
Some, at least, of Arthur's advisers believe what the
Christians tell him: that the only way to stop the
Saxons obliterating everything he has built is to com-
mit himself to their Empire of Faith—and then to

work with the utmost zeal for the similar conversion of the Saxons. The abbot is very fond of saying that Britain can only survive within Christendom, and that the idea of Britain can only become truly meaningful within the Christian faith. The Druids cannot accept that, of course, but the Romans exposed *their* impotence in the face of military might and no one has forgotten it.

"Taliesin has told Arthur that Christianity did not save Rome from Germanic invaders, but the abbot insists that if a man he calls Julian the Apostate had not betrayed his forebears and weakened the Romans' empire from within, the Vandals would never have reached Rome. Arthur cannot judge the truth of such disputes—but the mere fact that the abbot has such an intimate knowledge of things which happened so far away lends authority to his claims."

"What a busy spy you have been!" Morgan said. She said it sarcastically, but I was delighted nevertheless. Her eyes were still fixed on my face, but she relaxed slightly as she asked: "Again, the real question is: Does Merlin believe it?"

"I do not know what Merlin believes," I told her. "I know that he spends long hours with a mirror of black glass, trying with all his might to see the future—but he will not tell me what he sees, if he sees anything at all."

She softened then—or at least I thought so. She looked away, saying, "Don't doubt that he can see, Amory. I taught him well enough to see—but I thought I taught him well enough to know the treachery in what he sees, and to know that the security of a fixed future must be *made*, not found."

I could not say anything to that.

"Get up, Amory," she said, after a moment's pause. "I am not a queen; you may stand before me. Shall I tell you what I know of these matters, as one interested person to another?"

I must have looked thunderstruck, but I struggled to my feet regardless. "Don't worry, little spy," she said. "I ask for no pledge of secrecy. I will say nothing you cannot repeat to Merlin, if that is your will."

If that is your will. She said that to me! It did not occur to me to think that she was a faery, who cared not a jot for such ranks as king and commoner— all the more especially given what she knew about Arthur—and that she had probably judged me far better than I was able to judge myself. I only knew that she had spoken of *my will* as the arbiter of what I said to Merlin.

"I would be glad to know what your opinion is, my lady," I told her, very truthfully indeed.

"Political matters are of little interest to me," she said, "for reasons you may someday come to understand, but I am not so foolish that they are beyond my comprehension. I know well enough that before Arthur appeared on the scene, Britain was in a sorry state of chaos. The order that the Romans created fell apart when their legions left, although the British-born citizens they left behind tried with all their might to preserve it. Things had gone from bad to worse, in the eyes of those who valued what Rome had briefly brought. A king of kings was the last hope of the few who still remembered, and they were determined to create one at whatever cost—even at the cost of appointing Merlin their mastermind. It was he who persuaded them that the only king who could reign over kings was one found without the ranks of existing royal families, whose badges of office were mystical. It was he who devised the sword in the stone and the fiction of Arthur's strange conception. It was he who invented the notion that the idea of Britain existed even in Faerie, and that the fairy folk had some interest in its preservation. It was he who conceived the daring notion of making Arthur kin to *me*.

"I could see why Merlin thought it wise to invest his boy-king with an authority beyond that which petty kings had ever thought to claim; it amused me to lend my consent. I was curious, and I had liked Merlin as well as any other human I had seduced. I knew that he would grow old like all the rest, but the Unchanging are always looking for echoes of their own nature in those they love. I thought Merlin capable of greater loyalty than others of his kind— though I can see why he might think it advisable to substitute the authority of Christendom for the authority of Faerie. A nonexistent God is a more flexible instrument than a world which actually touches the world of men, however obliquely and infrequently. Perhaps, knowing how little I care for old men and political matters, Merlin thought that I would not care about his infidelity."

"Do you, my lady?"

That, alas, was an impertinence too far. I saw a fleck of green flash briefly in her gaze before it settled once again into golden tranquillity.

"If I were to offer you a gift," she said, ignoring my question, "would you do a little spying for me?"

"Yes, my lady," I said.

"Would you spy on *Merlin* for me?"

I did not hesitate. "Yes, my lady." I did not ask what the proffered gift might be; I thought the reward was likely to be greater if I trusted her honor in the matter.

"Good," she said. "I am a better spy-master than Merlin; I will give you two magics to help you remain undetected." She crossed the room to a trunk which contained the bulk of her luggage and rummaged beneath the cloaks and underclothes as any human woman might have done, eventually producing a sealed vial of clear liquid and a gray cap of the soft indoor kind.

"The cap will not grant you invisibility," she said, "but it will make you unobtrusive even to Merlin's heightened senses. The vial is the truth serum with which I threatened you earlier. It is rare and precious, even among my kind, and its power will be exhausted much more rapidly than anyone could wish. I would not want a single drop to be wasted—but I want to know what compact *really* exists between Merlin and the Church. When your master visits the eastern tower tomorrow, you must prime him with this dose—and you must listen very attentively to every word he speaks thereafter."

Like Merlin, she was content to leave the vulgar sleight of hand to my own contrivance.

"Thank you, my lady," I said, as she gave me the two magics.

"The cap is yours to keep," she said, "but the gift I promised you is still to come." She began to turn away then, but she turned back as if struck by an afterthought.

"You have never seen a faery before, have you, Amory?" she asked, as I bathed once again in the light of her regard.

"No, my lady," I replied.

"Six men out of seven would reckon this meeting a curse rather than a blessing," she said, "but I believe that you are the seventh. I believe, too, that you know full well that if I had known of a messenger who carried news injurious to my cause, I would not have hesitated a moment before slaying him—and would *never* have allowed him to reach the drawbridge of Camelot with an elf-bolt in his back."

"Yes, my lady," I said—although, for once, the words did not seem answer enough.

"In that case," said Morgan le Fay. "Tell me who shot the messenger, and what his message was."

"I think he delivered his message, my lady," I told her, keeping my voice quite steady. "His purpose was to say that there was a message, and then to die of elf-shot, thus proclaiming loudly that there was a secret which Faerie would kill to keep. The Churchmen wanted that message sent, but they could not contrive the precise manner of its delivery without magical assistance. The Druids would not help them, and the Saxons could not—which leaves my master Merlin, unless there are magicians hereabouts of whom I know nothing."

I would have given anything for the smile which that answer won. Her lips were so red and her teeth were so white: unhuman in their redness and whiteness alike. I would have given anything to win another smile like it, and she knew it. It was the greatest power she had, and the only one which did not diminish with use.

I knew that it would not be easy to make sure that Merlin drank the truth serum, and that it would be more difficult still to make sure that he would drink it at the right time. If each drop could only generate a single truth, I had to be careful not to waste it in the production of platitudes and trivia. Fortunately, my master liked a little wine with his early bread, and I was careful to make sure that he had salt and spice enough to generate a thirst as soon as he had to expend any considerable effort.

The task before me became doubly difficult when Merlin—who woke, as usual, in a foul temper—told me that I must be off to the king's own chamber, to listen in on all his conversations.

"Morgan will come to me before she tries to go to him again," he growled. "I shall not be here, but I cannot avoid her forever if I hope to keep her from Arthur indefinitely. In the meantime, Taliesin and his surly friends will be knocking on Arthur's door to make one last desperate plea, and the idiot will probably think himself honor bound to hear them out. The Saxons will have to wait for his summons, but if he talks to Taliesin, he'll probably think it necessary to soothe their fears immediately afterward. I need to know exactly what half-promises they winkle out of him."

I assured him that I would be in position as soon as I had taken care of my master's ordinary needs and seen him safely to whenever he intended to be when Morgan le Fay came looking for him.

"I'm not incapable of walking," he assured me waspishly.

"Far from it," I agreed, "but if, for instance, you were to take yourself off to the one place Morgan would be certain not to look for you—by which I mean the eastern tower—you might be grateful for certain preparations I might make."

"What preparations?" he demanded.

"The Abbot of Glastonbury has an attic room like yours," I told him, although he must have known that. "Whether it brings him closer to heaven or merely separates him more completely from the earth I don't know, but I do know—having spied on him at your request—that he burns incense incessantly. His abbey must be far less crowded than any castle, else he could not be so sensitive to common odors, and he must be so long inured to the effects of holy smoke that he does not know how offensive un-Christian nostrils might find it. If you will pardon me, sir, I would be happier in my own mind if you would let me see you up the stair and make some preparation for the defense of your palate."

By this means, I obtained an escort to the very door of the Abbot of Glastonbury's apartment. I was also able to give my master a small stone bottle to keep in his sleeve.

"Best not to offend the abbot," I said, "but you'll find that the sweet liquor will mount some defense against his noxious vapors. Take small sips at regular intervals, and try to breathe mostly through your mouth."

He slapped me behind the ear and cursed me for an interfering foster mother, but had he been determined to ignore my advice, he would only have laughed or snorted. I waited until we were halfway up the stair of the eastern tower before I slipped the gray cap upon my head, and Merlin was toiling sufficiently by then to have not noticed if it had been salmon-pink and utterly unvirtuous.

When we arrived at the abbot's rooms, the Churchman dismissed his followers, evidently thinking his privacy worth protection. He made a great fuss about finding my master a comfortable stool—and Merlin made no real objection to the fuss I made in settling him upon it, although he cuffed and cursed me in such an offhand manner that I am sure he would hardly have seen me had I not been so insistent in my helpfulness.

I was able to choose the moment of my departure with such accuracy that I could have hidden half a dozen elf-warriors as well as myself while the abbot and the magician took it for granted that I was hurrying down the stair.

I knew that I had to watch with extra vigilance, because I had to know exactly when my master sipped from the liquor I had given him—the liquor into which I had poured all but a single drop of the serum which Morgan le Fay had entrusted to my care.

"Our trick worked well enough," the abbot said, wasting no time at all in conversational preliminaries. I had already gathered, in the course of my spying, that Churchmen are not much given to conventional pleasantry. "My brothers assure me that the castle is abuzz with the rumor that Morgan le Fay killed the messenger sent to warn of her approach and her sinister intention. Every farmer within three days' ride sent produce for last evening's feast, so the rumor will be everywhere from Cornwall to Worcester within the week. No one asks, *'Who sent the messenger?'* The question on everyone's lips is *'What mischief do the faery folk intend?'* " He rubbed his hands together as he spoke; he was a little man but rather fat and very mean of spirit. His face was shaven but it looked as if it had been done with a rusty paring knife rather than a well-stropped razor.

"I am glad that you are pleased," Merlin said— but he had not taken a sip of the liquor yet, although aromatic incense *was* burning in a pot by the window.

"You must not think that this constitutes a precedent," the abbot warned. "Our opposition to black magic remains implacable—but the faery folk represent a greater evil than you. When Arthur has sent Morgan le Fay packing, you must promise to forswear the use of any power save that of prayer. You must repent all your sins if you are to be granted absolution."

"I will," said Merlin, whose throat must have been very dry indeed by now.

"Morgan le Fay *can* be sent packing, can she not?" the abbot asked, warily.

This time, Merlin took a draught of the liquor before replying. "No human can tell Morgan le Fay what to do," he said. "Neither prayer nor magic can offer any insight into her future. The advantage we have is that she does not care overmuch what happens in the world of men. If she is terribly offended by what I have done, she might exact revenge from me—but my hope is to persuade her that I have become too silly to be worth the waste of her wrath. I will remind her that she promised me an extra gift after those she had given freely, and that I asked for the use of her name in the matter of Britain, without ever swearing that I would use it honestly."

My first thought, on hearing that, was that I was a wiser man than my master ever was—but I am not so sure of that now.

"Her kind must be banished from the earth," the abbot said. "Paganism must be extinguished, root as well as branch. Druid lore must be obliterated, and we must make men forget that there ever were such things as faery folk. The One True God must stand alone in the respect and affection of His subjects; His love alone can secure the salvation of the world."

Merlin sipped again, and said: "The only way to unity and peace is through a king of kings, in the world we know and the world beyond it. If unity and peace are worth fighting for—if *Britain* is worth fighting for—the idea of Christ is now the best hope for its preservation. If the faery folk are to be removed, however, it cannot be done by banishment. We have not the power to do that. They can only remove themselves, and that must be achieved by cunning. Pleas are as empty in their ears as threats, but eternal youth confers on them a certain childishness. Far the best way to insure their absence—at least until Britain is secure—is to persuade them that the British in general deserve a punishment, and that the only punishment which fits the crime is their re-

fusal to notice us, or to maintain the fragile draw-
bridges which they sometimes lower to our common
soil. Much might be achieved by a carefully contrived
insult, and I intend to exercise all my ingenuity in
contriving one. In the meantime, I shall keep the lady
waiting and do what I can to insure that she does
not see Arthur at all."

At the time, I took all of this at face value—knowing, of course, that it had to be true. You, however,
may be wiser than I was. You may already be asking
the question I did not think to raise. *Did Merlin know
that I was listening?* It is possible, you see, that he
knew all along that Morgan would catch me spying,
judged that she would do exactly what she did, and
judged that I would do exactly what I had done. A
man who knows that he is drinking truth serum
knows that he cannot tell a lie, but he also knows
that he still retains the power to select which truths
to tell. It is possible, I now admit, that Merlin had
already contrived the first phase of his insult, and
that I was part and parcel of it.

"I prefer to trust the power of prayer and the rite
of exorcism," the abbot said loftily. I almost wished
that I had put the truth serum in wine they might
have shared—but that would have been a waste. The
mark of a truly great charlatan is that he always be-
gins to believe his own pretenses; his faith consumes
him as it consumes his converts.

"I shall be grateful for such support as your pray-
ers and rites can provide," said Merlin—who only
then paused to take another sip from his bottle. "I
shall be more grateful still if your brethren can contrive the conversion of the Saxons—and I will pro-

vide such support as I can by guiding the king's hand in the treatment and disposition of the hostages in the northern tower. I think we can reach an accommodation with them, if we concentrate all our efforts on the matter. The real danger lies in distraction. We must maintain the unity of our own folk at all costs. Talisesin's Welshmen are dispensable, given that they live in the remote west while the Saxons are advancing from the east, but if any rift were to appear in Camelot itself . . . you have no idea, my dear abbot, how difficult it is to control a company of envious knights."

"Have I not?" replied the abbot. "Do you think knights are worse than monks?"

"Certainly," said Merlin. I knew from the way that he tilted the bottle that he had drained it to the dregs, and I knew that the supply of truthfulness in his speech must be running to its equivalent end. My own mouth was growing dry by now, and the fumes of the incense made me want to sneeze, but I contrived to keep quiet while my master went on.

"Monks are bound to consider pride, envy, and anger as deadly sins," the magician observed, "and must therefore avoid their naked expression. By contrast, chivalry commands knights to defend their so-called honor at any cost, bloody violence always being their first recourse. Arthur, alas, is not merely a king above many kings but a knight above many knights. That is his strength, and also his weakness: his hardness *and* his brittleness. The idea of honor made him, but it might destroy him as easily."

"Christendom is full of knights," the abbot said, breathing very easily in spite of the rancid atmosphere, though he was sweating rather freely under the pressure of the clever conversation. "In the work of conversion, knights are almost as valuable as priests. Their notions of honor are infinitely valuable. When needs must, they kill for Christ with as great an abandon as they ever killed for pleasure, hearth, and home. And when it is necessary that they be quiet for a while, they can be sent forth in quest of the Holy Grail—which gives them something to occupy their minds, keeps them from annoying one another overmuch, and makes sure that any mischief they do is not upon their—and our—own doorstep. Arthur's problem is not that he has too many knights but that he dare not send them away while the mass of the Saxons is within a month's march. If he would only trust the Saxons to us, and fill his loyal followers with sanctified lust for the Grail, all would be well in Britain—now and forever."

"I hope you are right," said Merlin, only a little hoarsely, "and I am prepared to believe it."

Old fool! I thought. *Is your pretended feebleness of mind and body but a mask, to hide the real feebleness you dare not acknowledge to yourself?* I thought myself a very clever boy for thinking it, as I slipped away from my hiding place into the warren of passages which were my habitat. The air in the corridors was stale and soupy, but it seemed clean to my educated nostrils after the incense-laden air of the abbot's attic. I danced as I went down the steps, supremely pleased my my own wit and newfound ambition. I think I could have stood on the very rim of the cesspit and breathed in naught but the sweet odor of freedom—but my work was far from done.

*   *   *

Perhaps I should not have gone to Morgan immediately. Perhaps I should have done as Merlin had commanded and transferred myself without delay to Arthur's council chamber, there to spy upon his patient argument with Taliesin and his equally patient soothing of our Saxon guests. In my arrogance, I thought I could tell Merlin what had transpired on those occasions on the basis of my ingenuity alone—and I was desperate to show Morgan le Fay that I could be trusted: that I belonged wholeheartedly to her and would for as long as she consented to treat me kindly, even if that were forever and a day.

I now wonder whether Merlin intended me to go to Morgan, having played me for a fool—but of one thing and one thing only am I as sure now as I was then: Neither Merlin nor Morgan le Fay could have known that I had kept a single drop of the truth serum in reserve, and even if one or both of them had suspected it, neither of them could possibly have guessed what would become of it. For all their wondrous cleverness, and all the assiduousness of their studies in shadow-glass, *they could not have known the fate of that last infinitely precious and accursed drop.*

Having descended to the castle grounds, I went stealthily to the southern tower, wearing my new cap every step of the way. I might have been able to creep past Morgan's elvish guards, but that would not have been a diplomatic thing to do. As soon as I was sure that my approach would not be observed, I took my cap in my hand and declared myself. They had orders to let me pass, which did not prevent their looking down at me with open disdain. I suppose elves must take what opportunities they can to look *down* on men, for their average height is a good two inches less than ours. Arthur or Lancelot would have towered over these two like an oak above a pair of holly bushes, but I was not yet come into my full height and was still shorter than they were.

I did not kneel before the mistress of Avalon this time, although I bowed when I was first escorted into her presence. I wasted no time in telling her everything I had learned. She listened very carefully, but made no comment. She seemed slightly troubled by my news, but I know now that she was not significantly annoyed; the golden glow in her eyes remained perfectly steady.

"An insult, you say," she repeated, in a soft voice, when I had finished my tale. "He wishes to insult the faery folk, on behalf of all Britain. Having used me in the making of his dream, he wishes me to go away, never to return. Why does he not simply *ask* me?"

"He is not that kind of man, my lady," I told her. "Arthur might be, were Merlin not the power behind his throne, but Merlin never works straightly. It is not his nature."

"It *was* his nature, once upon a time," Morgan said, curling her red lips wryly.

It seemed to me that the time had come to be brave. I knew my limitations; I was short of beauty as well as short of stature, but I *was* bold. "You should not count yourself responsible for what he has become, my lady," I advised her. "You taught him magic, but he has decided how to use it. As with the dead rider at the gate whose message was mere appearance, the past that a man does not know is a mystery enclosing a void. How it is with the Unchanging I do not know, but men are all self-made."

That speech was then the greatest achievement of my life; sometimes, I think it still is. It caught and held the speculative gaze of Morgan's eyes. It intrigued her; it made me more than a convenient spy. In ironic reflection of its own import, it made me what I am today.

"Thank you, Amory," she said. "You have done well. It seems, after all, that Merlin has *not* grown feeble. Mad in some convoluted wise, perhaps, but not merely feeble. One question remains. You know what that is, of course."

It was a challenge as well as a compliment. "Has Arthur nevertheless grown vain?" I answered—correctly. "Merlin has not confided the full extent of his spidery schemes to Arthur, and it might yet be that Arthur will have none of them. Arthur is, after all, a man of honor—and he has publicly acknowledged the fiction that he is your half brother. Merlin must fear that Arthur *might* grant you an audience in spite of his advice, else he would not be going to such lengths of ingenuity to prevent it."

"I have already asked to see my dear half brother more than once," Morgan told me, "but it seems that he has been busy with affairs of state all morning and will be busy all afternoon. Your master has requested your invisible presence at all these meetings, I believe—you had best be off, lest he take up his whip to punish you for dereliction of your duty."

She issued no orders and made no requests. I was lost in delight. We had an understanding, it seemed.

It was easy enough arriving at my appointed station. As the architect of the castle, Merlin had made especially careful provision for his spies to look into the king's private council chamber; that was, after all, the very heart of the Britain he sought to make and preserve.

There was more than one listening post available to me, but I was in such a bold mood I chose the one closest to the king's chair—from where I might have extended an arm to touch his sleeve, had I wished to do it. I was behind a silken screen, on which was embroidered in wondrous detail a cavalcade of animals, headed by a lion and a unicorn. I had never seen the picture from the other side, but I knew that my peephole was the eye of the more fabulous of the two. Merlin had designed the embroidery himself, imagining the lion as Arthur and the unicorn as himself.

I had missed Taliesin and I had missed the Saxons, too. When I arrived at my station, Arthur was in the process of dismissing Sir Kay, who had been pestering him with complaints about provisions and accounts. Sir Gawain and Sir Lancelot—who must have come in with Kay—remained to bother him with different petitions.

"You must not see the lady, sire," Lancelot said, as soon as Kay had gone, evidently picking up the thread of an argument already begun. "The dead rider bears witness to her perfidy."

"I *must* see her," Arthur said. "She is my kinswoman." He was seated, but he was not sitting comfortably. Lancelot was standing some short distance away, very stiffly indeed. Only Gawain seemed wholly at peace with himself, but even he was not standing squarely before the king.

"No one believes that any longer, sire," Gawain told him gently. "The gossips say that she put about that lie in order to ally her own folk with your great cause, in the hope that men might forget centuries of mischief worked by their whim."

"Gossips have short memories," Arthur said. "Merlin was once ambitious to welcome the faery folk into the community of Britain; now, it seems, he is anxious to replace them with the Church. It is fickle—and it makes me seem fickle, too. Magicians are expected to be fickle, but kings are not."

"Merlin was once in love with Morgan le Fay, sire," Gawain reminded him. "He had been to Avalon, and probably dreamed of going back and forth throughout his life, a man of two worlds—but that is not the way of the faery folk. It is Morgan who was fickle, Your Majesty; she withheld her folk from the community of Britain, forcing Merlin to turn elsewhere for spiritual support. The Church is constant and reliable; if Merlin says that it has the strength to endure for a thousand years and more, I am prepared to believe him. Who knows more of the future than he does?"

Morgan le Fay, I answered, soundlessly—but neither Lancelot nor Arthur said so.

"You must not see her, sire," Lancelot repeated. He was not a man for subtle argument. I believed then, as I know now, that Gawain's arguments were honest and well meant. Even then I thought that Lancelot was the lesser of the two, a mere stubborn echo—but it did not even cross my mind that he might have a reason of his own for keeping Arthur and Morgan apart.

"She is a guest in my house," Arthur pointed out. "I ought to hear what she has to say. No matter how delicate my dealings are with Taliesin's Welshmen and the Saxon invaders, I must in all conscience make time for her. Merlin must be present, of course, and you also if that is your wish, but she is entitled to have her say."

"And if Merlin asks you to send her away, sire?" Gawain wanted to know. "Will you do as *he* asks?"

"I am the King," Arthur replied, "and I am the one who has acknowledged Morgan as my kinswoman. It is my obligation, not his."

"Will you at least take his advice as to what you should say?" Gawain continued, forgetting to add any kind of formal address to his inquiry. I wondered how Merlin had won Gawain so completely to his cause, given that Gawain of all men should have recognized the obligation of which Arthur spoke.

I was behind Arthur's seat and to his left, so I could barely see his face at all. But I saw his grizzled head fall a little, in evident weariness. Coming as they did in the wake of Taliesin's pleas and the anxieties of the Saxon lordlings, the persistent efforts of the two knights were wearing him down.

"Pour me some wine, Gawain." Arthur said it so gently that it was hardly a command. Gawain must have known as well as I did that the king was playing for time, but he could hardly refuse.

There was a stone jug on a table on the far side of the room, and several goblets with it. Doubtless, the Saxons had enjoyed a little of Arthur's hospitality;

Gawain had to hunt among the goblets for one that was clean. When he found it, he poured a light measure of wine into it and brought it to the king.

Arthur took a long and leisurely draught but did not drain the cup. He set it down, not quite empty, on the smaller table set to the left of his chair, immediately in front of the screen behind which I was hiding.

I knew that my chance had come to use the last drop of the truth serum which Morgan le Fay had given to me. I had reserved it for a more selfish purpose, but whatever doubts my first meeting with the faery had left in my head had been utterly banished by my second. The truth I now sought more than any other in the world was Arthur's present attitude to Merlin, and it was for Morgan that I sought to obtain that truth.

I was not sure that the cap upon my head could protect an arm reaching out from hiding, but I was reckless of any danger to myself. As soon as I was sure that Gawain and Lancelot were not looking in my direction, I slipped my hand through a gap between the silks and let the last drop fall from the vial into the king's unfinished cup.

He picked it up immediately, but did not yet drink. He was still deep in thought, or mounting that pretense in the face of pressure to decide against his own inclinations.

I willed Gawain to take up the thread of his argument again, and to phrase the question exactly as I wished it to be phrased. If only I had had the magic to make him do it!

Instead, Gawain left it to Lancelot to say, yet again:

"I beg you not to see the faery, my lord. All her kind are mischief makers, and the kingdom has troubles enough. One crack in our ranks might . . ."

He would doubtless have continued, but the door opened then and the queen came in; Lancelot immediately left off his speech.

A year or two before I had thought Guinevere the most beautiful woman in all the world, but I had begun to notice signs of age about her cheeks and eyes—even before I first laid eyes on Morgan le Fay.

"Arthur . . ." she began—but the king interrupted her.

"I am glad to see you, my darling," he said, with all apparent sincerity. "My head is buzzing. I had never thought that there could be so much intrigue in the world. I wish you could advise me, my dear, as to whether I should see my supposed kinswoman Morgan le Fay. Everyone tells me that I should not. But how can a man refuse his acknowledged sister, even if it now seems she is not really his sister at all?"

The queen was startled, as she had every right to be. The giving of advice was not her public function.

"I hardly know," she said.

"You must not see her, sire," said Lancelot again—more vehemently than before. He took a step forward, to draw attention back to himself.

I could not see Arthur's face, but I could see the queen's—and suddenly I knew, without the benefit of any magic at all, why Lancelot was so anxious that Arthur should not consult the wit and wisdom of Morgan le Fay—who was also Morgan the seer,

Morgan the discoverer, mistress of the darkest properties of good black shadow-glass.

Guinevere was no quicker of wit than Lancelot, and confusion disturbed her. I watched in fascination as she fluttered her hands, uncertain as to what to do or say. It was simply for the need to do *something* that she reached out and took the unemptied cup from the king's limp hand, and simply for the need to gain time that she lifted it absentmindedly to her lips.

"Why should I not see her, if I wish?" said Arthur. He must have been speaking to Lancelot, but his eyes—which I knew to be puzzled eyes, although I could not see their blueness—were still on Guinevere. He did love Guinevere, with all his heart, and she must have felt his gaze as a form of command, for she felt obliged to answer in the tall knight's stead even though she could not have known what answer she would give, until it was uttered.

"Because she might tell you," Guinevere said, aghast at her inability to stop herself, "that your wife loves Lancelot far better than she loves you."

And thus the dream of Britain died.

The crack of which Lancelot had spoken was made in Britain's ranks, and in Arthur's overstressed heart. And Morgan le Fay was avenged for the treachery Merlin had planned against her—*although she did not intend it.*

I thought then—and I still say now—that Morgan could not possibly have known that I would keep a drop of the serum, nor when I would use it, nor how it would go so strangely astray. Yes, she was a seer—but all she could see of the future was writ in shifting shadows in a dark glass. I have looked into the future myself, and I know what Merlin never could accept: that what we see is always treacherous. He knew, of course, that the future must be made as well as found, but he could not quite grasp that the winding snake of cause-and-effect is *always* apt to swallow its own tail.

It was not Morgan le Fay who murdered Arthur's Britain.

Chance murdered Arthur's Britain: blind, stupid, horrid chance.

It was to Merlin, not to Morgan le Fay that I ran first with the news. For once, I did not tell him *exactly* what was said, lest he find a mystery in the peculiar circumstance, although the fact would probably have been enough to distract him from the fine detail of its revelation.

When I told Merlin that Lancelot was banished and Arthur broken by his shame, my master actually became what he had until then only been pretending to be: an old, gray man.

He did not groan or tear his hair, nor did he express amazement at his failure to foresee that what he had armored so well without had in the meantime gone rotten at the core. He did not hit or slap me, but when I made as if to go, he told me to stay. I thought at first he had a task for me to perform, but he had none. It was my company he wanted, and my sympathy, too—but the desire came far too late. I was his adversary now, the betrayer of his cause, and it was in that temper that I listened to him when he brought himself to talk.

"It is not ended, Amory," he told me. "Camelot will fall, I suppose, now that the Round Table is cleft asunder, but Camelot was but the prelude to a greater dream. I know, because I have seen it in the glass, that the idea of Britain will not die. I know, because I have seen it, that Britain will flourish and grow, and will one day be monarch of the earth's oceans, holder of an empire which will span the earth from edge to edge. I know, because I have seen it, that Christendom will endure as long, and that Britain will be great because Christendom is great. All of that is predetermined, and nothing can prevent it. Only Camelot is doomed: only the compact of Arthur and Merlin, the lion and the unicorn. It is a tragedy of sorts, I suppose, that the Church will have its way without my leavening influence, but it is *my* tragedy and mine alone, not Britain's or the world's—nor even yours."

"No, master," I replied sincerely. "Not mine."

"In a way," he said, "I will have won. I have *already* won. The detail of my scheme has gone awry, but not its grander sweep. *I have made Britain.* Nothing can take that away from me, Amory. I have made Britain, and it will endure. It will not know that it was made by me, for the Church will write its history now, and will ruthlessly stamp out such rival histories as Taliesin's bards and Arthur's own minstrels might contrive. But what does that matter? No man knows how he came to be made, and if Britons of the future have no memory of me, I will be the architect of their world in spite of it. Could any man have done more than I? Could any man have done better?"

"No, master," I replied, with less sincerity than before. "No one."

Perhaps he detected the waning of my honesty. "You do not know, Amory," he assured me. "You are young enough and silly enough to think you know better than you do, but you have no idea what a task mine was. When I came back from my sojourn in Avalon, the world I had known before was dead and gone. My little brother had lain in his grave a hundred years. Everything was new and strange. All I had to call my own were the meager gifts that Morgan gave me: a little sight, a little sleight of hand, a little lore. You have no idea how parsimonious magic is, Amory, nor how rare and precious its instruments are. Virtue does not last; it evaporates like summer dew as soon as it is used. What Morgan gave me was not a lifetime's legacy—it could hardly be reckoned seven years' good luck in any ordinary man's account. But I looked at that world gone strange, Amory, and I said to myself: *This is my clay; I am its architect. I will take this world and make another. I will take the shabby wreckage of the empire that fell while I was away and build another. I will take the ruins of a province and build an empire whose heart will be close at hand. I will build Britain, and I will build it upon the foundation stone of Camelot.*

"You have no concept, stupid boy, of the enormity of that task. Taliesin has a better idea, but *he* dared not even attempt to master history. You have no concept of the ingenuity which went into my work—the ingenuity that was required to wring every last drop of effect from the magics I carried back from Avalon. There was a time when I hoped and believed that

Morgan might give me more—or if not Morgan, some other faery enchantress—but that is not the way of the faery folk. They promise much, but flatter only to deceive. The are petty, selfish, narcissistic folk who care nothing for anything within the world while their anchorage remains outside it. Do you think I would have turned to the Church had Faerie offered more? Do you think I would have conspired with the Church to blacken the name of Faerie if Faerie had offered anything at all? What I received from Faerie was my due; I owe my ancient mistress nothing. What I did with the gifts she gave me, I did by my own effort and my own design.

"No one could have done more, Amory. No one could have done better. And I *am* the architect of the world I have seen in my glass. I *am* the maker of Britain, the true father of its empire, whether the empire of Britain remembers it or not. I am the Architect of Worlds, and no one can take that away from me: not faithless Guinevere, nor fickle Morgan le Fay, nor the fat and finicky Abbot of Glastonbury. Do you hear me, Amory?"

"I hear you, master," I assured him, noting as I said it that some truths are very easy indeed to say aloud, because they really say nothing at all.

I heard him, but I did not believe him. I knew that he believed it—or, at least, was trying very hard to make himself believe it—but I could not. I was anxious to be off, anxious to give myself to Morgan le Fay, anxious that she might not want me in spite of all that I had done for her. So I heard him out, but I did not really *hear* him at all.

It is rumored that all might not have been lost even

after Lancelot's fall. They say that the battle of Camlan might have gone differently but for an unruly serpent, and that Mordred might have joined forces with Arthur in the end, to keep the Saxons at bay a little longer. Perhaps, if that had happened, the Church might have saved the day.

On the other hand, perhaps not. Merlin was gone by then, I believe, reportedly imprisoned in an oak by faery magic; I do not know whether to trust the rumor. I do know for sure that the rumor is false which said that Morgan le Fay took Arthur to Avalon to heal the wounds he sustained at Camlan. Had that happened, I would have known it, for I was, of course, in Avalon myself.

Had Morgan le Fay not taken me to Avalon, I could not be telling you this story. She kept me there longer than she had kept my master Merlin, and eventually sent me back to a world more changed than I had ever imagined possible.

I thought then that she must have loved me far more than any other man she had ever taken across the drawbridge between the worlds, but since I have grown old, I am not so sure.

Morgan gave me gifts, as she had promised. I was right to believe that they would be greater in number and power if I trusted to her honor instead of making requests. She gave me answers, too, to a number of questions which came to seem more urgent with the passing of time in Faerie.

I asked her why she and her kin bothered to extend bridges to the human world at all, and why they chose humans as lovers in preference to their own kind. She told me that it was—and presumably still is—because humans die. Love, she said, is not eternal; it flares up and quickly turns to ash. Humans, she told me, can love anyone or anything at all, for they may die with their love if their love does not die sooner. The Unchanging, by contrast, can only love mortal beings, who can be expelled from Faerie when their moment is past.

I mention this in order to explain that there is no evil in the creatures of Faerie; they are *not* mischief makers by whim alone, and their fickleness is not a kind of failure.

I have no residual complaint against Morgan le Fay. I do, however, have a complaint to lodge against Merlin—knowing, as I lodge it, that I betrayed him and that he would doubtless hold me to blame for the failure of his schemes.

Merlin was mistaken in thinking himself the Architect of Worlds, too proud by half in declaring that no one could have done more than he, or better than he, with the start that he was given when Morgan cast him out of Faerie into a world far younger than he. I dare say that if he were somehow able to see me now, he would cling hard to his opinion, saying: "What have *you* done, now that you have duplicated my experience? What have *you* made that is the equal of Britain, or the equal of Camelot, or even the equal of Taliesin's bardic order?"

"Nothing," I would have to say, "except for my own happiness and wisdom."

But that would not be all I would have to say to my erstwhile master, because I would *have* to say— would I not?—that his estimation of his own achievements was very wide of the mark. You and I know—do we not?—that it was *not* because of him that Britain came to be, or that it came to be within the embrace of Christendom. You and I know that Merlin was an old, self-deluding fool whose last speech to me was a desperate attempt to snatch some crumbs of comfort from the embers of his ambition. You and I know, by virtue of what I have confessed here, that Merlin was not an Architect of Worlds at all, and that the only edifice he did design has passed so thoroughly from history into myth that no one nowadays knows exactly where it was built.

The reality, as I learned when I let fall that last precious drop of certain truth, is that the fate of a world entire may turn upon a whim. A world may be canceled as easily as a man's ambition, by a single stroke of petty and absurd misfortune.

Chance is the Architect of Worlds: blind, stupid, horrid chance. That is why the only future we can see is uncertainly sketched by shadows in a black glass; that is why the forces which forge the future in the crucible of the past are more shadowy still, fated forever to evade even the most studious eye.

You and I know now—do we not?—that I have done no worse than any other man, including Taliesin and my onetime master Merlin.

I have seen Morgan le Fay's eyes go from gold to green, from green to purple, and—once only—from purple to red. But I have also seen her smile, and laugh, and purr with pleasure.

If Morgan le Fay had smiled at you, could you have done differently?

Chance, I insist, is the Architect of Worlds.

THE BRIDGE OF FIRE

by Mike Ashley

Mike Ashley is a leading authority on Arthurian fiction, having edited *The Pendragon Chronicles, The Camelot Chronicles, The Merlin Chronicles, The Chronicles of the Round Table,* and *The Chronicles of the Holy Grail,* in addition to writing and editing numerous other books, including *Best of British SF, Who's Who in Horror and Fantasy Fiction, The Mammoth Book of Historical Whodunits,* and *The Mammoth Book of Comic Fantasy.* He has contributed to *Locus, Twilight Zone Magazine,* and *Fantasy Tales,* among numerous other periodicals. He lives in Kent, England, and works in Local Government.

"The Bridge of Fire" picks a most unlikely hero to play detective and clear the name of Lancelot, the archetypal Knight-in-Shining-Armor, in this magical whodunit.

It was one of those days Kamelin hated. All of Camelot was buzzing with the latest success of Sir Lancelot. The story of how he had rescued Guinevere from the mysterious island of Gorre, where she had been taken by Meleagaunce, was rapidly becoming regarded as Lancelot's greatest adventure. Kamelin had at first been entranced by the story, especially the part where Lancelot had to cross a bridge of fire. But he began to resent it as all the great and the mighty at Camelot surrounded the knight and cheered his achievements while Kamelin found himself pushed into the background and ignored—once again.

No one loved Kamelin—a truth made even harsher by the fact that everyone adored his twin brother Miroet who, even now, was dining and drinking in the court in celebration of his victory at the tourney which Arthur had promptly ordered to celebrate Guinevere's homecoming. Despite the similarity of the two brothers—both were tall with long dark hair, brilliant green-gray eyes, swarthy complexions, and athletic builds—the difference between their personalities was obvious. Miroet was talkative, alert, and always ready to be involved in the latest adventure, while Kamelin was reserved, reticent, and shunned attention.

No one really understood how Kamelin had achieved his knighthood. He had, in fact, been knighted by Lancelot himself, who had witnessed Kamelin's daring rescue of a young shepherdess who, in searching for a lost lamb, had tumbled down a cliff and was hanging by her jerkin from the branch of a gnarled tree which jutted out from the sheer rock face. Without a moment's thought, Kamelin had climbed down the cliff and carried the girl to safety on his back. Kamelin was wined and dined, he was the hero of the moment. He loved every moment of it. But his subsequent actions, or lack thereof, as he avoided adventure and daring, started some at Camelot thinking that Lancelot had confused Kamelin with his brother Miroet. As the months passed, many began to speculate that Kamelin had achieved his knighthood under false pretenses, and the young man became first an object of scorn and then ridicule at the court. He often wondered why he remained, though in his heart he was forced to accept that it was safer there than anywhere else. Although he dreamed of far-off places and adventures, especially in the world of Faerie, the idea of actually setting forth made him break out in a cold sweat. Miroet had once angrily declared that Kamelin suffered from a phobia of life and some days Kamelin was forced to admit that his brother was probably right.

Kamelin walked alone through the empty corridors and rooms of Camelot. He was hoping he might find Rhun, the only real friend he had at Camelot. Rhun was the son of Urien, king of Rheged, and the brother of the great Sir Yvain. Unlike his father and brother, Rhun was not a lover of battles and quests. He was quiet and solitary, very learned, and one whom Kamelin believed was destined for the church. Rhun, though, could not make up his mind what to do and on more than one occasion, he and Kamelin had spent the small hours of the morning talking about each other's mixed-up lives and what the future might hold in store for them. On this night, however, Rhun was nowhere to be seen.

Kamelin's aimless wanderings drew him inevitably to his favorite haunt, the seldom-used library of Camelot. Library is perhaps too grand a term. It housed the books which were presented to Arthur by occasionally humbled kings, but no one had cataloged them or even placed them in any order. Merlin had once browsed through a few of them, but found none of any interest. Rhun and Kamelin, however, found them fascinating. They were full of family histories and tales of long ago—days when the world was full of dragons and elves and fairies. Kamelin had never seen any of these creatures, and though he longed to experience the supernatural he had never so much as seen a ghost. In fact, he had never even seen Merlin perform any of the magic for which the wizard was renowned and Kamelin was half-convinced that Merlin was a charlatan. The only person whom Kamelin believed capable of things wondrous was Rhun's stepmother, Morgan. He'd only seen her once, but he was convinced she was a witch. She rarely came to Camelot, though Kamelin had heard whispers that she was here now. He certainly had not seen her, but that didn't surprise him. Rhun had once told him that his mother was capable of changing shape and imitating anything she wished. Her only limitation was that she could not change her voice; as a result she seldom changed into other people, thought she frequently took on the shape of birds and beasts. But Kamelin had seen none of these feats.

The library door was already ajar, which was unusual, but Kamelin found no one inside. He always left the door open when he was there in order to get some fresh air, since none of the windows opened. He was sure he'd closed it after his last visit, but maybe he'd forgotten.

Kamelin selected one of the volumes he most enjoyed reading, *The Tale of Blaedud*, and settled down into a corner of the room by the window. He found that as he read he drowsed and while he drowsed he fancied he heard voices, but whether they were real or part of his dream, he did not know.

Have you done it? said one voice.

I have, said another, slightly deeper than the first. *I did not fail you. Now get me out of here.*

There was a noise like the rustling of wings, and then silence. After a few moments Kamelin shivered with the cold and he shifted in his window seat. In that moment he heard another strange sound, rather like a cork being pulled from a bottle. He opened his eyes briefly and thought he saw a flash of yellow, the color of mustard, disappear behind one of the book racks, and there was another pop. Then Kamelin drifted off to sleep.

"Where have you been?" Miroet scolded Kamelin as his brother emerged into the courtyard the next morning.

It was a bright, clear autumn day and Kamelin realized he had slept all night. He had been awakened by considerable noise and agitation throughout the castle, with doors slamming and knights rushing everywhere. No one had entered the library—it was a room no one thought about—but the noise was evident everywhere. Kamelin's body ached from its unforgiving stone bed and he was in sore need of a wash, a meal, and some exercise, but for the moment his attention was grabbed by all the hustle and bustle. Merlin was standing in the center of the courtyard looking as confused as ever but endeavoring to control the situation, while Arthur stood looking saddened and dejected.

"What's going on?" Kamelin asked, ignoring his brother's question.

As if in answer, Sir Kay appeared through a far

archway and strutted toward the King brandishing something in his hands.

"Here it is, my Lord," he said in his usual smug voice.

Arthur took the object and studied it for less than a second.

"Where did you find it?"

Sir Kay seemed more than happy to answer and said, in his loudest and least sincere voice, "It was in the chamber of Sir Lancelot."

Shock echoed round the courtyard, while Arthur's shoulders slumped and his head drooped.

"What have they found?" Kamelin asked his brother.

"Guinevere's wedding ring. She was not wearing it when she rose this morning. The ring has never been off her finger since the day they were married. Arthur instigated an immediate search. I'm surprised you haven't heard it."

"What was the ring doing in Lancelot's room?"

"What do you think?" Miroet answered with a smirk and a wink, elbowing Kamelin in the ribs.

"Had she given it to him as a gift for rescuing her?"

"Oh, Kamelin, why are you so thick? Why would the Queen give Lancelot her wedding ring, surely her most treasured possession, unless it was a token of her love?"

Kamelin had heard some rumors about the affection between Lancelot and Guinevere, but he had dismissed it as castle gossip. He had never witnessed anything between them, and assumed those with unseemly minds had chosen to misinterpret nothing simpler than the inevitable gratitude between a Queen and her champion.

"But why would she do something so absurd?" Kamelin asked, still puzzled by the events. "It would bring into the open any relationship that was between them and seal their fate."

"You don't think she did it deliberately, you oaf," Miroet responded with his usual contempt for his brother. "She must have removed the ring during their lovemaking and forgot to collect it when she returned to her room."

Kamelin was about to continue with his protestations of disbelief when there was further scuffling in the courtyard. Lancelot was brought into the yard held tight by Sir Agravaine and Sir Lionel.

Arthur held out the ring in the palm of his hand.

"Do you recognize this ring, Sir Lancelot?"

Lancelot nodded. "It is the wedding ring of the Queen."

"And can you explain why it was found in your chamber?"

"I have no idea, my Lord King."

Kamelin looked on in astonishment. For all that he tired of hearing about Lancelot's heroic escapades, there was no doubting his brilliance as a knight and, as he stood there now before his King—tall, proud but not defiant, his long blond hair rustling in the strong morning breeze—Kamelin felt a surge of loyalty for him. Here was the one knight who had respected Kamelin and given him his knighthood. Kamelin could not believe that Lancelot would betray his king, and certainly he would not lie. If he said he did not know how the ring came to be in his room, then that must be true.

"I ask you again, Sir Lancelot. Why was this ring found in your room?"

"My Lord King, if I knew why, I would tell you. The first I realized it was there was when Sir Agravaine accosted me a short while ago. As you will recall, my Lord, I have been involved in the search along with everyone else. If I had taken the ring, surely I would not leave it open to the gaze of anyone entering my room."

"Where was the ring found, Sir Kay?" Arthur turned to his seneschal.

"It was on a table by the side of Lancelot's bed, my Lord."

Another wave of shocked whispers echoed round the courtyard.

Arthur looked about him.

"This is not the place to conduct such an inquiry. Sir Agravaine, Sir Lionel, take Sir Lancelot to the dungeon. I shall conduct a full trial three days hence. Sir Kay, please make the necessary arrangements. Sir Lancelot . . ." Arthur raised his hand as Lionel and Agravaine began to pull Lancelot away. "Whom do you wish to represent you at your trial?"

Lancelot looked about him. He was aware that all of those who had congratulated him on his daring adventure and celebrated his success a day ago were now only too keen to keep their distance. As his gaze moved around those assembled in the courtyard, faces were cast down or looked away. Those who had always envied Lancelot now sneered at him or looked on mockingly. Did he not have a friend in the whole of Camelot?

His gaze finally settled on Kamelin. Normally the young man would hide behind his brother at moments like this, but for once Lancelot found it difficult to be sure who was who. Kamelin's face was aglow, while Miroet looked as distant as the other knights. There was something in Kamelin's expression that reminded Lancelot of the young man he had knighted two years ago, and made Lancelot decide what would otherwise be unthinkable.

"I choose Sir Kamelin."

The consternation that now echoed around the castle was louder than ever, and even Arthur looked shocked. Kamelin was not even sure he had heard right, and certainly did not know what it was he had been chosen to do.

"Are you sure, Sir Lancelot?" Arthur asked. "You want Sir Kamelin to act as your advocate?"

"I do."

"Very well." Arthur motioned to Kamelin to come across to him. Kamelin walked as in a dream, not even conscious of his disheveled clothing, his morning stubble, or his unkempt hair. He knelt before his King, wincing slightly at his aching back.

"Sir Kamelin, you have been chosen to defend Sir Lancelot at his trial to be held in the Great Court in three days time. Do you accept?"

"Yes, my Lord," Kamelin found himself saying, though he felt utterly bewildered.

"So be it. You have my permission to interview anyone at court, and undertake such actions as you need, though you may only interview the Queen in my presence. Do you understand?" The last three words were spoken with a harshness and force that made Kamelin's legs quiver and nearly emptied his bowels.

Kamelin nodded. With that Arthur dismissed those present. Kamelin found himself looking at Lancelot as he was taken away, wondering why the greatest knight in all of Christendom had selected him. The expression on Lancelot's face, which looked like one of total hopelessness, did nothing to encourage Kamelin. Around him the whispers of the knights and courtiers made Kamelin feel even more uncertain. Surely this was going to be a farce. Kamelin had no idea what he was supposed to do. He wanted only to run and hide. Suddenly he felt a pain in his bladder and he knew that he had to run somewhere. With the sound of laughter at his heels, Kamelin fled from the courtyard to the nearest midden, wishing the world would swallow him up.

It was less than an hour later, when Kamelin had emptied his bladder and his bowels, and had washed and dressed, that Rhun found him, hiding in his room. That is if one could call a windowless six-foot-by-four cellar under the stairs leading to the courtyard, a room.

Kamelin was relieved to see his friend and hugged him until they both ached with the pressure. Rhun was taller than Kamelin and a year or two older. His hair, which was short-cropped almost to the point of baldness, had been a vibrant red in his childhood, but had dulled in recent years. With his hair so short, Rhun's head looked rusty. His face was round and his eyes and mouth permanently creased from always smiling.

"Oh, Rhun, what am I to do?" Kamelin whined.

"Your duty."

"But why me?"

"Kamelin, Sir Lancelot has put his faith and trust in you, as he did two years ago. He alone of all the knights of Camelot knows the inner strength that you have. Why do you think he knighted you? You are a man of justice and fair play who will help Sir Lancelot in his hour of need."

"But, Rhun, I'm hopeless."

"By what standards do you judge yourself? Is it because you don't charge off at the slightest whim to slaughter our fellow souls? Is it because you have not undertaken quests to seek out hidden treasures or avenge misdemeanors? Kamelin, we have spoken of this many times before. You judge yourself too often by others' standards, not by your own. Because you cannot match the courage and strength of other knights, you regard yourself as a failure. But you have many facets that others lack."

"What, a weak bladder?"

"Your knowledge. You have studied for two years in that library and have a deep understanding of what motivates people and how they live. Just because you've never chosen to use that knowledge does not mean that you don't possess it. Lancelot knows you for what you are. You must not fail him."

"But what do I do?"

"Seek the truth, Kamelin."

"How do I do that?"

Rhun sighed. "By asking people. By checking the facts. By investigating."

"But I've never done that before."

"You have, Kamelin, if only in books. Now's your chance to do it in the real world. It's your golden opportunity to prove your real worth."

Kamelin looked only half convinced.

"Look, I'll help you," Rhun ventured. "Between us we'll save him."

Kamelin's face split into a broad grin and he hugged Rhun again, who returned the gesture with more than his usual affection. Then for a moment Kamelin was thoughtful.

"What is it, Kamelin?" Rhun asked, sensing his friend's concern.

"It's something you said earlier. 'You must not fail him.' "

"What about it?"

"It's reminded me of something I heard . . . or dreamed . . . last night."

Kamelin told Rhun of the whisperings he'd heard as he slumbered in the library. "Do you think they have any connection?"

"Who knows?" responded Rhun. "Bear it in mind among all the other facts. But now, don't you think you ought to talk to Lancelot."

Kamelin felt fear run through him at realizing that he had to act. He remembered when he had rescued that young shepherdess—he had not thought then, but had acted on impulse. Had he thought, he'd most certainly have done nothing. Perhaps he should act on impulse now, before his imagination got the better of him.

"Come on, Rhun. Let battle commence."

*   *   *

The meeting with Lancelot lasted longer than Kamelin had expected. The knight was relieved to see Kamelin, but not out of any great sense of security. He had started to think the young man would duck out of his responsibilities. He was puzzled to see Rhun with him, but accepted his role as Kamelin's helper. In fact, it was Rhun who asked most of the questions.

"Sir Lancelot, before we can help you we must be sure of your innocence." Rhun produced a Bible from a deep pocket in his surcoat, and placed it on the bench beside Lancelot. "Can you swear on the Bible that you did not steal Queen Guinevere's ring?"

"Of course I did not," Lancelot spat vehemently. "Why should I do such a thing?"

"You tell me," said Kamelin. "There have been rumors, so I have heard, Sir Lancelot, that your relationship with the Queen is closer than is seemly."

Lancelot bristled and Kamelin shrank back. Lancelot was no man to anger, and such a question asked outside this dungeon cell would have resulted in Lancelot cleaving Kamelin's body in twain.

"I'm sorry if my question offends, Sir Knight, but I have to ask."

"My relationship with the Queen is none of your business, Kamelin."

"But it will be the court's business three days hence. I must say I was puzzled from the outset, that if there were a relationship between the two of you, why you should openly display the ring. My brother suggested that it had been left in your room by mistake."

"Don't you think I'd've noticed it?"

"After the celebrations of last night? How much wine did you consume, Sir Lancelot? Enough to cause you and the Queen to act with abandon and for you not to notice the consequences?"

Kamelin just managed to dodge the fist that Lancelot swung at him. Rhun stepped between them.

"Violence will not resolve this matter, my lord," Rhun admonished. "Perhaps you can tell us what happened last night."

Lancelot drew back and seemed to fold into himself as he settled back onto his cell's cot. "To be honest I do not remember much. On that, Kamelin is right. The wine flowed freely. I remember the celebrations and then nothing else until I awoke this morning."

"Did you awake in your own bed?"

"Of course I did."

"And were you in your bed, dressed in your night attire?" Rhun persisted.

Lancelot paused for thought. "No, I wasn't. I was dressed as I am now and as I was last night, and was lying on top of my bed."

"So it seems you staggered back to your room last night and collapsed on the bed until awoken this morning," Kamelin sought to summarize the position.

Lancelot glared at him at the use of the words "staggered" and "collapsed" but was prepared to admit that they were probably true.

"Were you on your own?" Rhun asked.

"Of course I was."

"How do you know?"

"I may have enjoyed the wine, but I ought to know if I was sharing my bed with anyone."

"I did not mean alone in bed, my lord knight," Rhun clarified. "Were you alone when you returned to your room?"

"So far as I can remember. I left the hall with Sir Lionel who was recounting a particularly saucy tale about the nuns of the Convent of St. David, but we parted along the corridor to his room and I stagg—, uhm, strode back to my room."

"What time was that?"

"I don't remember. Late. Midnight was past."

"How then do you account for the ring being in your room?"

"As I have already said to King Arthur himself, I do not know. I do not believe it was there last night, and I was rather too bleary when I awoke this morning to notice anything." Lancelot clasped his head, which throbbed in memory of the hangover.

"That is unfortunate," Kamelin noted. "If you were too drunk to notice, then your enemies could as easily claim that the Queen spent the night with you and left the ring by mistake. How do you know that she didn't?"

"Drunk or not, Sir Kamelin, don't you think I'd know if I was screwing the Queen last night?"

Somewhat abashed, Kamelin shrunk back, but Rhun persisted in his questioning.

"Then if neither the Queen nor you placed the ring there, someone else must have done so. But who, Sir Lancelot, besides the Queen herself, has access to her ring, her rooms, and your room?"

Lancelot sat and thought and at length shook his

head. "No one, other than the King himself, and perhaps Merlin."

Rhun and Kamelin looked at each other, both too frightened to consider the implications of what Lancelot had just uttered.

"And what motive might they have to plant the ring in your room?"

"None that I can think of," Lancelot responded.

"So who hates you enough to do such a thing?"

Lancelot gave a short laugh. "At one time or another, probably everyone at Camelot!"

Having uttered these words, the gravity of his position finally dawned upon Lancelot. He looked up at the faces of Kamelin and Rhun, two young men virtually untried in the world. "What have I let you in for?" he said in deep resignation. "Kamelin, I am putting all my trust in you to help me." Lancelot paused and took a deep breath. "And in so doing I must be fair with you."

He ushered the young knight nearer, so that he could whisper in Kamelin's ear without a chance of the jailer overhearing.

"The bond between our Lady Queen and myself is strong, but I can assure you that I have remained faithful and honorable. There is nothing but the combined love of our Lord and our King between us."

Kamelin felt his heart and soul rise as he heard these words. "If that is so, my lord knight, then I shall move heaven and earth to clear your name."

As Kamelin and Rhun left Lancelot, there was a disturbance from a neighboring cell. The jailer opened the slot and shouted at the prisoner to be quiet. Passing the door, Kamelin saw a glimpse of the prisoner inside and stopped dead in his tracks. The prisoner's surcoat was of mustard yellow. He said as much to Rhun, and asked who the prisoner was. Rhun had no idea, so the two asked the jailer.

"What's it to you?" The jailer clearly had not heard of Kamelin's commission.

"I am working on behalf of the King himself, who will not look kindly on anyone who hinders my work," Kamelin responded, trying to make himself look tall but barely reaching the jailer's shoulders. The guard looked down his nose at Kamelin and grinned.

"It's the villain Meleagaunce."

"What's he doing here?"

"Ah," interjected Rhun. "Lancelot had been all prepared to execute Meleagaunce on the spot, but his father, King Bagdemagus, pleaded for his life. Lancelot agreed to hold Meleagaunce in prison for a year and then his fate would be decided."

"May I talk to him?" Kamelin asked.

"How do I know what you're scheming?" the jailer responded. "You can talk to him through the bars, so I can hear what you're saying."

The jailer opened the grille, and Kamelin looked through at Meleagaunce. Much had been made of the villainy of this man over the last year, but Kamelin saw only a young man, scarcely a year or two older than himself, of thin build but tall and wiry. He hardly looked a rival for Lancelot, and Kamelin found himself feeling sorry for the man. Meleagaunce returned his gaze but said nothing.

"Sir Meleagaunce," Kamelin began hesitantly. "I hope you are well?"

"Who are you?"

Kamelin was struck by the voice. Surely it was the same as the one he had heard in his slumber! But how could that be so if Meleagaunce had been imprisoned here?

"I am Sir Kamelin."

"Never heard of you. What do you want?"

Kamelin was a little at a loss for words. "I," he began. "I was admiring your surcoat, my lord knight, and wondered . . ." his eyes latched on the device emblazoned across the surcoat of a bridge of fire, ". . . wondered if one day I may hear your story of Lancelot's rescue of Guinevere."

Meleagaunce spat at the door, causing Kamelin to jump back. "When I tell the story it shall be before my knights in my kingdom, not a little squirt like you."

Kamelin stepped back and motioned to the jailer to throw back the grille. His opinion of Meleagaunce had rapidly changed. Before leaving, he asked the jailer when the prisoner had been brought here. He learned that Meleagaunce had been imprisoned since Lancelot's return on the eve before yesterday, and had been in the cell ever since.

As the two walked away Rhun suddenly thought of something and went back to the jailer. "Has anyone visited him?"

"Not while I've been on duty, but you'll have to ask Cornubras who guarded him during the hours of the night."

"And where is Cornubras now?"

"Asleep in the guardroom." The jailer gestured a thumb down the corridor. "I wouldn't wake him if

I were you, unless you want to be spitting out of your arse for the rest of your life."

Rhun thanked the guard and hurried back to Kamelin. The guardroom was itself guarded and neither Kamelin nor Rhun felt sufficiently strong of heart to risk entering there and waking a man of undoubted strength and assured ill-temper, so they left word to be contacted when Cornubras had awakened and hurried out of the dungeons.

Kamelin felt ill at ease about talking to Queen Guinevere and was not convinced he would learn anything, though Rhun reminded him that he did need to know when the Queen had missed the ring and whether she could support Lancelot's story.

"Later, Rhun, later," Kamelin prevaricated. "I'd rather talk to the Queen when I know as many facts as possible. If we need to substantiate Lancelot's story, why don't we talk to Sir Lionel, the last person he was with before he retired."

They found Lionel out in the practice yard matching swords with Sir Renoart. They approached cautiously. Lionel was an ill-tempered and violent man who never needed an excuse for a fight. Renoart was silent and mysterious. No one really knew his background, though he would tell tales when drunk about his adventures among the fairies. The man had once been passionate about Rhun's stepmother, Morgan, but otherwise Rhun knew little about him. Rhun was surprised to find him at Camelot, however, as Renoart usually only arrived on the key feast days and vanished for the rest of the year.

The two young men waited patiently for Lionel and Renoart to finish their practice only to be ignored as the two men shook hands and went their separate ways, though Renoart gave Kamelin a parting quizzical glance. When Kamelin called after Lionel, the knight still ignored him and Kamelin was forced to hurry after him. When he caught him by the sleeve, Lionel drew his sword and held the point tightly against Kamelin's throat.

"Keep out of my way, you runt," he spat into Kamelin's face.

"I am acting under King Arthur's authorization," Kamelin gasped, fearing that the sword would slice his Adam's apple as it throbbed in his throat.

"I don't care if you're acting under the authority of the Lord God himself."

Rhun placed a hand firmly on Lionel's shoulder, causing the knight to swing round and confront him.

"You might care if the Lord God withered your sword arm, or turned you blind, or ripped out your tongue, for taking his name in vain." As he spoke, Rhun pulled out a small cross from around his neck and held it before Lionel's eyes.

The knight pushed Rhun away from him, but thought twice about striking him. Instead he shook a fist at him. "No one threatens me, least of all a young whelp like you."

"Were you with Sir Lancelot last night?" Kamelin asked, ignoring the debacle.

"What of it?"

"We're trying to trace his movements, as you well know."

"You can wallow in his movements for all I care," Lionel chuckled.

"I believe you told him a tale about the nuns of St. David," Kamelin persisted.

Lionel continued to grin, remembering the story. "I probably did, though Lancelot's not the kind to appreciate the story. I doubt you two would either."

"Where did you last see him?"

Lionel suddenly thrust out both arms and caught Kamelin and Rhun by their collars.

"Look, you two little squirts. Don't try and cross-examine me and involve me in Lancelot's sordid little episode. We left the hall together. I began to tell Lancelot my story, but he wasn't interested and he staggered off to his room. That's it."

He thrust the two back with such force that both fell over. Wiping his hands of them, Lionel strode off toward the stables. Kamelin and Rhun helped each other up and dusted themselves down. They were more embarrassed than hurt and looked around rather shamefacedly at the knights who were laughing at them.

"Never mind," said Sir Breunor, who was crossing the yard toward the kitchens. "At least he didn't break your necks."

"Sir Breunor," began Kamelin, who had always held some affection for the ungainly old knight. "You have no reason to dislike Lancelot, do you?"

"None whatsoever. But don't expect me to help you. Lancelot's cooked his own stew this time." Breunor was never much with words. "If I were you, I'd look to his real enemies."

Breunor nodded across the yard to the stables where Lionel was joining Agravaine, who had a kestrel on his arm and was evidently readying himself for a hunt. There was no opportunity to talk to Agravaine now, and Kamelin and Rhun decided to retire to the library where they could think matters over.

"Right, what do we know?" Rhun encouraged Kamelin to consider.

"Not a lot."

"Come now. Be positive."

"If we are to believe Lancelot, we know that he went to bed alone and slept in a drunken stupor till this morning." Kamelin scratched his head. "That's it."

"What about Meleagaunce?"

"He is wearing a surcoat the same color as the one I thought I saw last night, but since he was in prison all night, I don't think that helps. Anyway, I was probably dreaming."

"What time were you here in this library?"

"About midnight. I'd had enough of the revelry and come in search of you. I couldn't find you anywhere, though. Come to think of it, Rhun, where were you last night?"

"Doing much the same as you. But I went to the chapel and prayed. Look, Kamelin, don't worry about what I was doing, I'm intrigued by this story of yours last night. Let's assume it did happen and wasn't a dream. You heard two voices. Were they in this room or outside?"

"I don't know. They were very clear, almost as if they were on the other side of one of the shelves."

"Where were you sitting?"

"Right where we are now." Kamelin held his arm out to take in the window seat and shelving.

"And where did you see this flash of yellow and hear the popping sound?"

Kamelin pointed to the end of the bookshelf. There was a small gap between it and the edge of the open door.

"I'd left the door open to keep the air fresh. It gets very musty in here."

"Was the door open when you arrived?"

"Come to think of it, it was."

"But there was no one here?"

"No. After all, it isn't a big room. You'd know if someone were here."

"Would they know you were here, tucked in this window seat and blocked off by the open door?"

"Perhaps not, but they'd hear me coming in."

"Suppose they'd been in here, came out, and then returned. They wouldn't think twice to look behind the door, and wouldn't be surprised at it being open."

Kamelin nodded in agreement. "But who were they?"

"Well, one must be Meleagaunce, if you recognize his surcoat and voice."

"But he was in his cell all night."

"We don't know that yet."

Rhun pushed back the open door and moved to the other side of the shelving. Other books and papers were piled on the floor which was otherwise covered in dust. The signs of Rhun's and Kamelin's footprints around the doorway and the shelves were very evident. There were also marks in the dust closer to the far wall.

"Did you come over here, Kamelin?"

"Not last night, but I probably have on past visits."

"This dust looks freshly disturbed."

Kamelin joined Rhun and the two peered at the prints. Most of the dust was well scuffed, but in several places there were very clear footmarks. Rhun placed his own foot alongside one and it was clear that the mark was larger than his foot by at least a finger's width. Kamelin's feet were even smaller. Another mark was almost exactly the same size as Kamelin's foot but slightly narrower and the mark was more well defined. There were no clearly distinguishable features about the foot marks, although Rhun was convinced that the larger print had some design in the center of the heel. He wondered whether it might have been a crest, although it was too smudged to be sure.

"What's also interesting," Rhun noted, "is that these marks look as if the person was standing. Whereas this mark," and he pointed to a less-clear one nearer the wall, "looks like someone was moving." To demonstrate he stamped his own foot down in the dust. Not only did he leave a clear mark, but the force of his foot caused some of the surrounding dust to shift, thus leaving a slightly larger and less clear edge.

"Well, we know they were moving, Rhun. Otherwise they'd still be standing here."

"You miss my point!" Rhun sounded exasperated. He continued looking at the marks, and followed others until these became merged with their own footsteps. "I can't be sure, but it looks to me as if you can see two sets of footprints leaving through this door, though some are blurred by our own footprints, as well as by the same set coming back through the door. I'm pretty sure by the way the prints overlap each other that the people went out first and then came back in, not the other way round. The last set of clear prints are these stationary ones. I can't be sure what happened then."

"But that doesn't make sense, Rhun. Surely whoever I saw must have come into the room first and then left. How could they have arrived at this room without leaving prints. You must have it back to front."

"Do I? Remember the evidence of your own senses. You heard voices and then saw a flash of yellow as someone came into this room, and then you heard that strange popping sound. You may have later fallen asleep, but you did not tell me you were aware of anyone leaving."

"But they must have. I haven't really given the episode much thought. I suppose I assumed whoever had come into the room had perhaps selected a book and then left."

"I wonder . . ." As Kamelin was talking, Rhun looked around the piles of books and papers, and also the shelves. "None of these books show any less dust, so I don't think anything's been taken from this pile. And there's no space on the shelves where there isn't also an accumulation of dust. So I'm fairly sure no book has been taken."

Rhun continued to look along the books and at length pulled out one. "This book is the only one without a noticeable deposit of dust on the top—*The Tale of Blaedud*. It also looks like it was replaced in a hurry, as it's jutting out from the other books. I presume this was the book *you* were reading last night."

"That's amazing, Rhun, you're right. How clever of you. Do these shelves tell you anything else?"

Rhun continued to peer along the shelves and at the books. "I'm not sure."

As he checked the shelves by the window, Rhun occasionally muttered to himself and tapped a volume, as if recognizing books he had once read. Suddenly he made a louder noise as if in triumph and pulled a large tome from the top shelf.

"Now this is interesting, Kamelin. Look: This book has been replaced upside down. It still has an accumulation of dust on the top (which is really the bottom) but very little on the real top of the book. Clearly this book had been studied at length at some stage, but not recently. It's not one I've ever read. Have you?"

Kamelin opened the book and studied the front page, which read: *The World of the Faery*. "No, I've never read this book. If I'd seen it I'd certainly have read it, as I'm fascinated by fairy legends, but I can't reach that top shelf easily."

Rhun laid the book down with its spine resting on the floor, then eased it open to see if it fell naturally at a certain place. The weight of the book did not make this easy, but after repeating the exercise five times, he was certain that it was opening more readily at a place about a third of the way into the book. Rhun checked through the headings. He stopped suddenly and read intently, with Kamelin peering over his shoulder.

"Do you read what I read?" Rhun asked after a while.

"Entrances from this world to the world of Faerie," Kamelin said in a disbelieving voice. He had read several books telling of adventures with the fairies and elves, but never a book which suggested there was a doorway between this world and theirs.

"If I understand this properly," Rhun said, "there are various locations where the barrier between our world and the land of Faerie is very thin and it is possible to transfer across provided one knows the appropriate signs and words of magic. This picture here of a stone circle, it's up on the hills south of Caer Leol in my father's kingdom. I've always felt that place had a mystical significance beyond what the priests tell us."

He turned over a few more pages. "I'm surprised this book isn't one Merlin kept for his shelves. He can't have realized its significance."

"Perhaps the book hasn't been here long, but was once kept elsewhere."

Rhun paused for a while, thinking through the implications of his words, then continued leafing through the book, searching for a section he hoped was there. "Ah, look, Kamelin. It mentions Camelot here: 'built on the site where all the lines of Faerie meet.' I wonder what that means."

Kamelin's imagination took over. "It means that Camelot is the central connection to the land of Faerie! Lines must radiate out from Camelot like the spokes of a wheel, and probably the doorways to Faerie are positioned along these lines. This may well explain how the fairy folk could shift instantaneously from one place to another by traveling magically along these lines. I wonder if Merlin knows about this?''

"I'm sure he does," Rhun responded. "But more to the point, who else knows about it? And does this have any connection with this library?''

"You mean, might this be an access to the doorway?''

"Why not?''

"Yes, but why here? No one comes here. You'd think such an access point would be in a more obvious place, such as in the courtyard or the Great Hall.''

"I don't think this was always a library, Kamelin. It became a convenient storeroom for all these books Arthur was given, but what about in the days before Arthur? It's quite possible the significance of this room has been forgotten by many, maybe even by Merlin himself. He's so old and doddery these days, I don't think he knows his way to the lavatory half the time. We've no idea how old Camelot is . . . ?''

"Oh, I have," Kamelin interjected, delighted that for once he knew something. "I read it once in one of these books. It was a castle of some kind or other way back in the time of the Romans, when the great King Cymbeline ruled the land, hundreds of years ago. It's been rebuilt and strengthened many times, but the original site is centuries old. The name Camelot means *curved light* in the old tongue.''

"Curved light . . ." Rhun mused over the phrase. "I wonder . . .''

He stood up and replaced the book on the shelves. "I think we've done almost all we can do here, though there's one more thing I'm going to try. Let's assume that there is a doorway to Faerie in this room. If so, someone might use it again fairly soon, and I'd like to know who. I have some very fine powder in my chambers which I'm going to sprinkle over the floor here by the far wall, and then we'll see what happens."

It was an hour or two later that a young boy found Rhun and Kamelin eating in the kitchen to tell them that Cornubras was awake, and if they still wanted to talk to him, they must see him now as he was about to go on an errand. They found the guard by the city gates making the final adjustments to his horse's bridle. Rhun had brought a few coins with him to help ease the man's memory, and Cornubras' expression mellowed the moment Rhun held them up.

"We won't delay you, my good man. I understand you were the guard outside Meleagaunce's cell last night."

"That is true."

"Was he there in his cell all night?"

"Of course he was! There's no way out of the cell all the time I'm on the door."

"How do you know he was always there?" Rhun asked. He held up a hand to the guard's protestations. "Did he talk or make noises?"

"Oh, he was always doing that. I doubt whether he slept all night, there was always something going on."

"Such as what?"

"He was muttering strangely and moving about. I told him to shut up or he'd be muttering through his arse." As if to demonstrate his meaning, Cornubras held a mighty fist up to Rhun's chin. Rhun carefully pushed it aside, concluding that all jailers must delight in inflicting anal locution upon their wards.

"Were there any other noises?"

"Well, there was that bloody bird squawking for some while."

"Bird? What bird?"

"A kestrel. It was his pet, I gather. Sir Agravaine brought it down to him, saying it was fretting and missed its master and asked whether it could stay in the cell for a while."

"What time was this?"

"In the middle of the watch, just about midnight."

"Excellent, Cornubras, you've been very helpful. Now, just one more thing." Rhun held up another tempting coin. "Were there any other noises shortly after you left the kestrel in the cell?"

Cornubras scratched his head for a while. "There *was* this strange swishing sound. I thought it was the straw being moved around and didn't take too much notice of it. But there was a popping sound, like this . . ." Cornubras placed his finger inside his mouth and flicked it out against his inner cheek with a pop. "Heard that a couple of times. The second time I looked in the cell to see what he was playing at, but he was sitting quietly on the bench talking to the bird as if it were some sweetheart of his. No accounting for some people." He looked up suddenly. "Now, have you finished with me? My errand is urgent."

Rhun gave Cornubras the second coin and thanked him again. "Will you be on guard again tonight?"

Cornubras nodded.

"Do you mind if we accompany you?"

Cornubras looked a little less easy. "That's not up to me. You'll have to talk to the Captain of the Guard about that."

"Of course, my good man. Have a safe journey."

As Rhun and Kamelin crossed back over the courtyard, they saw Sir Renoart watching them from near the exercise yard. He did not move as they approached, so Rhun decided to speak to him.

"Good day, Sir Renoart, I trust you are well."

"Well enough. How is your work going?"

"Well enough," Rhun responded, not sure how much to say. He looked for a while into Sir Renoart's eyes, which seemed to have a distant, faraway look. He'd never understood this man who had occasionally appeared at Rhun's childhood home in Rheged and who, for a while, seemed to have an attachment with his stepmother, Morgan, before Rhun's father, Urien, sent Renoart away. Rhun had heard some story about Renoart nearly drowning at sea and blaming Morgan for it, but he never knew the full story. He did not know whether to trust the man or not, but felt it might be worth testing. "Is there anything you know about the affair?"

"That depends on what you know."

"Look, Sir Renoart," Kamelin interjected, trying to impose what little authority he believed he had. "We are acting on behalf of the King in this matter, and if there is anything that you know, you should tell us."

Renoart turned his eyes on Kamelin and the young man became spellbound. Here were eyes that had seen more horrors than any man deserves, but had also seen wonders beyond imagining. In that instant Kamelin found himself both fearing Renoart and wishing he knew the man better. He felt as if Renoart's eyes, maybe even his mind, were boring into Kamelin's. Renoart's face suddenly relaxed and a smile cracked his otherwise dark features.

"You know of the portals of power?"

"We do," Rhun answered quickly, only half certain that they did.

"Then you know all you need to know."

Kamelin was exasperated.

"What do you mean? I don't understand you."

"You have the imagination, Kamelin. You have the knowledge, Rhun. Use them."

With that, Renoart turned on his heels and marched away, but after a few steps he stopped and looked back.

"You may need my help tonight. If you do, just call my name and shout *cymorth*. But you must pronounce my name correctly."

He smiled and went on his way.

Kamelin and Rhun watched him go with mixed feelings. His last remark and the general gist of his comments puzzled them, but they felt that they had at last found an ally. He also seemed to suggest they were near the end of their quest, but how he knew that was beyond them.

"It was almost as if he saw into our hearts and minds," Kamelin said as the two walked back to Rhun's chambers which were rather more spacious than Kamelin's. Safely ensconced in the room, they reviewed what they'd learned.

"Now let's think this through," Rhun said methodically. "And you can bring your imagination to work on this.

"The way I'm interpreting events is that Meleagaunce has discovered the secret of the portals of power, as Renoart calls them."

"I bet that's what the bridge-of-fire symbol is on his surcoat," interrupted Kamelin. "Remember that Lancelot had to cross such a bridge to reach the castle at Gorre. Maybe Meleagaunce already has access to several of these portals, though if that's the case, I wonder why he is still in his cell and hasn't escaped."

"I was wondering that, but maybe he doesn't know the right words of power or the right gestures to open the way. He'd need help in doing that."

"Agravaine," Kamelin shouted. "When he brought the kestrel to Meleagaunce, maybe there was a message hidden in the bird's hood or jesses."

"Possibly," Rhun mused, "though Meleagaunce might not get the right pronunciation from that. He'd need someone who could speak the words for him, who was almost certainly the person you heard him with."

"But that was in the library, not in his cell. He only had the bird with him. Unless . . ."

The two looked at each other in a sudden surge of inspiration.

"*Morgan.*" They spoke in unison.

"Who else?" Rhun emphasized. "Isn't she supposed to be the greatest of all shapechangers?"

"I've heard this," said Kamelin, "but never witnessed it."

"But who does?" Rhun responded. "I've known

her about as much as anyone except my father these last few years, and she keeps herself very much to herself. She's hardly likely to change into something before your very eyes, but I'm sure when she's on her own, she turns into whatever she needs to for her purposes."

The two sat quietly for a moment, comforted by what they had deduced and feeling rather smug. Then a frown creased Kamelin's face.

"Hang on, though, Rhun. Where does all this get us? We're trying to prove Lancelot's innocent of either stealing Guinevere's ring or of having had relations with her last night and the Queen leaving the ring in Lancelot's chamber. What has this to do with Meleagaunce and Morgan shifting between the cell and the library?"

"Because it was probably Meleagaunce who stole the ring and put it in Lancelot's chamber."

"But how can we prove that?"

Kamelin's question echoed in the ensuing silence. The two sat quietly for a while.

"It's a pity he wasn't doing it again tonight," Kamelin mused after some moments, "because then we could follow the chalk footprints he'd make."

"Maybe we should set a trap for him. If we could find a way of luring him to Guinevere's rooms again and could trap him there, he'd be forced into confessing."

"But why would he go there a second time? In fact, how do we know he did the first time? It could well have been Morgan who acquired the ring by changing into the form of one of Guinevere's ladies-in-waiting. She would have slipped the ring to Meleagaunce, who put it in Lancelot's chamber, probably while Sir Lionel waylaid Lancelot with his bawdy story."

"Sounds very feasible, Kamelin. But if we tell that story to Arthur or attempt to use it in Lancelot's defense without any evidence, we'll get nowhere. Meleagaunce will merely deny it."

"There is one reason why Meleagaunce would need to go again to Lancelot's room," taunted Kamelin, with a smile lighting up his face.

"What's that?"

"If he was led to believe he had left some evidence there."

"Such as what?"

"I don't know, but perhaps we ought to look. You do realize that in our investigation the one place we haven't visited is the scene of the crime itself!"

As the day had progressed, word had spread around the castle about Kamelin's and Rhun's investigations, and though most of the residents of Camelot treated them with scorn, they were nevertheless followed to Lancelot's grand apartments by a curious few. They had to ask for the help of a guard on the door to stop people coming into Lancelot's rooms.

They closed the door behind them and stepped cautiously into the room, only too aware that there might be some crucial evidence there that they might unwittingly spoil. Kamelin looked enviously about him. It was not just the sheer size of the room, but the magnificence of its furnishings that made his jaw drop. The two stood and admired them for several minutes.

"Come on, Kamelin," Rhun nudged him back into reality. "Let's check for clues thoroughly."

"Before we do," Kamelin pondered, "let's think what Meleagaunce might have done. He needed to get in and out of this room as quickly as possible, and would have made the most direct dash. Where was the ring found?"

"On the cabinet by the bed, Sir Agravaine said."

"That's not the most direct route. It's on the far side of the bed. To get there, Meleagaunce would have had to cross this beautiful soft carpet, part those draperies (assuming they were closed), mount those few steps, and move around the bed. That would be difficult to do in a hurry."

And as if to demonstrate it, Kamelin stepped forth onto the large rug by the door and promptly slipped, as the rug shifted on the highly polished marble floor.

"If he did what I just did, he'd almost certainly have stumbled."

Kamelin and Rhun carefully trod the route they imagined Meleagaunce would have taken. It was not long before Kamelin pounced on something in triumph and held it aloft.

"Look, Rhun, a buckle, and see the insignia—a bridge of fire."

Rhun clapped Kamelin on the back.

"You've done it, Kamelin. We have our proof. Now we must plan our strategy. We can't just say we found it here, because Meleagaunce will claim it was planted."

"But we have witnesses aplenty outside this door."

"No, we don't want anyone to know, otherwise

word will get back to Meleagaunce. Only the King shall learn all we know. For Meleagaunce, we can lay our trap.''

As night fell, Kamelin and Rhun went to see Cornubras, who had just taken up the watch. They had spoken to the Captain of the Watch and had permission from the highest authority to accomplish whatever they needed. They asked to see Meleagaunce in private.

Meleagaunce eyed them suspiciously as they entered his cell. There was only the one bench upon which he remained seated, and so Rhun and Kamelin stood together by the doorway. Rhun turned and spoke sternly to Cornubras to close the grille and not to listen.

''Come to admire my surcoat again?'' Meleagaunce taunted.

''In a manner of speaking,'' Kamelin responded. ''I was fascinated by the bridge of fire and wanted to know more about it.''

''Well, you won't learn its secret from me.''

''I wasn't so interested in the secret of the bridge as in the stories about it. I love the tales of adventure and knightly intrigue. There must be many adventures about the bridge.''

''Until Lancelot came along, they were all stories of knightly doom,'' Meleagaunce puffed himself up with pride. ''Gorre is a special land which has long remained distant from the world, as you well know, Rhun, since your father once laid claim to it.''

''Indeed he did, but neither he nor Yvain ever found a way to cross the barriers to the island.''

"Nor will they. With Lancelot's death, his knowledge dies with him. Only my father and I know how to pass."

"And whoever told Lancelot," Kamelin taunted.

"Aye, well, maybe no one told him. That lad is part fay himself. Perhaps he learned its secrets by his own devices."

"I've often wondered if my stepmother knew," Rhun suggested.

Meleagaunce had been gazing at the floor as his mind drifted over past deeds, but he now shot a glance directly at Rhun.

"What makes you say that?"

"I don't know. Just guessing. Who knows what Morgan knows and what she might reveal."

"Morgan is no friend of Lancelot."

"Maybe not. You know her that well, do you?"

Meleagaunce tightened his lip, which was answer enough for Rhun.

While they had been talking Kamelin had been studying Meleagaunce's footwear. "I see you have a bridge-of-fire buckle on your left boot, but not your right," Kamelin said. "Is that significant?"

Meleagaunce's hand shot down to his right boot, and he felt where the buckle was missing. He shot his feet out before him, giving Rhun enough opportunity to see that there was another bridge-of-fire device engraved into the leather in each heel.

"As you know," Meleagaunce fumbled for words, "the left side signifies the more sinister route. The buckle there is symbolic of a dark and dangerous road."

"Very clever," Kamelin commented, knowing that

Meleagaunce was lying, but admiring his quick fabrication. "Well, if you won't tell me any more about the bridge, I'll have to wait for a better opportunity."

With that, Kamelin and Rhun called for Cornubras and left the cell. Now they needed to wait. Kamelin remained with Cornubras, though hidden in the darkness, while Rhun hurried to the library. It was not long before Meleagaunce called for Cornubras and asked for his kestrel, concerned that the bird might be fretting. Cornubras was about to tell Meleagaunce where he could stuff the bird when he caught sight of Kamelin nodding in the shadows and grudgingly agreed to see what he could do. It was perhaps half an hour before Agravaine appeared with the bird and was allowed to pass it to Meleagaunce. Kamelin kept himself well hidden from Agravaine, who looked as surly and angry as ever. Kamelin wondered what deep inner resentment fired people such as Agravaine and Lionel, and how they ever became knights.

After Agravaine left, Kamelin emerged from the darkness and stood next to Cornubras, signaling him to remain silent, and listened closely at the door. He could hear a whispering which was clearly Meleagaunce, followed by another voice, in a higher register, which was speaking in a strange tongue. Cornubras was all for opening the door and entering, but Kamelin restrained him . . . for the moment. Shortly the whisperings ceased and there was a sudden swishing of air and a faint pop.

"Now," Kamelin shouted.

Cornubras unlocked the door and whisked it open. For a split second they saw the outline and image of a tall, thin woman, dressed entirely in black and with long dark hair. Then she was gone and in her place was the kestrel which immediately spread its wings and fluttered around the cell, diving at Cornubras and Kamelin until it could gain access to the door. Kamelin quickly pulled the door shut. Realizing she was trapped, Morgan was forced to speak her own magic words. It was weird to hear the woman's voice coming from the bird's beak. Cornubras had drawn his sword and was trying to strike the bird, but without success, though his actions clearly delayed Morgan. Kamelin guessed she had not spoken the words properly the first time.

The second time she got them right. Again there was the swishing of air and this time only a small pop, and she vanished. Kamelin pulled open the door and rushed out, anxious to reach his friend.

Rhun had positioned himself in a dark corner of the library behind the shelving and waited. In due course he heard, or rather sensed, a whoosh of air and a faint accompanying pop. From his position he could see nothing, but he heard someone open the door and hurry out into the corridor. Rhun waited a few moments and then emerged from his hiding place. He lit a lantern he had brought with him and peered at the floor. He was delighted to see the chalk marks in the dirt leading through the doorway and he followed them. Though they grew fainter with each step, he knew where they were going. What he was not aware of was a second whoosh of air in the room behind him and the emergence of Morgan— but she was aware of him.

It was not far to Lancelot's room, though it did

require passing along two corridors and up a flight of stairs. As on the previous night, Meleagaunce trod carefully, hugging the walls, and thus it was that Rhun gained on him more rapidly than he expected and had to douse his lantern and hang back. In the darkness he did not know that Morgan was close behind him.

Meleagaunce reached Lancelot's room. Rhun held back and observed him from round a curve in the corridor, knowing it would not be long now. Meleagaunce opened the door and entered. Rhun hurried across the corridor in time to see lights ignited in the room and Meleagaunce surrounded by knights. Arthur stepped forth from behind the wall drapes and held out Meleagaunce's shoe buckle.

"Is this what you are seeking?" he asked.

Rhun was standing in the doorway, delighted by the outcome of events, when a hand suddenly covered his mouth and he felt cold steel at his throat. A voice spoke sharply to Arthur: "If you harm Meleagaunce, my young brother, then Rhun dies."

"Morgan. I should have known you were behind this. I don't care what you do with Meleagaunce. Have him, for all I care. My relief is that this proves Lancelot's innocence."

"Believe what you may. Now release Meleagaunce."

Such was the scene that Kamelin encountered as he hurried toward Lancelot's room. He realized that once Meleagaunce was at Morgan's side, she could speak the magic words and vanish along the channels of Faerie. She could not let go of Rhun or the knights would rush her, so they would take Rhun with them, and probably kill him.

This was the moment that Renoart had somehow envisaged. In the moment's panic, Kamelin could not remember what he was supposed to say, and he knew he had to get it right the first time. With Morgan's hand over Rhun's mouth, his friend could not help. What was it Renoart had said? To make sure his name was properly pronounced and to call for help—*cymorth* in the old tongue. Rhun had pronounced the name as Renort, but perhaps that was wrong. Kamelin had never seen the name written down, so had no idea how it was spelled. How else could it be pronounced? And then he remembered. As he said the two words over in his mind he recalled the old way of pronouncing it so that the two words actually rhymed.

"*Ren-orth cy-morth,*" he said as loudly as he could.

At the sound of Kamelin's voice Morgan turned, and in that moment Renoart materialized between her and Kamelin. Morgan was sufficiently taken off guard for Rhun to wriggle free. Meleagaunce, however, was already moving through the doorway, and he caught Rhun and drew Rhun's sword. Sir Tor and Sir Dinadin, who had been closest to Meleagaunce, had moved forward to recapture him, but now they hesitated.

Everyone stood motionless except for Renoart. With a speed that defied the eye, he drew his sword. It was not a blade of steel but a blade of white fire. It dazzled those who beheld it, though Morgan had eyes that reacted to such light.

Meleagaunce retreated along the corridor still holding the sword to Rhun's throat. Renoart pointed his blade and Meleagaunce became frozen in his steps.

Even though he was several yards distant, Renoart twisted his blade, and both Meleagaunce and Rhun collapsed to the floor.

This had given Morgan time to prepare her defenses. However, Renoart held her eyes with his gaze, and she found it impossible to concentrate on the spell she was seeking to invoke. She could not escape using the faerie lines, but she could transform herself.

In the space of less than a second, the corridor was filled with fire. The heat forced Kamelin back around the curve, while Dinadin pulled Rhun into the safety of Lancelot's room. Renoart stood his ground and Morgan's fire became focused onto his blade and was channeled back along the corridor. For what seemed an eternity, an arc of living flame coruscated along the corridor. It was a bridge of fire.

Too late, Kamelin understood what Morgan had done. She had used Renoart's power to her own purpose. A cackle of laughter filled the air as a pulsation of light moved along the bridge. As it reached the midpoint, however, Renoart suddenly sliced his blade down, breaking the arc. The laughter turned into a scream, vibrating along the corridor and threatening to burst Kamelin's eardrums. Renoart continued to brandish his blade and Kamelin became aware that Renoart was spelling out certain sigils through the air, though he had no idea what they meant. The last few passes almost looked like Renoart was tying a knot. As he finished, the screaming stopped abruptly, and the fire faded.

Renoart replaced his blade in its scabbard, stepped back into the shadows, and vanished.

*   *   *

This episode was the talk of Camelot for months. Kamelin found his status had risen remarkably and everyone wanted to know how he and Rhun had established Lancelot's innocence. Only Sir Lionel and Sir Agravaine continued to treat them with contempt. Although the king severely reprimanded both knights, there was no hard proof of their part in Meleagaunce's plot. Lancelot's trial was canceled. Meleagaunce had miraculously survived the fire in the corridor, though his face was scorched by the heat. Lancelot was released and demanded trial by combat with Meleagaunce. The result was a foregone conclusion and Meleagaunce's headless body was returned to his father in Gorre.

Questions were asked about Renoart and his part in the episode, but no one knew what had become of him.

"Now there is a challenge for you and your detective skills, Kamelin," Miroet said to him a few days later. "You may have solved one mystery, but you've opened up two others?"

"Two?"

"The whereabouts of Renoart and of Morgan?"

"I'm not sure I want to know. Doesn't Merlin know?"

"Apparently not, but Arthur wants to. He wants to reward Renoart and punish Morgan."

"I suspect Morgan is where Renoart wants her, and she'll be there for as long as he wishes. I think Arthur should leave well enough alone."

But as Miroet left Kamelin sitting on a bench by the jousting yard, the young man began to wonder about Renoart and Morgan. Where were they, and would he see them again?

There was a world of Faerie out there, after all, one that he had longed to see. Maybe he would go in search of Renoart. One day.

THE FEASTING OF THE HUNGRY MAN

by Ian McDowell

Ian McDowell is the author of two Arthurian novels, *Mordred's Curse* and *Merlin's Gift*. His short fiction has appeared in *Asimov's Science Fiction*, *The Magazine of Fantasy and Science Fiction*, *Amazing Stories*, and *Deathrealm*, as well as various anthologies such as *The Pendragon Chronicles* and *Love in Vein*. Thirty-nine years old, he lives in Greensboro, North Carolina, with Oz, his huge and perpetually morose iguana.

"The Feasting of the Hungry Man" concerns one of the most famous relics of Arthurian lore, and is on its surface a simple adventure. In McDowell's hands, however, this story is also a fascinating exploration of Mordred's relationships with his father, Arthur, and his stepmother, Guinevere, and their various disparate ways of thinking and acting.

"It's not quite the Earthly Paradise, I'll grant you," said my father as we clattered down the Isca Road that ran from Camelot to the uplands of Northeast Gwent. "There's sin aplenty if you look for it, as there will always be when men come together. My soldiers carouse and whore and sometimes stick blades into each other, and if they thought they could get away with it, many would gladly abuse the local townsfolk and farmers, not to mention their wives and daughters." A buxom wall-eyed woman with green ribbons in her red hair gave us a gap-toothed grin from where she leaned against a graffiti-scratched storehouse wall, while the two equally red-haired Gaels she'd been haggling with shot Arthur awkward salutes, their regulation harness jingling as they snapped to embarrassed attention. Arthur reined in his roan gelding and nodded his head sadly at them. "I'll not order you to stop, but I'll pray for you in chapel," he said softly. "Whatever business you're about to conduct, keep it off the street and out of public view, else you'll earn more than my disapproval. You lads understand me?"

"Ave, Imperator!" said the taller of the Gaels, his embarrassment causing him to treat Arthur with more formality than was the norm among the troops. "Your Highness, we were just buying some ribbons from this woman," stammered his shorter companion, whose left earlobe looked like it had been chewed in a brawl. "For our wives, that is."

The taller man kicked him in the ankle. "Shut up, Sion. One doesn't lie to the High King. That only makes things worse."

"Are you Christians?" asked Arthur mildly. Both men nodded, the taller crossing himself. "Well, that's something. Whatever you do, say confession afterward."

"That's hypocrisy," I said when they were out of earshot, for even I had more tact than to chide my father where his men could hear. "You'd let them sin all they want, as long as they mew an insincere apology to your god afterward?"

Arthur sighed with practiced patience. "Better I

should scold them for whoring, Mordred, than have
to hang them for rape. I've tried to build a fortress
of Roman law and Christian virtue here at Camelot,
but all men are flawed, including myself. Half mea-
sures and compromises are sometimes necessary."

Time's softened you a bit, I thought. *The old Arthur
would have either sent those men back to their barracks
with an angry word or gently preached to them until his
pious homilies took all the stiffness out of their dicks.
You're more able to accept others' failings now. Maybe
your own, too. Too bad; I used to enjoy seeing you squirm
in the hair shirt you'd made of your own body.* But was
that really true? There was, perhaps, some filial part
of me that, despite past woundings, was not un-
happy to see Arthur finding a modicum of peace
with the world and with himself. Artorious Imperator, the High King of All the Britons, was a different
man from the one who recoiled from me in horror
when I first told him I was his son as well as nephew,
and I sometimes wondered if any vestigial resentment I might feel was only a balm for my guilt,
something to ease my conscience when I fucked his
wife.

But this was no day for a bramble maze of equivo-
cations. It was a glorious autumn afternoon, with
woolly clouds scudding across a deep azure sky,
tumbled by a gentle wind that smelled of crisping
leaves and fallen apple blossoms. Behind us, the
white-mortared, red-picked walls and polished slate
roofs of Camelot were washed in the kind of crisp,
clear light that I associated more with the coast than
the Severn Valley, gleaming on the gilded canopy
and glittering from the yellow clerestory windows of

the palace that Arthur had built above the foundations of the old praetorium. We passed storehouses and barracks, where more soldiers saluted us as they looked up from their dice games and cook fires, their blowsy women and near-naked children pointing and chattering as they beat laundry or fed chickens, then huts and cottages and haystacks, beyond which cornfields nestled each other in sun-dappled waves and black cattle grazed among gorse bushes and the jagged outcrop of mossy blue rocks. When we veered from the old paved thoroughfare that tracked the looping gray-green Usk, the fields and grassy meads gave way to tall heather, resplendent in its autumn purple, lit up here and there with patches of light gorse or terraced with queer pink limestone, beyond which blue-black hills and bare crags beckoned.

We rode without an escort, a testament to just how safe the southlands were these days, with the Saxons keeping to their borders since their crushing defeat at Badon twenty-two years ago, and no Irish or North British raids in over a decade. I'd not intended to go riding with Arthur when I set out for the stables after a lazy morning spent eating black bread and hard cheese in the inner courtyard, where my hangover had made me lose two successive chess games to Guinevere and, more gallingly, one to my half brother Gawain. However, when I looked up from saddling my horse to see him saddling his, I could hardly refuse the invitation to join him. Truth be told, he was not bad company.

After some more idle talk, in which I refrained from further baiting and instead kept my manner pleasant, we rode in blessed silence, our otter-lined cloaks flapping behind us as we galloped toward the beckoning bare heights, those wild uplands of Gwent whose pinnacles scraped cloud, where the barren vistas and turbulent air reminded me of my boyhood in wave-bound, storm-swept Orkney. It was a route that I doubt Arthur would have chosen for an afternoon's gallop, for he did not share my love of empty places, but he seemed content to let me lead the way, and a perverse impulse made me want to see how long he'd follow without protest, even as more and more bare stone peered through the rolling slopes that tumbled upward into sky-piercing crag and ominously darkening cloud. It was probably foolish to ride so far from help, for falling boulders and treacherous pathways don't know high lords from common peasants, but Arthur said nothing, and, if anything, his presence made me more careless than I would have been alone.

All was not yet starkness, for we crossed hollows where lush hillsides descended to buttercup meadows and salmon rivers wound their way through mountain shadow, and there was much variety in the slopes that rose up on all sides. Some were long and gentle, some sharp and rugged, some dark with trees, some green with grass, and others bare and brown. Indeed, we never made the greater heights, for with no more than a single thundercrack of warning, a storm came sweeping down from the rock-ribbed upper reaches, like something poured over giant battlements to repel our intrusion. The crag-framed sky turned from blue to a leaden gray to a muddy, roiled black in scarcely more time than it took to rein in and reluctantly suggest we turn back, and then came the sweeping gusts of rain that we stood no chance of outracing. Blotting out mountain, sky, and even the path before us, the torrent seemed a separate element, one as easy to lose yourself in as a sea fog, the kind of rain that runs round corners with the wind and even blows upward over the edges of high places. Needless to say, it soon found its clammy way up my woolen sleeves and down my neck, and despite my quickly sodden cloak I could feel it in the small of my back and even the crack of my bum. "We must find shelter," I croaked above the downpour to the dim shape that was Arthur.

Despite the forty-some years that had lined his beaky face and grayed his peppery hair, his eagle's gaze was sharper than mine. "That way," he said, and I rode after him, although I was not entirely sure which way he meant. The ground rose and I wondered if he was foolishly leading us back the upland path, but no, it was the ridge we'd previously crossed. There, just below its summit, I could make out a dim shape that could have been anything from a natural mound to a building. Fortunately, it proved to be the latter, a squat, turf-roofed stone-sided affair with a thatch-and-timber barn. Smoke curled from a roof-hole, the gray wind-torn tendrils pierced by darker spears of rain. The barn was small and partially collapsed, but provided just enough shelter for two horses, although they seemed uneasy at being led inside. There were no proper stalls, just a couple of posts to which we tied their reins. I stroked my mare's neck in the damp hay-smelling gloom while Arthur similarly calmed his gelding, then I followed him out into the torrent, for there was no door connecting the barn to the hut.

The door proved to be on the opposite side, which was damned inconvenient, and was nothing more than an opening half-covered by a rotting cowhide. Arthur attempted to knock the pommel of his sword against turf and stone, but I was too wet for such pleasantries and pushed my way past him and inside, my own sword held before me, lest I find myself unwelcome. Not that I could imagine anyone who dwelt in such a place being well-armed enough to be much of a threat. I'd lived too long amid civilized comfort and material things, you see, and had forgotten what I should have learned from my sorceress mother, that there are things more dangerous than blades.

At first, the hut seemed as empty as the barn, with straw underfoot and dripping turf and rotting timbers overhead, and smoke that burned my eyes while the wet straw tickled my nose. But no. The interior space was roughly oval, and at the far end of it, something stirred before a small pit in which a few embers burned.

"Welcome, good gentlemen, although I fear my hospitality is meager," said a dry, high voice in rusticated British.

"Pardon our intrusion, good cottager," said Arthur behind me. "We need no hospitality other than brief shelter. Indeed, we can go back to the barn if you'd prefer it. I am Arthur of Camelot, and this my son Mordred." There had been just a moment's hesitation between the words "my" and "son," although I suppose that's better than the old days, when he would

have called me "nephew" if he cared to claim any
relation at all. *Don't be so free with our names,* I
thought. *Naming gives power.* My sense of supernatural peril was not entirely atrophied, not that it was
likely to do us any good now.

"No one, not even a king, should cross a strange
threshold without a gift," continued the voice. "Camelot has rich lands and fat cattle, and is bordered by
woods full of deer and streams full of trout. It is said
that folk do not often hunger there. Have you
brought me anything to eat? I have been hungry for
a long time."

I could now better make out the form that
crouched above the coals. The matted beard indicated that he was male, despite the high voice, and
I could see eyes that glittered like the embers below
them, shadowed under a bare brow as wrinkled as
a turtle's neck and lumpy as the back of a toad. He
wore a mantle of rags, from which his arms and legs
stuck out like leathery sticks, his hands clasped over
his scabby knees like pale mating spiders. Behind the
tangled veil of his beard, his smile was very wide,
and I wondered that such a small, thin person could
have so large a mouth. Indeed, it spread even wider
as I watched, so that its corners seemed to disappear
around the back of his head. "Guests should feed
their hosts," he tittered, "and that's the truth of it,
for all that most folk claim it should be the other
way around. I have nothing to give to Camelot, and
have not asked Camelot to come here. Now, I think,
Camelot should give to me."

"We have no food with us, I am sad to say," said
Arthur gently, with no trace of offense or wariness in

his voice. "However, once the rain stops, and we've returned to Camelot, we can send some back here to you. Or you can go back with us, if you're strong enough to travel."

Christ's balls, but I dearly wanted to kick him. *I'm not taking this insulting and probably malodorous creature up behind me in the saddle*, I thought to myself. *Your offer of sending food was kind enough; there's no need to make a prideful spectacle of your generosity.*

The thin figure that crouched over the fire seemed just as amused as I was irritated. "Would you tie me to the back of your horse like a bundle of kindling?" it tittered. "Now there's a happy thought. But no, I can travel well enough, when I choose to do so. Tell me, do you dine heartily in Camelot?"

Arthur seemed to treat this as a serious question, for all the apparent mockery in the reedy voice. "The Lord has seen fit to bless us with His bounty, yes. It looks to be a good harvest."

"And may I come to your harvest feast, then?" asked the form before the fire.

"He said we would have food sent to you," I growled. "If the rain stops soon enough, we might have a wagon back here by early nightfall." That wasn't likely, actually, for I doubted that any servant or soldier we sent with provisions would quickly find this place, and wagons did not travel as swiftly in these hills as horses. Still, there was no point in saying that. "His Majesty has made you a generous offer. There's no need to be insolent. Another way to keep you from worrying about your empty belly is to relieve you of your head."

My hand was already on my sword hilt, but Arthur, who'd somehow seen it out of the corner of his eye and in the gloom, stayed it with a touch, his callused fingers gently brushing my knuckles. "Hush, Mordred, there's no need for that."

"No, Mordred, no need at all," said the huddled shape. "Especially since my head does not easily come off."

Hairs were rising on the back of my neck, for I greatly feared that we faced something more than a mad, starved peasant. I found myself wishing Arthur would pray, for while I scorned his religion I knew that it was sometimes potent against the darker powers; indeed, it had once allowed him to stand against Merlin, old Uther Pendragon's sorcerous catamite, not long after his coronation. Merlin now lived as a hermit in the Caledonian Wildwood because his magics weren't proof against Arthur's faith. But no, nothing about my father's voice or dimly perceived bearing indicated that he sensed any danger. Not that this meant much, for he'd always been able to calmly stare down death and worse.

"Arthur," I said very softly, "take care. This creature may not be what he seems."

The dim form emitted another high-pitched cackle that, rather unexpectedly, turned into something resembling a sob. "Not what I seem? Who among us is ever what he seems? Yet that is no reason for the high and mighty princeling to fear old Huarwor! How can one who has so much be frightened of one who has so little? I have nothing but my hunger, my constant hunger, my belly like an empty pit that I would fill with all the world if I could." He farted loudly in the gloom and began to rock back and forth on his haunches. "Of course you would not have such a one as me at your table. Indeed, the very sight of me would likely spoil your feast."

"That is not true," said Arthur, although more hesitantly than before. "You will be most welcome at the harvest feast. I give you my word on this. Come, and your belly will be well filled."

Huarwor, if that was the creature's name, bent over the remains of the fire, blowing on the one coal that still glowed. "Well filled? Oh, Highest of High Kings, do you think my hunger can ever be assuaged?"

"If you are indeed so hungry," said Arthur softly, "I really do think we should send you food before then. The feast is not for another month, and you don't seem to have anything to sustain yourself here." *Damn you, Arthur*, I thought, *if you again offer to take this wretch back with us, I really will kick you, I mean it.* But I needn't have worried. "Let me have soldiers bring you food. That way you will be fit for the journey, when the feasting day comes."

Huarwor daintily picked up the final glowing coal, his bony fingertips sizzling as he lifted it, and palmed it, looking at us through the oily smoke that rose from his blistering flesh. "I will be well enough till feast day. I am always well enough, even as I am always hungry. Now, I think the rain is about to stop." Saying that, he popped the coal in his wide, wide mouth and swallowed it, his thin throat pulsing like that of a snake that's downed a frog.

In the suddenly increased gloom, I couldn't tell whether or not Arthur actually crossed himself, but I heard him mutter a prayer. Indeed, I could hear much more than I could a moment ago—my own heart pounding, Arthur's even breathing, the creak of Huarwor's spindly frame and gurgle of his belly, and the rustle of straw underfoot—yes, the rain had stopped.

"We'll be going now," I said inanely.

Arthur didn't say anything, but I heard him moving after me toward the doorway. Behind us, Huarwor gurgled and shivered and tittered and made a strange sound like flints being struck together. *Can that really be the clacking of his jaws?* I thought as I gripped my sword hilt tightly.

Overhead, the clouds were breaking up, with shafts of reddish-gold light spearing the sodden hills and haloing the high crags. Our horses nickered in the half-collapsed barn, impatient to be out of there and off. Needless to say, I was, too.

"Some wizard or fairy spirit," I said to Arthur when we were well away from there, the hut out of sight behind a succession of rocky rises. "You shouldn't have told it our names. You don't want things like that knowing who you are."

"There's a lot of things in this life I shouldn't have done," said my father in a grimmer voice than I'd heard him use in a long time. "Many things, indeed. I do not, however, think that offering my name and hospitality to a starving cottager is one of them."

I snorted derisively. "What, you think that was just some half-mad hermit?"

He pulled ahead of me, looking back for a moment over his shoulder. "And why not? A conjurer's trick with hot coals doesn't mean that we were in any danger. If Huarwor shows up at the harvest feast, he will be most welcome, just as I told him. You've been

too touched by the dark world, Mordred; it's made
you start at shadows." But he sounded more like he
was trying to convince himself than me.

"The only time I've ever seen a richer feast is when
I guested in the hall of Manadan Mac Dirwnach,"
said the rotund little trader with the satisfaction of
one who'd filled more than his belly on Camelot's
bounty, although in all fairness his mercantile con-
nections in Less Britain and Greater Gaul had contributed significantly to the kingdom's wealth.

Guinevere put down her joint of mutton and used
only slightly grease-stained fingers to brush red hair
out of eyes that gleamed like emeralds in the firelight. "Really, good Brennetach, I'm not sure it's entirely polite to call your host second best, even if it's
true." The deep music of her voice took the sting out
of her words, and as the tilt of her head followed the
line of her crooked smile, I once again marveled at
the way the hearth glow limned the tiny hairs on the
swan curve of her neck and picked out the delicate
tracery of veins in the pale hollow of her throat.
Fourteen years younger than her graying and much-
weathered husband, she looked even younger still,
scarce changed from the freshly budded woman
(even then too wise and worldly to be truly called a
girl) in whose green, green eyes my heart nearly
drowned when I first saw her in the sun-dappled,
apple-scented palace courtyard, a moment now nine
years past, but with all the bite of a newly sharp-
ened blade.

Brennetach nodded, using a soggy corner of his
bread to scoop up some stewed ham hocks that were

flavored with onions and delectable chunks of jellied eel. "Ah, Manadan has the Cauldron of Plenty, which makes the fact that Arthur almost matches his generosity all the more impressive."

"The Cauldron of Plenty?" said Gwen with bemusement as she gnawed on her mutton with strong white teeth unusual even in nobility. "How did an Irish pirate chieftain come across such a thing as that?"

"His father stole it from another chieftain, whose grandfather had wrested it from the Otherworld," said Brennetach, gold and copper rings flashing on his fingers as he reached for the bowl of minced sheep's liver and porridge that a serving girl held out to him. "Which is why Manadan and his clan are no more pirates than I'm a prelate. They don't need to be, not any more, with the cauldron providing them an endless supply of good food and wine, the latter of which they can put in casks and sell to brave traders such as myself, while still having enough to keep every clansman drunk beyond a less fortunate Irishman's dreams. It's a marvel, right enough. Food cooked in it replenishes itself, so that the cauldron never seems to empty, not unless it's tipped completely over. Put a few drops of ale in it and it fills to the brim and stays filled, even though a Saxon army were to dip their cups in it. I've seen no miracles to match that, for all the blatherings of priests."

Arthur's gaze had been far away, looking past the flames that cast their glow upon his peppery hair and furrowed brow and shone on his bronze neck torque, adding an unwanted luster to it and the other

bits of metal that gleamed amid the affected plain-
ness of his well-worn wool and leather. Now, his
attention came back to the great hall and those gathered in it. "That's no greater power than that which
wore my body like a cloak at Badon, where those
poor Saxon devils fell before me like sheep. At the
end of the day there were over three hundred dead
at my hand, a figure I'd scorn at if I heard it of a
hero in a story. But I was no Bran or Cuchulain, but
an instrument of His will, shedding heathen blood
that Christian Britain might live and prosper. I felt
that same power in this very hall, when I faced down
Merlin, that poisonous ancient boy who'd once held
my father in his thrall. I could not have defied that
demon's whelp on my own, but when I became an
instrument of Divine Will he could not stand before me."

Merlin had not, by all accounts, held the late Uther
Pendragon in thrall, having instead been so smitten
with my grandfather that he would have wriggled
naked over caltrops to avoid displeasing him. But
there was no point in reminding Arthur of what he
considered the depravity of our family history.

Arthur's face then mellowed in the dancing firelight. "Ach, and now I'm sounding the pompous
braggart, aren't I? Forgive my mood; the harvest feast
is not time for such posturing. I shall do my best to
make merry."

Gwen laughed her deep laugh. "My love, you
sound like a man bracing himself to lift a heavy
weight. I'm surprised you didn't spit on your hands
and take a deep breath before declaring your inten-

tion of being happy. Is it really such an onerous burden?"

He looked at her and became, there in the softening firelight, the happy champion of my youth, whom I'd loved like a father before he or I knew he was my father. *That's how she makes me feel, too*, I thought with surprisingly little bitterness or envy. "Not any more," he said, taking her by the hand. I looked into the roaring fire and tried not to think of the smoothness of her skin.

Oak logs cracked on the open sandstone hearth that filled one end of the great hall, which was also lit by several dozen lamps and braziers. The smoke curled in ghostly serpent shapes beneath the holly-bedecked roof beams, while the fire-flung shadows danced on the blue-and-white slabs of floor stone and climbed the rich tapestries that hung on plastered walls, giving an amusingly calculating and even sinister cast to the image of a beardless Christ with a Chi-Ro monogram in his halo, an icon that by daylight looked guileless to the point of imbecility. The tapestry hid a quite lovely mosaic of Faunus, which Arthur's love for Roman craftsmanship would not let him have removed or defaced, even while his Christian faith demanded that it be covered up.

The feast was indeed sumptuous. There were trout and salmon pies; stewed otters; salads of onion, leek, and watercress; shags and shearwaters spit-roasted with their guts inside; porridges flavored with eel and turtle meat and sheep's kidneys and fat dormice; trenchers of fine bread, boars' heads, and trotters; haunches of venison; and a pair of roasted oxen, over which the poor cooks had been laboring since before yesterday morning. Outside, tents had been erected all along the Via Principalia, their pegs driven between paving stones, serving those who could not fit inside the rectangular, four-story palace, for tonight all Camelot was fed from Arthur's larder, although those not actually inside the palace got rather more porridge, leeks, and lentils and less roasted or stewed flesh than those lucky enough to dine in the great hall.

Movement caught my eye on the stairway at the other end of the hall; I wouldn't have given the dim form a second glance out on the colonnaded walkway, but it was shabby enough to look out of place descending from the upper stories. Even the lowest servant would be wearing freshly cleaned clothing tonight, so who was this hunched figure clad in a ragged mantle? Across the feasting assembly, its gaze met mine, and I found myself staring into two red eyes that burned above an impossibly wide mouth and the longest, filthiest beard I'd ever seen.

It was Huarwor, of course, scuttling sideways into the light like a hairy crab or perhaps a crippled spider. Indeed, I wondered if that's how he'd gotten into the palace, clambering up the outer wall spider-fashion, to scramble in a window and bide his time watching us from the dark landing. How thin he was, with arms and legs like sticks, and ribs showing through the rags and tangled beard. Yet he did not move like a feeble thing, but with a lurching quickness, and was halfway across the room before anyone else spied him.

"Hold, beggar, what do you here?" snapped a man-at-arms, lowering his spear. Huarwor paused and seemed about to collapse, but no, it was simply a grotesque bow.

"I am here at your King's bidding!" he said, his reedy voice somehow carrying over the din. His glittering gaze fixed on Arthur. "Do you know me, King of All the Britons? Is there no honor in your word? I have come a long way, and am very hungry."

Arthur stood, his right thumb on the hilt of the Imperial Sword of Maximus. "Of course I remember you," he said easily, "and you are indeed welcome here, for all that we prefer our guests to come in by the front door."

"Feed me, then," said Huarwor.

"Arthur, who is this person?" asked Guinevere, rising to stand beside her husband, the fire shining on her hair and through her green linen robe.

He held out his arm in front of her, as if he feared she would approach Huarwor, although the table lay between them. "Someone whom Mordred and I met when we were riding on the high moor. He sheltered us from the storm, and so I told him that he was welcome at my table."

"I am Huarwor the Hungry Man," said the gaunt and filthy creature, "and never truly welcome anywhere, for all your pretty words. But you gave me leave to come and I have come, and now I will feast and you will see why I am well and truly named." His smile widened like a chasm, spreading past his withered ears and almost bisecting his face, and as his black lips drew back the whole assembly gasped as one, for his stony gray teeth were like old flint knives dug out of some ancient mound. It did not

seem that any human mouth could hold such teeth,
not so many of them and so large.

"This is no man, my love," said Guinevere, touching Arthur's left arm with right hand and my right
wrist with her left. "I fear we have a visitor from the
Otherworld."

Arthur, unlike Gwen and myself, had never actually been to the Otherworld, and perhaps did not feel
the chill of the wind that blew from that place that
is no place. "Perhaps his unnatural air is just a trick.
If he proves a danger, he will be dealt with, but for
now he is an invited guest. Let a place be made
for him."

That last sentence was much more loudly spoken,
but Arthur had to clap his hands before anyone
obeyed. A place was cleared at the left end of the
horseshoe-shaped formation of tables and food was
brought. And so the Feasting of the Hungry Man
began.

Pardon me if I lapse into bardic solemnity, but I
haven't the language for this kind of thing. Although
I grew up in far storm-swept Orkney, I had the advantage of my mother's books, which she'd inherited
from her uncle Ambrosius, who'd owned the finest
library in Britain. Stately Seneca, Cicero with his
windy sonorities, passionate Ovid, and brittle, bawdy
Catullus (my favorite of the lot) have all given me the
words for many things, but not this, nothing like this.

He ate and ate and ate, devouring meal and meat,
marrow and bone, porridge and bread, grain and
gruel, his hard gray teeth grinding with the inexorable rhythm of millstones. We all watched in dread
fascination, none of us speaking, those who were

seated staying that way for such a timeless time that many must have pissed themselves (I know I did at one point), with only the servants moving, for despite their obvious fear they needed no prompting to pile more food before him, as if they were terrified of what he might turn his appetite upon should his bowl be left too long empty. He ate his entire weight in food as easily as a hungry child eats a sweetmeat, and then that quantity again, and again after that. We breathed to the rhythm of his chewing, and the working of his corded jaw muscled set the tempo for our hearts.

I don't know how long it took until there was no more food. The fire was out, and daylight was shining through the opaque yellow window set above the hearth. I ached all over from my long sitting, as Arthur and Guinevere and everyone else surely must have ached, but no one made so much as a groan. But now that the food had stopped coming, we looked furtively at each other, and I stretched my legs and drummed my heels on the floor stones, although I had no idea what action I might be readying myself for.

"So, your bounty is not inexhaustible," said Huarwor, who looked just as emaciated as always, despite having devoured enough food to fill a decent-sized storeroom. "Now, whatever will I dine on next?"

Arthur rose somewhat unsteadily, blinking in the morning light. The Imperial Sword of Maximus flashed from its brass scabbard, the blood-red ruby on its hilt the only jewel my father ever wore. "I rescind my welcome, Huarwor" he said in a thick but steady voice. "I invited you here because I thought you one of God's creatures. Now that I see that you are not, I order you be gone, in the name of the Creator, of His son, and of the Virgin whose image I wore on my shield at Badon." With a grace that belied both his long sit and his years, he leaped atop the table and walked down its length toward Huarwor, striding like a proud commander atop a wall. "Go now, creature, and quicker than you came. I did indeed invite you here, and so I would not destroy you while you are my guest, no matter what foul fiend you may be, but slay you I will if you don't depart."

That stirred the men-at-arms to life, and within an instant the ragged seated figure was ringed by spear-points. Feeling I should play some part in this, I clambered over the table and stood just below Arthur, although I felt really naked when I realized I had no weapon but my knife.

"You can't command me, Arthur," said Huarwor, picking his flinty teeth with a horny nail. "Nor can you call on your God to do so. That fire doesn't burn in you any more. You are too much at peace with the world. Those Christian sorcerers who work what you call miracles—why do you think so many of them are half-crazed hermits? You cannot be a king and call on the power of your crucified god, not for long. And your cold steel is nothing to me."

Saying that, he turned gracelessly but serpent-quick and grasped one of the spearheads, which he pulled to his great gaping mouth, bit off, and swallowed before the startled guardsman could wrench it away. The others were not so paralyzed and closed in on him, stabbing, but their points could not pierce his seemingly frail flesh, and he ignored them, his grip shifting from broken spear haft to the quivering arm that held it, and then he had the poor bastard's hand in his mouth and was chewing on it, and the sound of bones crunching was audible even above his victim's screaming. Arthur ran at him, shoving his way through the shocked warriors, and began to hack and hack and hack with his polished sword. Imagine a thick, strong root, the kind that's as big as a man's thigh, and yourself a small weak child armed with only a toy sword made of some soft wood; that's as little damage as Arthur's fierce blows did to Huarwor's arms, head, and torso, which is to say, no damage at all.

Huarwor ate the man as he stood there. Well, before he was half-done, his victim wasn't so much standing as slumping, first unconscious and then mercifully dead, while those jaws did their remorseless work, pulping flesh and bone but still managing to leave one connected to the other, so that the corpse was mangled but essentially swallowed in one piece. At one point Huarwor seemed to unhinge his jaws like those of a snake, so that he was able to get his victim's entire head in his mouth, but unlike a snake's, his jaws continued to chew and chew and chew.

The other soldiers broke away from him then, understandably wanting to stay beyond the reach of those spindly, pockmarked arms, those dreadful chewing jaws, and I stepped forward and pulled Arthur back by a loop of his belt, lest he become the next course. There was a mad rush for the door and the stairway, servants and soldiers and high lords and ladies overturning stools and tables and trampling each other in their haste to be gone, so that only Arthur and Guinevere and me and a few doughty warriors were left, with me and Gwen both trying to hustle Arthur out the door.

Huarwor began to laugh. "Now what sort of host leaves his guest unsatisfied? You told me I should have my fill in your hall and have my fill I shall. Even if you and all you command flee Camelot, I shall eat the contents of your granaries, the herds in your fields, the very stones of your palace. I shall eat and eat until there is nothing here but bare earth, and should you build another fortress elsewhere, I shall come and eat that, too. I am Huarwor the Hungry Man, and nothing can assuage me."

"And what if something could?"

It was Guinevere, brave beautiful Gwen, who had not built Camelot but loved it as much as Arthur, who said that. Her back was very straight and her voice was amazingly calm, although I caught a hint of the tension underneath it. "Answer me that, Huarwor, what if something could?"

Huarwor knelt down and tore a chunk of shale from the floor as easily as one tearing off a piece of bread. He put it in his mouth, chewed it twice, and swallowed. "Lady, there is nothing in this world or out of it that can fill my belly."

"You're wrong," said Gwen, her voice still steady, me and Arthur both stupefied behind her, looking blankly at each other and wondering what to do. "My husband the king invited you here thinking you were a man, and offered you his bounty. Knowing you are not a man, his queen says this. Leave us now, but come back in three months' time, and your belly will be filled. I swear this, both by the One God of my husband and all the gods my mother worshiped."

Huarwor cackled again. "I am not as easily tricked as that."

"Can we get some archers in here?" I whispered to Arthur.

He shook his head. "What good could they do? Perhaps we could barricade the hall, and burn it with him inside, but I fear not even that would work."

"Listen to me and know I speak truly," continued Guinevere. "Can you not find us wherever we go? What is the point of trickery? Come to us in three months' time and we will feed you such as you have never been fed before. If we cannot do this, we will not flee from you, but stand there like Christian martyrs facing hungry lions and let you eat us one by one. Arthur and I can even draw lots to see who you will eat first." Arthur made a sound that was more growl than words, but Gwen paid him no heed. "However, if we fill your belly, you must promise never to return, not to Camelot or anywhere else in Britain. Are you afraid to accept this challenge?"

Huarwor cocked his head to the side, regarding her like an emaciated hawk, his hands twitching as with palsy and his red eyes blinking. "I fear nothing," he said at last in a lower voice than he'd used before. "But you will fear my hunger when I return in three months' time." And then he was simply gone, vanishing like the flame of an extinguished lamp, leaving nothing behind him but the blood and juices that had dribbled from him and stained the floor as he'd feasted.

Guinevere turned and collapsed into our arms. "It worked," she said with a shudder, her voice much smaller now. "That wasn't the hardest thing that will have to be done, but it was hard enough. I so wanted to turn and run."

"But you didn't," I said, too stunned to even resent sharing her embrace with Arthur. "You saved Camelot."

Arthur, surprisingly, was the one who broke away first. "Bought us some time, at least. But what can we do?" He righted an overturned bench and sat on it. There were garbled sounds outside, and faces peered in at us, but we gave them no heed. "I am not holy enough any more, it seems. Perhaps Gildas was right when he denounced me from the pulpit at Glastonbury."

"I was not bluffing," said Gwen, sitting close beside her husband but looking straight at me. "There is a way to slake this monster's appetite, and at little or no cost to the kingdom."

Too tired to find a chair, I sat on the floor, which was sticky with spilled wine. At least, I hoped it was wine. "And what way is that?"

Gwen took the burnished circlet from her hair, which tumbled down her shoulders in an unruly red cascade. In the morning's pale light she almost looked her thirty-one years. "It's simple, really. All we have to do is fetch something back from Ireland. The Cauldron of Plenty that Brennetach spoke of. I dearly hope that he wasn't merely entertaining us with a baseless traveler's tale. I like the man, and would hate to see him tortured, but if this miraculous cauldron of Manadan Mac Dirwnach doesn't really exist, I'll heat the irons myself."

The hall of Manadan Mac Dirwnach was shaped like a huge double oval, or maybe two squashed-together tits. Although it covered as much ground as Arthur's palace, it was at no point higher than six or seven feet, with a herd of bristly fierce-eyed pigs rooting in its sod roof, and I was afraid the ceiling would be oppressively low. But no, for much like the Picts, these Irishmen constructed such buildings partially underground, and although the dim and smoky interior was a maze of ceiling posts, barrels, and cowhide partitions, there was plenty of space above our heads.

"All right, I've done what the queen made me promise to do and brought you this far," whispered little Brennetach in Continental Latin, which our hosts almost certainly didn't understand. "But I fail to see what you hope to accomplish. Manadan wouldn't sell his cauldron even if we had something of good value to offer him, and there's no way you and a half-dozen men can wrest it away from him. Why did you bring so few?"

"More would have made him suspicious," I hissed back, thinking of my last conversation alone with Guinevere before I sailed. "Arthur is often wise but only occasionally clever," she'd said to me, my head resting in her lap and her glorious hair tickling my face. "You on the other hand are often most unwise, else we'd never have become lovers.

But you're almost always clever. It's that cleverness we need now."

Well, now it was time to see if her faith in me was justified. I might die here, but it would be the kind of death I could understand, and at least my feet were on solid land. I'd spent the voyage from the mouth of the Severn Estuary puking over the rail of Brennetach's sturdy little two-masted cornship. In my mind I still loved the sea and all her moods, but somewhere down the years I'd lost my stomach for riding on her.

Spring had shown no inclination to come early this year, and I wore cowhide leggings over woolen trousers, a leather tunic over two woolen ones, and a hooded cloak lined with fox-and-otter fur. However, the interior of Manadan's hall was so warm that my eyes had scarcely adjusted to the peat smoke and torchlight before I was sweating as heavily as if I'd just marched five miles in full armor under the July sun. Many of the leering tribesmen surrounding me, Brennetach, and the six uneasy soldiers I'd brought with me from Camelot wore nothing but orange, black, and green plaid blankets, fastened at their hips with bronze or silver brooches, and silver torques that gleamed about their necks.

Those necks were very thick, and their waists thicker still, and many of them had great sagging sweaty man-tits. Their long hair was tied with green-and-red ribbons and their heavy mustaches were stiffened with lime and cow dung, such traditionally warlike decorations seeming quite out of place on men who waddled rather than walked and had more chins than pampered Roman matrons. Still, their swords and spears were sharp enough, and they seemed as pleased by my company as lazy barnyard cats that have just spied a crippled mouse.

Besides peat smoke, the mazelike interior smelled of beer, sweat, piss, and vomit. Many of the Irishmen lay sprawled in the shadows or propped up against the roof posts, as if they'd been carousing. Of course, given their endless supply of drink, it was unlikely that they ever stopped.

Manadan's throne was a blocky chair carved from the trunk of an oak tree and draped in sheepskins. His hair was not red like so many of his warriors, but an oily black, and his squashed-looking nose was venous and crimson. His neck torque was gold, of course, with more gold coiled in serpent shapes around his meaty arms and a silver pendant hanging in the hairy hollow of his sagging chest. His crown was of gold-enameled boars' teeth and he held a sloshing silver goblet in one meaty hand.

"Why do you come here?" he asked in lilting British.

I drew myself up to my full height, although that wasn't terribly impressive, and stuck out my chest, which at least was not as heavy-breasted as a woman's. "To drink and drink and then drink some more," I said in the Irish of my youth. "I am Mordred Mac Lot, Prince of Orkney, and happy to be among kinsmen again."

"Orkney is no more," growled Manadan, "and you are no kin of mine."

I looked offended. "Am I not *Scotti*?" I said in mock indignation, using another word for the Irish that was now more commonly applied to their descendants who'd settled in North Britain. "And as for Orkney, those islands still stand, but the Jutes rule there now. That is why I took service in Britain, but now I find myself sick of the place, and wish to be among men who truly know how to drink." I looked at the open barrels of wine, beer, and mead, and then at those men who were unable to stand. "Perhaps I've come to the wrong place. At least a third of your war band appears to be incapacitated, and yet most of those barrels are still full."

Manadan burped and picked at his flaring nose, but his eyes were crafty. "No man could consume all the drink that is to be had here, not if he'd been drinking since the beginning of the world." Then he switched back to British. "But you know that, don't you? Brennetach has surely told you much about us, Mordred Mac Lot. Or should I say Mordred ab Arthur? Do you think I'm such a fool as to not know the name of the British High King's son? We're not ignorant savages here, whatever you may think. But there's plenty of time to find out why you're truly here. If you want drink, you shall have it."

He clapped his hands and oaken benches were set before us. I unpinned my heavy cloak and spread it on the rough wood before sitting, Brennetach fidgeting on my left and three men on either side of us—not that they'd do us much good if this lot got nasty. Two huge Irishmen emerged from the gloom bearing a plain black cauldron by the iron rings set in its lip. Grunting, they tipped it completely over, spilling a stew of eels, leeks, and boiled swine flesh out onto the straw, then righted it again.

"You must eat well here, that you can pour a good dinner on the ground," I said with mild reproach.

Manadan laughed. "Oh, we eat well, indeed," he said, slapping his sagging belly, which jiggled like a wine-filled goatskin. "And now you shall see how we drink." He held up his silver goblet. "I have but to pour this wine into the cauldron and it will fill to the brim, and stay full as long as we do not turn it over."

I nodded. "So I have heard, but I have something better than wine. Brennetach, please hand me that jug I gave you to carry."

His hands so shook that, fearing he'd drop it, I quickly snatched it from him, whispering, "Calm down, you fool" in Latin. "Do you know what heart-of-wine is, Good King Manadan?"

He shook his head suspiciously, but said nothing.

"It's a drink that will put any Briton under the table," I continued, standing up and unstopping the jug. "It's the liquid that's left behind when you pack a bottle of wine in a cold cellar with salt and snow, then strain out the ice. You don't get much, but its potency makes it very precious." It also tasted pretty vile, but I doubted this lot had refined palates. "May I pour this into your cauldron?"

Manadan's eyes narrowed. "How do I know you aren't planning to poison us?"

The idea had occurred to me, but this should work even better, providing it worked at all, for you can't poison so many men and have the potion work upon each of them at the same time, and when the first start to convulse, those who drank last tend to become suspicious and then violent. Besides, they'd expect me to drink, too.

"Not at all," I said. "I will be the first to try it. My cup, please, good Brennetach."

He handed it to me more steadily than he had the jug, which was a good thing, as I couldn't afford them to be suspicious of my drinking vessel. If they examined it, they'd surely notice the purple gemstone set in its bottom. Amethyst is commonly believed to be proof against drunkenness. It doesn't really work, of course, not unless you say the right spell over it. Fortunately, I'd learned a little of my mother's arts.

I poured the contents of the castorware jug into the cauldron. Without a sound, and with a speed that surprised even me, who'd grown up among small household magics, the liquid filled the container to the brim, as though it were being pumped through clever Roman plumbing. Filling my cup, I drank it in one gulp.

It burned on my tongue, and in the back of my throat, but it was a pleasant kind of burning, and it tasted much better than I'd expected. Apparently the cauldron's magic not only effected the quantity of that which was poured into it, but the quality as well. "I think I'll have another," I said, flashing my best grin. "After all, you lads have been drinking since you arose this morning, and I have much catching up to do."

Many in the throng laughed at that, and flashed their yellow teeth, and before much longer they were all drinking, too, marveling at the headiness of the draught. They sang rowdy songs and swore fierce oaths and filled their cups again and again, and soon Manadan's eyes lost their suspicion and he peered at me in bleary-eyed good fellowship. My men did not join the carousing, but the Irish were too deep in their cups to notice. For my part I began to feel bloated from the liquid I'd consumed, but the charm did its work and my head remained clear.

Eventually, only myself, Brennetach, and my men were left seated upright. Manadan lolled on his throne, eyes shut and chins buried in his flabby chest, and all about us his warriors were stretched out on the straw like basking seals. Despite the fact that we were not yet out of danger and that my belly was as heavy as that of a parched horse that's been allowed to drink too much too quickly, I had to laugh. "Buck up, Brennetach," I said, clapping him on his quivering back. "I told you it would work." Leaning over, I stuck my thumb into my throat and vomited a bucketful of heart-of-wine onto the already quite soiled straw.

"Arthur owes me much," muttered Brennetach, ignoring my convulsive puking. "I'll never be able to trade with these folk for wine again."

Wiping my mouth on my sleeve, I stood, taking deep breaths and shaking my head to clear it again, the regurgitated spirits giving a particularly vile taste to my own bile. With the help of one of my men, I got the cauldron turned over, spilling out the heart-of-wine, the level of which had not dropped an inch until now, despite so many cups having been filled from it. The now empty and rather lighter cauldron set right again, I made Brennetach grasp one of the iron rings set in its lip, for I needed to leave as many of my men with free hands as possible, as there'd likely be some fighting between here and the moored ship. We'd had to disarm before descending the crude stone steps that led down into Manadan's hall, but there were plenty of swords and spears lying about. Fortunately, most of the folk outside were slaves and not likely to be much of a threat.

It was a feast in name only, with just me, Arthur, and Guinevere seated at the center table, two dozen men-at-arms flanking us as more of a symbolic comfort than a practical precaution. It was warmer here in Southwest Britain than it had been on the cold Irish sea, and the fire on the great hearth had been reduced to glowing ashes. On these, the cauldron sat, its contents steaming. A simple soldier's porridge of grain and lentils and scraps of mutton had been cooked in it. Arthur and Guinevere weren't hungry, but I'd already tried some. No seasoning had been used, yet the flavor was far richer and more satisfying than should have possible with such humble ingredients. But that, of course, was part of the cauldron's magic.

"It would be a fine thing if Mordred risked his life to bring the Cauldron of Plenty into Britain, yet Huarwor doesn't come," said Gwen softly. "Although to be truthful, I would be happy not to see him again."

Arthur ran a callused thumb along the bridge of his broken nose. "There's no need for you to be here. I would prefer that you weren't in danger."

Gwen took his hand. "Hush, love. I'm in the thick

of it, and have been, since goading the creature with this challenge."

I looked at the darkening yellow glass above us. "It's nightfall. I wonder how long it will be until he comes."

With her other hand, Gwen squeezed mine under the table. "It won't be soon enough. I'd have this over with."

And then Huarwor was there, not descending the stairs this time, but standing in the shadows beneath them. "I have come as you bade me, Queen of Camelot," he trilled, his hungry eyes ignoring me and Arthur. "And I've brought my hunger with me."

"That is good," said the woman my father and I both loved, "for we have something to assuage it now." At her signal, trembling servants leaned over the hot ashes, shoving a stout pole between two of the cauldron's iron rings. Grunting, they heaved it off the hearth and set it down before the table, then quickly got as far away from Huarwor as they could.

Guinevere rose and came around the long table. Arthur followed, trying to pull her back, but she shook him off. My guts in a knot, I clambered gracelessly over the table, trying to head her off, but she pushed her way past me as well, and the two of us could only stand behind her, our hands on hilts.

In her hand she held a wooden ladle. "Here, Huarwor," she said with a tight smile. "Eat your fill."

He grinned that preternaturally wide grin again, exposing all his large stony teeth, of which he seemed to have more than a man, although I had no inclination to actually count them. And then he began to eat. We stood there, watching, while the ladle rose and fell and his jaws worked. He didn't need to chew the porridge, but his teeth clacked together anyway, and although I'd never seen him drink, I expect he even chewed water.

And the night wore on, and Huarwor chewed and swallowed, chewed and swallowed, raising the ladle to his mouth and dipping it again, and the cauldron remained full almost to the brim. He took no notice when we returned to our chairs and sat there watching him eat, like spectators at a Roman play. Finally, so inured had I become to marvels and danger that I lay my head down on the table and drowsed, and when I lifted it up again a faint predawn light was seeping through the far window, and Huarwor was still eating.

Now, however, he was not so gaunt, for his belly was beginning to bulge, and his ribs were no longer visible. How much had he eaten already? Each ladle contained at least a half-pint of food, and how many of these did he consume in each minute of his rhythmic eating? At least a score, I thought, and possibly more than that, which meant that he swallowed close to a hundred gallons in an hour. And how many hours had passed? Ach, even if I had an accurate count of the time, the arithmetic made my head hurt.

The guards beside us changed shifts, servants brought us food and drink, I rose and stretched and would have rubbed Gwen's shoulders and had her rub mine, had Arthur not been present, and still Huarwor continued to eat. By midday his stomach was as large as that of a woman near the end of her pregnancy, and still he ate and ate and ate.

By the time the first evening candles were lit, he

was as swollen as some huge bearded tick, his belly
sloshing out before him, making his arms and legs
seem more skinny and insectile than ever. There was
now a huge crowd gathered in the hall, with soldiers
tramping in from the barracks and folk even coming
from the civilian settlement that sprawled between
Camelot and the looping Usk. The palace guard became more concerned with keeping order than with
watching Huarwor, and the assembled throng grew
bolder as the hours took the edge of their fearful
awe, and began to take bets as to how long he would
continue to eat from the cauldron's inexhaustible
supply. I had a mad vision of him going on like
this for weeks and months and years, of his feasting
becoming a marvel that brought folk from all over
Britain and across the channel, of us growing old
while he filled his stomach.

Some time before the morning, he simply burst,
with no warning or preamble. I was reminded of the
time I attended the funeral of a fat bishop who died
of the infection from an internal rupture. He'd lain
in state for too long in the summer heat, and when
the lid was pressed down on his coffin he'd exploded
from pus, splattering the rich vestments of the on-
lookers. This explosion was even more vile. Fortunately, so many people had pressed their way in
front of us that we were spared the worst of it. There
was another scramble for the door, the guards at the
rear trying with little success to restore order, and
much screaming. In moments, the hall was almost
empty.

Gwen looked at me with mingled relief and disgust. Arthur rose, his face unreadable, the mask I

remembered from my early days at Camelot, when he was still struggling with what we were to each other. He looked down at the remains, which seemed to be melting like lard in a skillet, and then at the plain black cauldron, which appeared to be just as full of porridge as ever. "Some time in the bath house is in order, I think," he said at last. "Have the floor scrubbed with lye, and then anointed with holy water."

"What will we do with the cauldron?" asked Guinevere, eyes watching her husband trudge wearily from the room but her hand touching mine.

"We'll worry about that tomorrow," I said. "Right now, I've had my fill of marvels, as surely as Huarwor had his fill of porridge."

BUILDER OF KEEPS

by Gregory Maguire

Gregory Maguire is the author of many novels, including *Wicked: The Life and Times of the Wicked Witch of the West*, *Seven Spiders Spinning*, *I Feel Like the Morning Star*, *The Good Liar*, *Missing Sisters*, and *Oasis*. He lives in Concord, Massachusetts.

"Builder of Keeps" is a tale in which the myth of Camelot in all its splendor, that idealized palace, exists even before the first stone is set in place, before its familiar characters have come together, or become legend. It is a tale of looking toward the future, of holding on to hope and looking for one's Destiny—or one's past, if you're that wizard cursed to live life in reverse, Merlin, who here puts in a comical appearance reminiscent of T. H. White's incarnation, anachronisms and all.

The vision was primary—well, visions are. By their nature they usurp the mundane. Visions bleed their out-of-context energy into the field of coordinates, warping expectations, shifting proportions, collapsing equations. No wonder saints roll their eyes up into their heads, virgins elevate, cows give birth to baby bears, clouds assemble into airy armies from the west. The here and the now is all we have, unless we have visions. The here, the now, and the story,

that is, and this is the story of the architect of
Camelot.

Mendorix came upon the promontory on an early
winter afternoon of vengeful winds accompanied by
a desultory small rain. Logres was behind him, by
seven days' hard travel. Behind him—and good riddance to the noise and the clatter of foreign tongues,
and also to the harlot who had tricked him out of
his sobriety, his sleep, and his purse. He might not
have all his fingers, but he still had the significant
digit, and was at some mercy to its needs. So, to
rejoin a dissolute remnant of his clan, now that his
productive times were behind him, he was making
for the wastes of Cornwall, and figured it still a few
days ahead. Cornwall of the scrubby furze, the red
water, the sandy strands that burn gold even in the
height of sour weather.

Therefore Mendorix was surprised at first by the
prospect on which he stumbled. Cornwall already?
Seven league boots could not bring it this near, this
fast. But no, it was a mirage of a sort: That was not
silent sea roiling beneath the lip of the long as-
cending slope, but mist. Rags and tendrils of water
spun into air. Mendorix was surprised at his mistake. Overtired?

But what a pleasant prospect, this lenient
hillside. . . .

He began to stride up the slope, which in some
accident of tectonic shift had been arranged in a natural half coil, like an arm curling away from a body,
its hand elevated on a pillow. The very crown of the
slope had a faint depression, just like a palm in a

hand, and it was beyond the fingers that the mist was playing at being the sea.

As he mounted the slope, the wind grew fiercer. His head began to pound, but it wasn't the exertion, for the slope was gentle enough—a natural approach for horses, he thought. Not too steep that, in full mail, the horses would be exhausted, but steep enough for adequate defense as well as a prospect suitable to a warlord or a chieftain. No, the pounding came from the outside, not the inside. He considered at first that a distant drum might be beating; or could it be his heart? Or the sea, maybe nearer than he thought?

Or was it perhaps the realization that there was nothing clammy about the mists? There was no sour miasma of any Oxenford, not the choking chill of the highlands of the Scots. The gray-silver-green cloud that pummeled the air in slow-motion fists, in blank tossing heads, like a sea of decaying souls, didn't lend its moisture to the air. In fact, Mendorix found he was warm from his walk, and he had to throw his cloak back.

On the top of the hill he stopped, his feet firmly planted in the palm hollow, which was much larger that it had looked from below. And here the vision descended upon Mendorix, the sorry traveler, who for his pains and labors on behalf of the foremen of an irate potentate had one hand seared closed in a fire, and the other burned so badly that he had cut it off himself with an ax. To carry a staff he had to squat and slip the unopenable ring of his fingers and thumb around it from the top, and push down until his hand was positioned correctly. He shook his head. For years there had been no hair in front to negotiate away from his eyes, but he tossed imaginary hair away out of habit, because he could not believe what he was seeing.

The mist below had no noise of its own. It was not a sea. But it was a sea, and though here and there the spiky leafless tops of stag-head oak showed through, the mist moved in successive waves like a tide pushing against the shore. He was on a spit of land, standing on a Hand of Britain reaching out into the west, into the land of the spirits, where the future and the past mingle without distraction. Tears started in his eyes, for reasons he could not understand. Through the tears he saw the coracle approaching.

In later years, and when he could not sleep, he imagined that the coracle had been pure gold, as if it had been launched from the doors of a mighty cathedral built on a canal. But a pragmatist above all, and an atheist except in times of terror or peril, more often Mendorix kept himself to his original impression: It was only a weatherbeaten and somewhat abused vessel, a bit lopsided if the truth be told. Without stateliness or particular efficiency it rode the crests of the sea mist. The lone passenger seemed in danger of being thrown out. A stout, cowled figure, Mendorix could see as the coracle approached, possibly a friar.

Without a word, the squat man in the coracle reached for a coil of rope, and when near enough, he made to throw one end of the rope to Mendorix. "I am without the appropriate appendages," called Mendorix, but that message didn't mean much to the approaching man, who threw the rope anyway.

Mendorix was not able to loop the rope with his staff, but he threw himself on the rope before it slithered off the cliff edge back into the impossible sea. Then, by rolling on it and tucking it beneath his right armpit, he was able to help draw the coracle up to a safe berth.

For an instant—perhaps a throwback to the sourgut wine he'd had the week earlier?—his eyes cleared, and he saw that the coracle was plainly harbored in midair, perpendicular to a cliff face without visible support, as an arm can be held perpendicular to a spine. Then—what tricks exhaustion and pain can play!—he saw the ocean of mist spume again. The newcomer alighted, with some difficulty, with a grunt and an oath, dragging a heavy sack on his shoulder.

"I had intended a month of solitude for my ruminations," said the newcomer, a bit grumpily. The diction was educated, but the accent was a man of the western hills. "How do you come to be in the cloister of my mind?"

Mendorix did not know what he meant. "Do you often travel on cloud seas?" he said.

"Private oceans of thought," said the visitor, "with the emphasis on private. I'm losing my touch. Who are you?"

"Mendorix, builder of keeps."

"I had guessed you might be a convenient boatwright, anyway, to help repair the loathsome vessel. It lists like a randy goat."

"Who are you?" said Mendorix.

"Oh, well, then, I need hardly introduce myself to the figments of my own dream world!" cried the man. "The rudeness of the psyche! I would strike myself on my own forehead if I thought it would help."

"I am hardly a figment of anyone's dream world, including my own," said Mendorix coldly.

"How could you know whether you were in your reality or mine, one way or the other?" said the newcomer.

"You tell me," Mendorix replied, holding out the one hand encasing the staff, and the other arm that ended in a stump. "Which of my limbs gives me the more pain? If I am a fiction in your mind, you should know as much as I do about myself, or more."

"Hmmm," said the man. "A clever bastard. Well, clearly your left arm must pain you more, for I see it is burned into a closed ring of flesh. There is more of your left arm. The right arm ends abruptly, and there is no hand there to feel, so from a quantitative point of view, you have fewer resources for feeling there, so less capacity for pain."

"Stand corrected," said Mendorix. "The missing right hand was thrust in a fire the same as the left, but burned so much more horribly that I chopped it off myself, only to learn that losing the actual flesh is not the same thing as losing the memory of the pain, which I endure with every moment of waking and sleeping. So with the pain of the fire and the pain of the ax, my right arm suffers the more. Why do you not know this?"

"I'm a magician, not a fortune teller," said the man. "Is there anything to eat in this vision?"

"I do not share my parcel of provisions with dream-creatures who conceal their names."

"Oh," laughed the short man then, a bit hollowly, "it appears that my holy visions need to find a way to crawl up my skirts and bite me on the ass! Well, then, if it is only to feed me, why, I'll tell you: I am Merlin, none other."

He looked out of the corner of his eyes at Mendorix for recognition, approval, delight. Mendorix couldn't oblige; he had no memory of anyone named Merlin. "I have a small loaf," said Mendorix, "some dried salted fish, Merlin, some old greens that would be better in soup. You haven't got a kettle in your sack?"

"You should know what I have in my sack as well as I do," said Merlin, peering at the builder with suspicion.

"I do not know that," said Mendorix. "You may have arrived out of some magic transport, and from who knows where, but it seems to have addled your brains. Have you a pot we can stew some greens in, or have you not?"

"It's not a question of whether either of us knows where I came from," said Merlin, "but do either of us know where I have arrived?"

"Well said, that's the question in my mind, too," said Mendorix. But Merlin looked more puzzled now than before. He set down his sack and turned his chin to one side, looking at Mendorix out of one iron-gray eye. Then he turned his chin in the opposite direction and examined Mendorix, blinking a nut-brown eye several times. And as Mendorix was scrutinized, so he looked back. The self-named magician scarcely came up to Mendorix's shoulder blades. He was old but not especially wrinkled; he had the

slightly doughy look of a eunuch, only not so much
so. Was it possible to be a half-eunuch, Mendorix
wondered, and decided from an arithmetical point of
view it probably was.

Merlin's cloak slipped from his shoulders, and a
tunic of old blue-brown cloth showed beneath. It was
pinned by an ornate, dirt-encrusted broach of the sort
worn by royalty, but royalty generally kept such
things in better condition. Merlin's hair was thin on
the sides, and shorn close; there was a pattern of
scars on his forehead in the exact formation of the
constellation that some called the Pendragon. Extraordinary. And his eyes, when they both looked
upon Mendorix at once, had a mesmerizing quality,
perhaps due to their contrary coloration: But Merlin
was difficult to look back at. He seemed to recede
and advance in focal depth at once.

Mendorix, though a simple man, was not untrav-
eled and not untimid. He knew how to sight a solient
wall going up, how to put his cheek to the first stone
and gaze at the highest point in the heavens to deter-
mine if the stone was set true; he knew how to tread
upon treacherous ramparts in high winds to gauge
the width of the moat such a height would require
to prevent breaching. Being able to see the up and
the down of a keep, the inside and the outside at
once, is perhaps not the most exotic of talents, and
no match for magic; but it is not inconsiderable either, and Mendorix was a master builder. He relied
on his skills at sighting to examine Merlin, at least
intently enough so that the man grew uneasy and
dropped his gaze.

"Fair enough," said Merlin, kicking at his sack

until it opened and a pot rolled out. "I have gone off course and ended up in some nook of the world I did not intend to grace with my presence. Unless I have suffered a demonic blood bubble of some sort and am revisiting the dotage I thought I had left behind. You seem to be real enough, if you can keep your identity separate from my own."

Mendorix farted, not unkindly, but to make a point. Merlin winced and said, "Yes, separate, I concur. Any dramatic personae of my own invention are better behaved than to break wind in my presence."

"You'll need to get water for that pot and prepare a cook fire," said Mendorix. "I could do it but it would be several hours, with such addled hands as I do have."

Merlin clapped his hands once. Though Mendorix hardly could believe his eyes, the cookpot stopped rolling and shuddered to attention. Merlin clapped again, and a few live coals popped out of the top of the pot. They scraped against each other in midair, like a couple of cats stretching and nuzzling, and in a moment a small fire hovered in midair, for all the world like a bird in flames.

"This perverse land," muttered Merlin. "Come to ground when I call you, Fire!"

Fire refused, though—if Mendorix could credit it— the refusal was accompanied by a deferential flicker, like a curtsy or a genuflection of some sort.

"Pot," said Merlin, "collect some water, then, so we may stew our provisions into some semblance of a digestible state."

Pot had three stumpy legs on which it hobbled. It reminded Mendorix of a crippled badger who had lost his hair from mange. Nothing short of grotesque. "Saints preserve us," muttered Mendorix, against his better judgment, and he crossed himself out of childhood habit.

"Saints permit us," murmured Merlin, arguing across the grain somehow, but Mendorix could not follow the arc of logic. He watched Pot make its way over the sere grass of the knoll, and, with a little contortion of its stumps, launch itself off the brow into the mist that still pulsed on three sides of the promontory, making it a peninsula of Britain jutting into the world of magic. They heard Pot splashing about, and it returned, dripping wet, its cavity filled to overflowing with a water that seemed to have been wrung from the mist.

"Salt," said Merlin, "extract Thyself."

A funny sound, as of vellum scraping along vellum. Then up from the pot rose a string of graywhite crystals. Or perhaps it was multiple strings in tightly arranged parallel lines; Mendorix couldn't tell. It was about a foot long, and it hovered at shoulder height, like an edge of light in a window showing through a window improperly shuttered. Mendorix had an impulse to rush at it and push open the window he just then imagined there, and see what he could see inside the fantastic room—or outside it, perhaps—but before Mendorix could move, Merlin cupped his hand beneath the strand. The salt fell into a heap in his palm. He threw away most of it, but returned a small portion of salt to the water and patted Pot on its tummy or its bottom. "Let the water boil," said Merlin.

Pot reared back on two of its stumps and appeared

to be assessing the problem that Fire was five feet in the air.

"I know, tiresome," said Merlin. "Fire has gotten uppity for some reason. Can you manage?"

Pot took a lunge, and a healthy portion of water sloshed out, but Merlin said authoritatively, "Water!" and the water heeled and returned to Pot. Pot scrambled on an invisible hook and hung over Fire, twitching its stumps in apparent pleasure.

"There," said Merlin, and turned to Mendorix. "Your turn. What can you conjure?"

"The wallet is bound around my waist," said Mendorix. "It would serve our purposes more neatly if you just take from it what you want. I can manage, but it will require your patience."

"Do not strike me with your staff, then," said Merlin, "and I will find what you have to offer. I hope it's dried pheasant and an appropriate complement of herbs."

"Desiccated turnip," said Mendorix heavily.

Merlin cursed, and rummaged through the leather satchel. He was just pulling out a couple of forlorn carrots wrapped in some leaves that had long since lost their will to crispness when there was a sound from the mist out beyond the promontory. "Hail!" cried a voice, "hail, and rain and snow for all I know, and if there's an able-bodied soul out there to call in this infernal beast, do your work, for my talents of persuasion have no impact here!"

"A most annoying habit of interruption in this meditation," snapped Merlin. "Go save yourself!" he cried.

"Here," said Mendorix, more kindly. "Here, cour-

age and forbearance, came forward and find us, whoever you are!''

"I resent your pretense to authority in this situation," said Merlin, but he turned with Mendorix to
see who was approaching. Pot and Fire both tilted
expectantly out over the mist sea.

A wreath of charcoal smoke made its way across
the silvery mist-waves. The vessel, whatever sort it
was, seemed to be hung with its own attendant vapors, as if it were bearing a smoking cauldron in
need of a good scrub and rinse. "I launch a javelin,"
cried the newcomer in a husky voice, and both Merlin and Mendorix had to leap back as suddenly, with
ferocious power, a javelin trailing a rope plunged
dangerously near. Mendorix would have tumbled
onto his back without the help of his staff, but Merlin
reached up and plucked the passing javelin out of
the air as if it were a snowflake rather than a deadly
weapon. Then he and Mendorix pulled at the rope,
and dragged in the portable cloud.

"There we are, that's it now—you useless waste of
timber!" cried the voice, and the newcomer leaped
out of the dark smoke onto the palm of the land.

"Oh, the Morgana," said Merlin. "I might have
known. The one among us who can't keep her house
in order."

"You!" said the Morgana, who was a striking
woman with tumults of coal-black tresses coursing
about a narrow and fiercely beautiful face. "I prepare
myself a touch of charmed sleep to restore myself to
essentials, and I come upon you, of all people? Not
even powerful enough to be my nemesis? I surely

am losing my touch. Please, depart from my vision—
this is too tawdry."

She reached out and snatched Mendorix's staff out
of its setting of seared flesh. He roared with pain.
She took no notice.

"I am persuaded this is not a vision," said Merlin.
"I had made the same journey, and landed here instead of in the sacred silence of my magic. I find a
much abused journeyman builder instead of a celes-
tial guide."

"Even my visions prattle," murmured the Morgana, not convinced. She had turned back to her
cloud and was sweeping at it with both hands. The
shreds of darkness began to dissipate, and the outline
of an antique vessel showed through. It was a small
and elegant floating palanquin of some sort, with a
carved dragon head on its prow. Then the dragon
head puffed one last snort of smoke and batted its
eyes balefully, and the Morgana hit it across the forehead with Mendorix's walking stick.

"That'll teach you to chew tobacco and lose our
way," she said. "You are this close to being firewood,
do you hear me? Ungrateful lout."

"Would you happen to have any onions on board,
or a paste made of wild garlic?" said Merlin eagerly.
"I mean, as long as you're here . . ."

"Where is here?" said the Morgana. She looked
quite bad-tempered.

"Your guess is as good as mine," said Merlin.
"Maybe a few dried mushrooms?"

"You can't conjure a mushroom?" said the Morgana witheringly. She made a gesture in the air with
the end of Mendorix's staff. No mushrooms ap-

peared. She looked at the staff and threw it to the ground in disgust.

"That's mine," said Mendorix.

"Don't cross her, she's a vixen," said Merlin in a low voice.

"A vixen with a talent for the cookpot," said the Morgana playfully. She fixed her dragon with a close and meaningful look. The beast closed its eyes as if concentrating, and a minute later it opened its mouth and spit out a dozen onions, three bulbs of garlic, an assortment of mushrooms already scraped of soil, and a ham bone with some clean, unrotted scraps of meat still clinging to it.

"Display artist," murmured Merlin.

"We may as well eat," said the Morgana. "Garlic, one bulb is enough. Go to your work."

The supplies mounted the air as if on an invisible set of stairs and plopped themselves, one by one, into the pot. Almost at once there was a smell as of a stew that has cooked for eight hours under the loving attention of a master chef. Merlin threw in the dried turnip and the carrots and lettuce leaves as an afterthought. "Bowls, darlings, come and be useful," cried the Morgana, and some well-oiled wooden Bowls appeared in the air, mercifully not through the dragon's mouth, for the Bowls were of a size that would have caused the dragon some distress.

"Dish up, then," said Merlin, and the Pot obliged, pouring its succulent stew in three even portions. Fire died down a little and played with itself, without shame, like a cat bathing itself in full view of an attentive audience.

Merlin, the Morgana, and Mendorix settled on the

ground and set themselves to the task of eating a worthy meal. It was like none other Mendorix had ever enjoyed. Every mouthful seemed to him to restore some hollow, to answer some hunger he had forgotten since childhood to register. From such humble ingredients, it was a feast fit for kings and magistrates.

"Now tell us, what might be the cause of our having a repast together in our separate spiritual excursions?" said the Morgana at last.

"Not just us," said Merlin. "And perhaps not entirely spiritual. This mortal appears to be quite solidly at home in the world of heavy flesh. So either he is here on sufferance or neither of us ended up where we set out to be."

"Strange and troubling," said the Morgana, and belched with satisfaction. "To what end this barbarian, of all sorry errors of magic? When is a mortal ever of any use to us?"

"Oh, it has been known to happen," said Merlin. "Or it will be known one day, perhaps."

"The decay of the system," said the Morgana, sighing. "I preferred it when we could manage our own affairs without all these—well, you could call them domestics, I suppose—"

"Enough," said Merlin. "Let us not affront the man. He has a name. It is Mendorix. Builder of castle keeps, most recently for King Olaf the Mighty."

Mendorix had not yet mentioned his most recent employer, so he was startled—though why should he be startled after such other marvels? Perhaps, he thought suddenly, this was his dream, and he had invented a Merlin and a Morgana himself. When might he have fallen asleep? Could the harlot in London have slipped him some narcotic, and was he even now still prone upon her flea-choked mattress while she rifled his clothes and wallet?

Merlin continued, almost as if speaking to himself, working out the terms. "Mendorix," said Merlin, "is a builder. A builder of keeps. The Morgana," Merlin continued, "is a breaker. A force of decay."

"And what are you?" said the Morgana, poking Merlin in the jowl with a long, faintly putrescent finger. The finger seemed to have turned green at the idea of decay, but if it was a gesture, the Morgana didn't seem to have her heart in it, for it went rosy-pale almost at once when she retracted it from Merlin's chin.

"Neither a builder nor a breaker," said Merlin, a bit pompously. "You could call me a translator, an interpreter."

"Fence-sitter!" snorted the Morgana. "Why do I waste my time?"

"Let us waste no more time," said Merlin, suddenly serious. "We have met and we have eaten, and though we had set out to take other journeys, our journeys seem to have been intended to cross. Tell me, old foe," he said this with the nicest of smiles, "what were you about, so that we may see where the ley lines lead tonight?"

"Oh, a little of this, a little of that," said the Morgana crossly. "A plague on a friendly little village south of here; a sudden lightning storm on a tor. I'd considered I might set boulders rolling upon a band of unsuspecting travelers. Perhaps a mild earthquake if the mood strikes."

"I hardly think—" began Merlin, but the Morgana interrupted and said, "Well, what about you?"

"Prayer and penitence," he said, and lowered his head.

The Morgana shook with laughter. "I suppose I deserve it!" she chortled. "The idea of you doing penitence, you who juggle bishops' balls in your right hand . . ."

"Tell me the truth about your intentions today," said Merlin. "This may be serious."

"Truth is paid for by truth," she answered, and an astonishing look of power and, Mendorix thought, fear passed over her face. "If we enter into a pact, you fiend, you pay up honorably or I'll—I'll—" She looked about, and seemed to notice Mendorix for the first time. "I'll eviscerate the time-lubber and feed him to my dragon."

The dragon looked faintly nauseated at the prospect. Mendorix was hardly more interested.

"Agreed," said Merlin dismissively.

"AGREED?" shouted Mendorix.

"It's a formality," said Merlin, "I keep my bargains, don't worry."

"All right, then," said the Morgana. She positioned herself as a tripod, balancing on two knees and on her heels clenched close together. She opened her palms outward on her thighs in a position of acceptance, or, perhaps, deferentiality. Her sharp chin lifted and her eyes lowered. "If you must know, I was out and about at a little reconnaissance work. I was looking for a place to establish a foothold in the temporal sphere. The coming and going between dimensions is taking its toll on me." She belched again. "Even my digestion suffers. Ah, Merlin, age takes its toll."

The magician rocked on his haunches and looked worried. "A foothold in the temporal sphere? That is hardly your style."

"We all change, and our needs change, more's the pity," said the Morgana dismissively. "An outpost among the barbarians, I know, but barbarians can be amusing." She smiled in a wincing way at Mendorix.

"Don't avoid me," said Merlin. He stood up and fixed her with a gimlet gaze. "Don't you avoid me, or you'll be sorry. You're hiding something."

"The ages change," she said. "You don't notice, you fool, because you slide backward among them, and what seems like premonition to us is only memory to you; but change they do, and the time of beasts and spirits decays, and the time of barbarian human strength emerges. I am clever enough to want to play a part, old though I am."

She didn't look old, to Mendorix; in her limbs she seemed no more than nineteen. There was a spry and supple tenderness to them, an adroitness that seemed as much animal as—well, as whatever she really was. But her eyes were ancient ones.

"And you?" she went on, with a challenge in her voice. "Give me the same honor of honesty, or you pay the price."

"I am of a different order than you," he said. "So any bargain made between us is false. I owe you nothing. Even the Morgana cannot expect to negotiate with one who pipes the melody that the stars march to."

Mendorix was, to say the least, taken aback. The

Morgana however seemed to expect no better than this from Merlin, and she merely replied, "You will tell me what you are about, and dismiss such bombast from your pronouncements. We have made a bargain, and, my old foe, we have a witness." At this she shrugged in Mendorix's direction. "I can have him off to the Adjudicator at once, and he will have to tell the truth before the Adjudicator. Then you will suffer for deceiving me—not a nap, but banishment. And then I will yet have the entrails of Mendorix as you promised."

Merlin seemed disbelieving for the first time. "You cannot introduce a time-bound beast into the court chamber of the Adjudicator!"

"This is what comes from having second sight, darling," said the Morgana sweetly, "you don't pay attention to your first sight enough. Didn't you hear what I said? I am staking myself here, in this little corner of history, on this blurt of green land newly drifting off from the coast of the continent. I have refined a few skills. Who says you can't teach an old dog new tricks?" She made a sudden lewd motion with her hips. Merlin averted his eyes, but Mendorix suddenly started with recognition. For all her inattention to him, she knew the builder full well, and he knew her: the girl in London who had succumbed to his advances, and stolen his money.

"I have seen you before," said Mendorix.

"You think you come here of your own free will?" said the Morgana. "Mere mortals don't walk this aspect of Britain without invitation."

"Why have you brought him here, then?" said Merlin. "To trick me into revealing my intentions?"

She merely lowered her eyes at the compliment.

"Very well, then," he said at last. "It seems we are working at the same purpose from different angles. I am answerable to the Adjudicator, and if you can deliver a mortal witness into an immortal zone, I have no recourse. I am, incidentally, impressed at your skills, assuming you tell the truth."

"I promised the truth," she yawned. "I delivered it, too."

"Then so will I," he said, beaten. He sat backward and crossed his legs and leaned his elbows heavily upon his knees. "I am seeking a place in which to sequester myself for a long sleep. I am looking for a close chamber, a magic cloister, to rest my head, to dream the dreams of the world's past and my future. In short," he said, "you might say I'm in the market for a retirement cottage."

"Halfway between the worlds," said the Morgana. "So you may hope not to be bothered by do-gooders of any stripe."

"I am a seer," said Merlin, "but to be productive, I must spend my time dreaming, and I have gone too long in my travels among the stars."

"Fair enough," said the Morgana after a while. "I even believe you. Now what can it be that has drawn us together? You to remove yourself from the temporal world, I to busy myself the more deeply in it? And here we meet, on a green hillock that is part Britain, part Avalon?"

They both turned and looked at Mendorix.

"I have no idea," the builder said. His hand was still smarting from the Morgana's rude removal of his stake.

"You are a loser when it comes to doing the rowdy," said the Morgana, "but perhaps you have other skills. After all, something about you appealed to me."

"I have made no promises in this conversation," he said. "I owe you nothing."

"No," said the Morgana, and Merlin nodded and shrugged his grudging admission of the fact.

"Still, we could pay you handsomely if it turns out you are the missing ingredient in our understanding," said the Morgana.

"What? By not killing me?" said Mendorix dourly. "By not introducing me into the hall of the Adjudicator? I can live with death—in a manner of speaking. Kill me or not, it makes no difference." He held up his bad hand and his stump. "You wonder I am unsatisfactory on the mattress when I am so bereft of limbs?"

"Oh, it always comes down to the mattress with you lot," Merlin angrily declared. "I agree with the Morgana at that: You are all barbarians."

"You have all time ahead of you and behind you," said Mendorix, "and the only timelessness allowed us barbarians is twofold: Our children who are still us though not us, and our human pleasure, which distracts us from death by its fleeting magnificence. Why should I be bereft of pleasure, I who am without children and now am likely to remain so?"

"Is that all you want?" said the Morgana. "A passel of brats? Simple enough to manage. If you have the key to why we have stumbled together in unintentional colloquy, I can manage you brats. We've even slept together already, nothing easier."

"I do not want bastards of magic," said Mendorix. "I do not want an arrangement of children. I want to be desired."

"I will do what I can," said the Morgana.

"I want to be desired," said Mendorix, "and not by you."

"No problem there," she said.

"Be careful, Mendorix," said Merlin. "She's canny."

"I want nothing more or less than the full shape of life. Barbarian life, if that's how you call it. With its proper end when it comes, and untinged by magic."

"You want me by magic to give you something untinged by magic?" said the Morgana. She frowned at Merlin and rolled her eyes.

"You're the expert at barbarians," Merlin, grinning, said to her. "Nobody said they were going to be easy." He made a big show of collecting Pot from the air. "Fire, enough already," he said. Fire rubbed itself out, and the two hot coals tucked themselves back into Pot.

"So what are we talking about here, then?" said the Morgana. "You want, say, your hands back to full use?"

Mendorix came to the feeling—both sinking and instantaneous—that this was indeed no more than a dream born of ale and indigestion, for only a dream could promise an impossibility. Still, even in a dream or a vision, one has one's commitment to honor, and with little enthusiasm he said, "Hands, yes, hands would be nice."

"Humans and their hands," said the Morgana, examining hers distastefully. "Like mordant little crabs, they are. Getting into everything. Myself, I prefer the claws of an eagle or the talons of a leopard.''

"Even so,'' said Mendorix.

"Well, then, tell us why you are here,'' said the Morgana, and Merlin nodded at Mendorix.

"I am on my way to Cornwall,'' he said. "I have some family there, and they will take me in and feed me, as family must. Perhaps I can find myself something to do on the water's edge, hauling nets with a hook fastened in this ring of flesh left to my left arm. Anyway, I will not starve there.''

"But your trade was building?'' said Merlin.

"I am the best stone man in the business,'' said Mendorix. "I can draw a tower in the air based on the shape of the first stone they bring me for the foundation. I can throw a keystone on an arch before assembling the supporting toothstones. I have mathematics in my fingers and toes and can count to four hundred using my ribs as a memory system. I can put windows in walls,'' he said, "where there will not be suitable views for five hundred years, but when the view sees fit to arrange itself, the walls and the windows will still be there.''

"You can?'' said the Morgana. "Perhaps you are meant to supervise the construction of my little pied-a-terre here on Earth.''

"More to the point,'' said Merlin, "perhaps you can build a stone bower in which I can sleep and recover my childhood.''

"None of this is possible,'' said Mendorix. "I cannot use my hands now, and who cannot draw a little cannot show others how to build. Also a foreman needs to haul stones and plane timber and wield an

adze and a chisel to show workers what he wants. I
can do none of this. With a hook, I might do a little
fishing. Without hands, I can never build again."

"Interesting," said the Morgana. She looked sideways at Merlin. "But into whose vision did he really
creep, then? Mine or yours? Does one of us have a
prior claim on his abilities?"

"I cannot give him hands," said Merlin. "But it
may be that he isn't willing to make you a home if
he knows your true nature."

"My true nature," said the Morgana, pouting,
"is—how shall I put it—?"

"—trauma?" suggested Merlin.

"—intense," said the Morgana. "Let's say intense,
and leave it at that."

"I don't know," said Merlin, grinning. "Truth is
truth. Show the barbarian your very civilized ways,
why don't you."

"A little famine, a little pestilence; well, someone's
got to do the cleaning up around here," she said,
making a derisive gesture with her arm. "At least I
take a stand, I don't just mince around being all
things to all people, thanks to the illegible stars,
which by the way can be read to mean something
entirely opposite if you get far enough on the other
side of them to see it."

"Hands or no hands," said Mendorix, "I don't
want to build a hideout for a witch."

"Oh, moral purpose, how vile." The Morgana
made retching sounds in a juvenile way.

"Nor do I want any part in organizing your bier,
even a temporary one," said Mendorix to Merlin. "If
you are truly a seer, then we need you to see for us.

That's the nature of us barbarians, I think: When we're not bewitched, we're blinded."

"A phil-o-soph-er!" cried the Morgana, singsongingly.

"Then," said Merlin to Mendorix, "perhaps my ancient foe and I are present in your vision rather than you in ours. What a surprise. One might even say an omen. Why should we be called to the service of a mortal? I think unprecedented in my experience, or do I mean unrepeated?"

"I wasn't called here, I came of my own accord," snapped the Morgana, but when the dragon head behind her went into a coughing fit she said to it, "Oh, do shut up. Perhaps I did have some trouble with the tides. I figured it was merely that time of the month."

Mendorix stood. If this really was his dream, there was no cost to telling the truth.

"I have no life left," he said. "I was building the keep of a warlord who had imported horses into Britain and mounted an army of murderers upon them. It was the best job I had, for the size of the wallet he promised, but when I was nearly done I began the better to see what manner of villain he was. I had not made him so, but I had strengthened him by strengthening his house. I had provided him with toothy crenellations so that defending archers could hide and shoot at the same time. I had proposed a hidden dungeon without an exit, into whose hideous rank depths prisoners could be dropped, and whose snaking tunnels twisted in such a way that even if the entire castle were razed by battering rams, no daylight could ever again penetrate the deepest pit. I had conceived stables suitable for horses in armor,

so animals could be suited up inside and leave the
stronghold with the sun emblazoning on them. It was
my work of genius, and it was for an evil end. When
I had finished the plans, and the last bit of stonework
was about to be laid in place, the warlord made to
maim me so I could not share my inventions. First
he burned both my hands, and then was about to
sever my tongue, when a wandering minstrel began
to warble a song predicting his downfall. The miscre-
ant turned his rage to the minstrel momentarily, and
I in my pain overturned a table and escaped in the
confusion."

Merlin had a funny look on his face. He began
to warble.

"Sing hey! For the life of Olaf the Mighty,
Who keeps his wife happy and keeps his drawers tidy;
He might be a cretin, or maybe just flighty,
But strong house or not, a long life he's not got,
For he's ball-tired and walleyed and—"

"No," said Mendorix, in a whisper of recognition.

"You?" said the Morgana. "Playing the part of a
minstrel in some oaf's castle?"

"It was a good party," said Merlin. "And didn't I
save the man's tongue?"

"You might have started singing a bit earlier," said
Mendorix, holding up his limbs.

"I couldn't get the harp in tune. A devil of an
instrument," said Merlin. "Sorry."

"So where does that leave us, in whose realm?"
said the Morgana. "Apparently we have both inter-
fered in this man's life, you as a minstrel and I as a
mistress—to put a rather pretty term on it, but never
mind. This still doesn't answer what we're doing

here, and my dragon is looking a bit jumpy and needs to get on."

The dragon was at this point sound asleep, and snoring.

"Well," said Merlin, "if, indeed, the time of the barbarians is in the ascendancy, perhaps we should ask our resident barbarian what he would build, did he have useful hands as well as proper assistance?"

Mendorix thought about the long range of clients who had hired his services. Olaf the Mighty was only the latest in a string of boors. The problem was that the boors were getting more populous as well as more intelligent. They understood that their domination depended on adequate fortresses, on mounted calvaries, on pillaging and terror. Cornwall was far away, and its residents as much in thrall to their Lord of Sea as to any knock-kneed county chieftain, but sooner or later the climate of oppression would reach even to Cornwall's weary, wind-beaten reaches.

"I should like the chance," said Mendorix, "to build a castle keep for a champion instead of a thug."

"Whyever would you want to do that?" said the Morgana.

He held up his arms again, the conclusive point in any argument he had made since losing his hands.

"I certainly don't qualify as a champion," said the Morgana sniffily, "nor would I want to. Really. Smacks of sentimentality, if you ask me. Why don't you build a chapel while you're at it?"

"I'm not the chapel-building type," said Mendorix.

"Well," said Merlin, "I'm not a champion either. I am far too judicious to take sides, and am needed by agents of subtlety far beyond your comprehension, or beyond that of the vernacular to describe. If a vision has meaning to me, I will follow it at naptime rather than rouse myself and prevent the Morgana from scouring a valley with red-hot lava. In this you could call me amoral, I suppose."

"A champion of the pillow!" snorted the Morgana. "Well, if we are in Mendorix's vision rather than he in ours, for some bizarre reason, Merlin, we ought to be paying attention. If this is what he wants, could the want be so strong as to pull ourselves from our own concerns and into this terrain of his?"

"This isn't my terrain," said Mendorix hastily. "I hardly know where we are."

"What could be built here?" said the Morgana, looking about.

"Well," began Mendorix, getting to his feet with difficulty, since his staff still lay several yards away where the Morgana had thrown it, "this would make a handsome prospect for a castle keep. Look at the lilt of the land. You can tell even by how the boulders are thrown that there are ribs of rock stretching away like this—" Even now he could forget that his right hand was gone, for he found himself trying to attenuate his stump into fingers and articulate the rock ridges beneath the grass.

"And a great hall, here," he said, striding about and stamping on the ground. "With doors that could open into a courtyard here, and doors forty yards on—" he was running now "—that, just parallel, might deliver the entire prospect of this entrance slope to the throne room, so that any king who sat here could see anyone coming without fail! And a moat to run here to here, and windows here, tall mullions, and the soaring buttresses that could support the thinner walls, the higher roof, and the turrets that could be planted like stone torsos atop massive solients sunk into the ground, here!—and here!—and again here!

"A man with a passion," said Merlin quietly.

"Obsessive behavior," opined the Morgana, but admitted, "I rather like obsessive behavior."

"If this magic mist sea should ever retreat, and Britain's forest bloom here as usual, this would be an aspect high enough to oversee the entire world!" cried Mendorix. "From here would ships on the Solent be observed blinking their pale sails; from here could the fires of the brown-toothed Scots clans be read and responded to! This is the magic and mighty arm of Britain, and it should have a castle in its palm!"

"Quite delightful, wouldn't you agree?" said the Morgana.

"Words fail me," said Merlin. "But then, words have never been my strong suit. Stars have."

"A home for a champion without a champion is a bit—well—perhaps premature?" said the Morgana. "I'm merely asking."

"I don't make champions," said Mendorix. "I build castle keeps."

Merlin and the Morgana exchanged glances. "If I am heading for a lengthy entombment," said Merlin, "a champion on site might be something of an asset, I suppose. Especially if the Morgana is planning on more regular visits among the barbarians."

The Morgana blushed at the compliment. "Call it a bad habit," she said, "but human distress does so amuse me. For that matter, a local champion would be someone for me to pit my strength against. Not that I need the exercise . . ."

"A champion might benefit the barbarians," said Mendorix, and then it was his turn to blush. "I mean—might benefit us."

"Oh, well, I could use a champion myself," said the Morgana in a suggestive way, arching her back and closing her eyes, "especially since old Stumpy here has lost his way with women, if you know what I mean."

"It wasn't that bad," said Mendorix. "Really."

They sat in silence for a few moments, and it occurred to Mendorix then that it was beginning to get dark. The dragon's eyes had opened and they shone, two orange sparks in the blue dusk. Pot stirred itself a bit, and stretched its single lip in a kind of pouting yawn. Then the two live coals that had made Fire came up and sat watching, like two red eyes to match those of the dragon head.

"A champion," said Merlin dreamily. "Where to find one?"

"You don't find them," said the Morgana. "They find you. If you're lucky."

The mist was beginning to dissipate as the night came on. Mendorix expected to see the coracle and the dragon lose their bearing in the air, but they stayed prone, gently rocking in the disappearing waves. The wooded slopes beneath the brow of the hill showed through, a thousand million spring leaves at their work of unfolding, noisier than stars, could they be heard. There was a smell of thawing soil, and the tired odor of old ice about to melt away.

Spring leaves? But it had been early winter when Mendorix had strolled upon the uprise of land.

"I should get on," said Mendorix. "If this is one dream or another, a vision, a mistake, or just a blot of indigestion, it is time for it to be over. Release me, whoever holds me in thrall, even if I am just speaking to myself. Release me!" he cried.

He looked up, as if to see a figure of himself sleeping in the sky, or perhaps of Merlin, or the Morgana. The arch-rivals only laughed to see him struggle, but they looked up, too. So all of them saw the thrill of light, a falling star stitching its white thread against immortal blue light. It fell slowly, so they could all say "Look!" and still look, and it was still there. Even the dragon and the coals that were Fire looked. The dragon gaped its wooden jaws and its tongue lolled stupidly. Fire blinked, and Pot tried to clap two of its stumps in applause, but they were too far apart to reach.

"A javelin right through the Pendragon constellation!" cried the Morgana. She sat bolt upright.

"No," scoffed Merlin, though he seemed equally agitated. "Not through it. From it; can't you see?"

And the bolt was so slow, so majestic and serene, that, breathless and hushed, they could still follow it until it disappeared beyond the horizon to the west. It left a greenish scar in its wake, a green tendril against the ice-blue of space.

"Like a bolt of lightning from your brain," said Mendorix, pointing at the Pendragon sign that adorned Merlin's forehead.

"Not anything he's known for, bolts of lightning

from the brain," murmured the Morgana, but the mood had changed and she fell silent then.

Merlin sat with his head in his hands, as if gripped by a migraine.

"Could it be," he said, "that there was a fourth figure present in our conference?"

The Morgana understood what he meant, and drew her voluminous rags close as if someone had been peering at her without permission, but Mendorix had to be dull and ask, "What are you talking about?"

"Could it be, slug-brain," said Merlin, "that none of us has actually entered the others' vision-world, but that we are all of us called into someone else's?"

"But whose? And where?" said Mendorix.

Merlin pointed to the stars. "I can't say. But that stroke of brilliance up there seems to be for us. There is a House of Pendragon, you know, here on the island of rude kingdoms. Neither more prestigious nor less barbarian than that of Olaf the Mighty or Bryn the Beleaguered or Eldred-with-a-face-like-a-jug-of-ale. But if the world is changing, as the Morgana proposes it is, perhaps the House of Pendragon readies itself to deliver to us a champion, whether we ask for one or no."

"I am no handmaiden to a House of Barbarians!" cried the Morgana. "Really, I'd retire and write my memoirs first."

"I am not talking about the actual family, the scions of farmers who wrestle with mud and plead with clouds and must be grateful that one grain out of five goes uneaten by rooks. I am talking," continued Merlin, "about a House: about that strange and human structure that is part history and part story, in which barbarians take up their dwelling.''

''A keep?'' said Mendorix.

''If you will,'' said Merlin, ''a keep. Though not a castle keep, not the kind you build with stone, but the kind you build with legend.''

''Oh,'' said the Morgana, suddenly disgusted. ''Legend. Pfaah. Legend is to Existence as men's sexual boasting is to their actual prowess. Meaning that it bears no relationship at all.''

''Maybe not till now,'' said Merlin, worrying things over, turning his hands upon themselves, staring at the ground. ''But the House of Pendragon may have a legend in store for itself, and if barbarians are changing—are to change—perhaps legend itself is part of the structure of change. A new place in which they can live and understand themselves.''

''I am tired of this vision, whether it be yours, mine, or the stars,'' Mendorix told both of them. ''I know only how to build castle keeps. I want to move on with my life and suffer with my own. Strike your bargain with me now, or let me go. Look, the last of the mist is lifting up, like smoke from dying fires, and the ground is solid, and down I can walk, back into Britain, home to Cornwall. Say your farewells and let me go. I can wait for some misbegotten House of Pendragon to think up a legend for itself as easily in the huts on broken promontories lunging into the Atlantic as I can lollygagging about here with a couple of self-important magicians.''

''It's not quite all in place yet . . .'' murmured Merlin.

"Not that I have any stake in this," said the Morgana, "but I rather agree with you, for once."

At this, Pot suddenly shuddered as if in disgust, and the two coals that could rub each other into Fire fell to the ground. The coals rolled, one over the other, right through the triangle in which the travelers sat, across to the edge of the bluff. There they squirmed until they had ignited into Fire once again, and Fire leaped up into the waiting mouth of the dragon head.

The dragon gulped once or twice, adjusting, and turned its baleful eyes on the astonished three.

"For the love of all that's holy," said the dragon, speaking in little shoots of Fire, "does one have to rearrange the very stars to spell out what you are to do?"

"I refuse to be lectured by a mode of transport," murmured Morgana. "It's unbecoming." But the dragon spewed a scarf of Fire so far that she had to pull back and nod her reluctant acquiescence.

"Build the castle here," said the dragon. "Build the castle keep of the Pendragons. Build Camelot, build the stone house of it, build the walls and ramparts and arches. Throw together the stables, lean the highest walls you can imagine against strong buttresses, pitch the roofs steeply, drain the blood of the barbarian legacy into colored glass, so that there may be some future a bit different from the past! You have here with you the most talented person ever to think in stone!"

"I beg your pardon," said Merlin, stiffly. "I had my hand in the arrangement of Stonehedge, remember."

It was his turn to be licked by a little angry Fire.

"All right, all right," said Merlin. "Camelot?"

"Which Pendragon will live here?" said the Morgana.

"History takes care of itself," said the dragon. "Now keep your promise to the builder."

"A point of curiosity," said Merlin. "Are you the dragon speaking, or Fire?"

"I am neither the dragon nor Fire," came back the answer, "merely Legend waiting to be born, if you can bother to do your jobs."

The dragon closed its eyes as if exhausted. It panted a bit; the wooden sides of the vessel heaved. Fire reduced itself to two coals again, who returned, exhausted, to Pot.

"Very well," said the Morgana. "Perhaps the whole world is speaking the same thing to us, Merlin, and it is a universal vision we enter into, not yours nor mine nor our feeble builder's. Is there a Camelot to be built here, then?"

"You owe the man a pair of good hands," said Merlin. He fixed her with a penetrating gaze. "You know you do."

"I'll do the hands," said the Morgana at last, "you come up with a pair of gloves. This is going to be a long job and a hard one, and he may as well protect himself."

She stood up and straightened her robes about her. Suddenly she did not look nineteen any more, but a thousand years old, or more. She was not so much human as something catlike—but huge, like a lion. She moved her lips and mumbled something from deep within her, deeper than the voice box in the throat. Her hands twitched in a miniature way, as if describing the shape of hands in the air. Mendorix thought, *This is where my dream ends.* For he knew that dreams of desire mount right to the moment before delivery, and then fail.

He could not bear the frustration of waiting—the longer he waited to wake, the worse would be the disappointment. Rejoining the world in its sullen aspect every morning was one of his gravest sorrows. Out of old habit he made to strike himself, so as to bring this vision to an end, and accept the limits of life again.

But his hand, upon hitting his face, had five open fingers to it, and his other hand flexed the same.

By the time the tears had begun to slow, he could make out Merlin climbing into his coracle. The Morgana was already on board her dragon, making for a different direction. The sea they sailed upon now was not the white mist of winter but the haze of spring leaves. The moonlight was so bright that the leaves showed their green. "What, you leave me now?" he wept. "Just at the beginning?"

"We have done our job, you do yours," cried Merlin. His coracle was listing badly.

"We did do our job," answered the Morgana, in a voice like wind through leaves. She patted the head of the dragon, who rolled its eyes at her. The Morgana continued, "Nice working with you again, Merlin, you old reprobate!"

"I'll see you in the court of the Adjudicator!" he called.

"Not if I see you first!" she answered merrily. "Have a nice nap, if you ever get to it. Sounds like things are going to heat up a bit before they settle down."

"Easier for me than you," he answered. "I reclaim youthful vigor with every passing day."

"That's right, hit me where it hurts," she cried. "But maybe life among the barbarians will be better than I thought. You might even want to get involved before you nap."

"By the by," called Merlin, "can you really carry a time-bound barbarian into the court of the Adjudicator? Were you telling the truth?"

"Well, you lied about having just met Mendorix, when you had already saved his tongue from being ripped out at Olaf's castle-warming party!" She chortled wickedly. "You forgot to do the gloves, by the way."

Mendorix watched them disappear, the way the mist dissolved in the air, and the wind that caressed the green waves that had borne them up brought forth from the trees the scent of blossoms.

Then they were gone. And Mendorix turned to survey the ground. His hands were ready. His head was clear. His belly was full. The light was good. Cornwall could wait. King Olaf the Mighty had better beware. Someone or something was coming. The stars of the Pendragon said so. As for Merlin and the Morgana, they had played their part, and could retire from the stage. Probably no one would know of their agency in human affairs. Unless, of course, Mendorix chose to tell someone. To build a story with words— words that could flow from a pen that his hand was now equipped to hold. Unlikely, of course. There was the castle of Camelot to build first. Maybe someone else would tell the story. Maybe now he was not sentenced to aloneness, and could find a woman to hold, who would give him a child. And he had new hands to caress a child with, and a practiced tongue with which to tell a story. What a good story to tell a child.

THE SWORD OF THE NORTH

by Rosemary Edghill

Rosemary Edghill is the author of more than a dozen novels, including *Speak Daggers to Her, The Book of Moons, Bowl of Night, The Sword of Maiden's Tears, The Cup of Morning Shadows, The Cloak of Night and Daggers,* and *Fleeting Fancy,* among others. She has worked in publishing, and lives in Poughkeepsie, where she writes full-time.

Told in a high bardic style, "The Sword of the North" gives a startlingly different take on Arthur's wooing of Guinevere and the legend of Excalibur, in a historical setting.

Here is the story as it was never told. Here is the story as it was first laid down in all the garb of truth, for it is a story of the Elder Days, before the Dead God, called by his followers The White, had come much into the land Logres to burn the groves and the singers and to take our story from us. And though the story could not die, but would come back each spring as green as the salt-meadows of the Summer Country, this the tale was dressed anew in the garb of city-men and hall-feasters, in such wise that those who knew it first would not know it.

You who have heard the story will know it in other

wise than in its first truth, for in the telling it has splintered into a thousand tales, so that none but the North Wind could gather together all the strands of it and weave it once more into whole cloth now that Time and the White Man have unriddled it. Yet the tale needs be told, and here is a riddle: If I tell you this tale, what will you hear?

Listen.

The Bear King had been crowned in the River City at Wintermass, and all through the hard cold, when the River Tame had lain sluggish beneath the cold, had lain covered in ice so thick a man could dance on it, the Twelve Tribes and their Princes had sat quiet, wondering which way the cat would jump in the spring. No one of them wished to dare the Bear King's power, nor yet that of his Riders, and no two—or three, or five—of the Princes could agree on the terms of an alliance.

But come spring, things would be different. A man might make mistakes in the spring. A man must choose a bride.

The Bear Totem could marry where it would. On that the priests and the Princes agreed. The priests of the White Man, who had come lately to Logres from over the water, might hold their own opinions about this, as they did about so many things, but since neither they nor the White Man were related to anyone in Logres that anyone could discover, their opinions were entirely without merit. Hawk could not marry Hound, nor Horse marry Hind, for these were the laws set down from the ancient days, when the Great Beasts had come down out from the Heaven Houses and lain with the men and women of the Chalk, so that their children forever after might look to their kin-Totems for guidance and good hunting.

But Bear-kin might look where it chose for a bride. None of the other Houses were closed to the House of the Bear by taboo or custom, and the Bear King in the River City walked alone, without brothers or cousins to find brides for. The Bear King had no sister to bear his heir; who sat the High Seat of Logres after him must be the child of the woman he took to wife, and no child of his.

But the Bear King had known that this price was his to pay before he gathered his Riders and set them against the Legions, for he had had his doom of the Raven-wizard who raised him in a tower far from the Chalk. So he was reconciled to it as much as any man might be, and all that remained, now that he had gained the High Seat and taken the City of Legions that was the River City, was to name his bride, and see that she got with child.

It seemed that every Prince of the Twelve Tribes that spring had a sister, who brought a dowry of obligation and blood-feud, and who hoped to have the High Seat of Logres to gift to her son. A wise man would remain a bachelor in the face of such interest, and sleep among the Young Men for another year or even two.

But the Bear was not Bear alone, but also King. King by force of arms, King by luck and fortune and the kiss of the White Horse Goddess. He had learned swiftness from Stag and ruthlessness from Badger, cunning from Fox and long-sight from Eagle; all the

Great Beasts had given up some part of their gifts to him, so that he might rule all the Lodges fairly.

But most of all he was Bear—strong and slow to anger; terrifying in his fury . . . and stubborn in the working out of a puzzle.

The Legions had broken with last spring's rains, but the first frosts had come before they were all gone beyond the sea. He had wintered in the River City with all his court. The Bear King had been given much time to think that winter, with all the Princes of Logres camped in the city he had taken from the Legions and made his own. In his high tower he listened to the ice-songs of the Tame and thought of the spring, when the camps—spread upon the earth as the Wheel of the Great Beasts was spread against the sky—could become war-camps, and all that a man had won could trickle away between the stubbornness of men and the spears of the raiders from across the sea, grown bold now that the Legions were gone from Logres and Armorica and all the lands that a man might name.

He had no sister, so he must have a wife, bound to him with oaths and spells, so that any child of hers would be as true to him as any sister's-son, to hold the land and the Princes after Bear went to walk with the Mother of Bears in the Bear Lodge in the Silver Wheel.

But who would she be? And how could he hope she would cleave to him only, preferring him over her brothers?

"A man must marry," said Ancel the Hawk, who had been raised on the great horse-meadows of Armorica, meadows whose grass was so lush and long that it was mistaken by strangers for the shining surface of a vast inland lake.

"Perhaps she will not have a brother," said Cei the Horse—who had shared the High King's wet nurse in the long-ago time when Princes hid their heirs among the countryfolk in hope they would live to make old bones.

"As well hope she will not have a mother," Ancel said gloomily. He was promised to a woman of the Dove clan, for Hawk men always married with Dove women, and his bride's mother was much in his thoughts.

" 'A mother, a brother, a clan—three things every woman has,' " Cadal the Hound said.

"Do all women have clans?" the Bear asked, in much the same mild tone he had once asked, "Must the Legions sit in the city on the Tame forever?" His bladebrothers both gazed at him in surprise . . . and contemplation.

They had heard the tales, of course—all the Bear Court had—tales brought south by peddlers and horse-wranglers and priests of the White Man who tramped the land as endlessly as though they had no hill or barrow to call their own. In the North, far and far and far from the River City that had once belonged to the Legions, was a woman called White Shadow, who had no brother and no clan, a woman who struck with the silence of the Great Owl, and kept the Princes of the Bear from driving off the little red cattle and the swift black pigs. A woman whom the Painted People followed across the heather, calling her their Sword against the Legions, for that the

Legions were gone was not something well believed in the North, nor did the Bear King wish it so.

In the cold dark days after Hallowmass, when the food ran low and every man's mind ran much to the first green shoots of spring, the Bear's mind ran to the Bandit Queen in the North, whom Men called Guen-Hwyfar, White Shadow. And he thought of his Princes, and of the fact that quarrel though they did—and they quarreled much between Hallowmass and Wintermass—the one thing that all the Princes could agree upon was that the apple of the High Kingship to come should fall to the child of one of their Lodges, and that is should be bestowed elsewhere entirely was perhaps the one thing that could unite them.

Thus it was that the High King came to dream of a sword.

His dream was a public thing, announced at the High Feast of Wintermass. It was a politic thing as well, giving encouragement to the solitary priests of the White Man who had followed the Legions into Logres and remained after they had fled, as well as to the skin-clad priests of the Horned Lord who was both Hunter and prey and his Lady-consort who held the wheel of the twelve Great Beasts of Heaven in her pale hands and sent the White Horse Goddess to her chosen. Lord and Lady, and Motherless God, Bear's dream held out hope and deference to them all.

The sword Bear dreamed of was an invincible thing, sent by the spirits to put the seal of blessing upon his stewardship of the land. It held out the promise of peace through invincibility, for who held the sword held the land, and could be neither wounded nor defeated in battle.

Thus—Bear told them all—he had been promised, did he only have the courage to seek out this Cael-born, the Sword of Burning Stone.

A dream-quest was a sacred matter, and by such a quest had Bear first set his foot upon the road that had brought him to the High King's seat. Did the High King go forth on such a quest, the Princes would not look for him to choose a bride until he returned, nor, within reason, do that which would bring him back to settle their disputations with his quest unfulfilled. And—did the High King leave behind him in the City of Legions a sufficient force of loyal troops—the tribes who had acclaimed him at high summer, at Harvest, at Hallows, and at Win-termass would applaud him still upon his return.

So it was that King Bear rode out on the first day of the Feast of Lights, taking with him his Horse, his Hawk, and his Hound—Princes all and Lords of the Dance within their Lodges—to seek the sword that burned and would not break, the sword sheathed in the unremitting darkness of the North.

The four companions and their soldiers rode through lands that had bled for the taxes imposed by the Legions, and so were yet loyal; through lands that had feared the Legions in their absence, and so were grateful; through lands where the High King was a fable but bands of armed men were not, and so were prudent. And at last they reached the Wall that the Legions had set around the edge of their lands to mark the uttermost edge of their dominion, beyond the edge of which the edge of the world was not an unlooked-for thing.

Upon the way, the Bear had begun himself to believe in a sword.

As the rumors of the Court grew dim, so did the reports of White Shadow wax vivid. And for the first time did the Bear begin to hear tales of White Shadow and Black Shadow, of the horses which sped faster than the winter sun in the high places, of the sword whose burning blade was forged from the metal of the spear which had drunk the blood of the Dead God himself.

A sword forged in the blood of a god—even in the blood of a distant foreign god who had no mother and who sometimes died—was a sword with which to reckon. If a man's blood was let by such an edge, who was to say whether he could find his way to the meadows that lay beyond the Wheel of Heaven at all? It might be that he would be carried off instead into the Hollow Hills, or would wander hungry forever among the star-herds, unable to course his rightful prey. It was in the Bear's mind that men would avoid such a sword, and would twice avoid the owner of such a sword.

And so it was that it grew in the Bear's mind that to have such a sword would be a very great thing indeed. Did he return to the Court with such a sword belted at his hip, the Princes might take less notice of the fact that no daughter of their mothers was to sit beside the High King and bear the war-leader who would gather up all their allegiances in his two hands like the reins of a dozen chariots. The Princes might sit quiet for a season—or two, or three—and grant him time in which those who hunted and those who tilled might forget how Bear had come out of the forest with no mother and no sister to speak for him.

They might forget how the Old King had been of the Snake Clan, a man whom the Princes were accustomed to ignore and a King whom the Legions did not bother to fight. Old Snake had sat on the Chalk and sworn himself Lord of all the World, but Old Snake had been only the grandson of Nineve who had been sister to Meredin whose Lodge no man had known, for some said Cat and some said Hawk and some said Snake. And Nineve had said nothing at all, and her brother Meredin had been High King over all the tribes until the day his magic had failed. In that day the Legions had made his death between two oak trees, with him bound to both so that he could not escape the doom they crafted for him.

And Nineve his sister had fled away, living in the houses of the foreign governors and hiding among their women, until the son she bore was tall and strong, and a White Horse woman made him forget that he had been raised to be one of the clanless conquerors who broke the power of the Princes and ignored the necessities of the Land. But though his Blood mastered him, Nineve's child could not master the Princes, nor would any Lodge open to him, save Snake, and that only for the cause that Snake must always do what the other Lodges would not.

And did not Nineve's child buy his half sister Vivaie Nineve's daughter out of the houses of the Legions when she was yet a child and give her to his wife Graene the Hare to raise, the blood of Nineve would have vanished into the earth like the water from the rain. And so in his time was Old Snake born to the line of Meredin High King, and so did Bear come in the end to take back lands and power and High Seat all.

But Bear had no sister. And so, with the meats of the Feast of Lights barely cold upon his table, did he ride north.

At first he and his Horse, his Hawk, and his Hound came to lands where people made the sign against foul luck when the name of the White Shadow was mentioned, and next to the lands where men laughed when they were told who it was that Bear and his companions rode north in the cold and wet of Brightmass to seek. But in the last quarter of the spring moon, they came to a place where all that men said was that she was beyond the hill, did Bear aspire to speak to her.

And they spoke, too, of the sword Cale-born, which here they said was forged from the crown of the Daystar, which the Burning Prince had lost when he had been flung down out of heaven for his insolence to the Unconquered Sun. And for his safe conduct through the lands of the Beast Mother, whose silver castle held all Lodges, it had been that the Prince must surrender all his jewels, and from his iron crown had been forged the sword that held all the Burning Prince's power to sway the hearts of men. And thus it was that Cale-born was a sword that did not break.

Even without seeing it, the Bear came to want that sword as much as he wanted a kingdom for his heir. He'd fought with Legion castoffs and had them shear off at the hilt. He'd led his troops to victory with an iron sword forged on the Chalk by Weyland Smith himself, but it had shattered in his final battle, and in the end victory had been purchased with the spear that held his standard, himself wrapped in its blue cloth sewn with bright gold as if it were his winding-sheet, so that it should not be trampled under foot and lost to the eyes of men in the course of that grave battle.

The sword he carried now was good cold iron, tempered and browned and brought from far over sea, its hilt wrapped in braided horsehair and its pommel and scabbard encrusted with agates and pearls. It was a good sword, a King's sword, and it would serve him well, especially did he have the luck not to carry it into battle.

But it was not a legend-sword. And it was not such a sword as he'd sworn to all the Princes at their feasting that he'd dreamed of, back in the city of Legions. That such a sword was here after all made Bear wonder if some antic godlet had put the notion of this quest into his mind, knowing that against all expectation Bear (who hated magic) would find it true when he had journeyed to the ends of the earth in the service of no more eldritch a thing than guile and statecraft, conjured with no more sorcery than his own good mind that he might hold the Princes and the Tribes for a wheel of seasons more.

God-ridden or not, there was nothing to do here and now but go on, for god-sword or woman-sword or perhaps for his doom entire.

"What shall we do?" Cei the Horse asked, and Ancel Hawkwing and Cadal of the Dog Clan looked as though they would like to ask the question as well. *How shall we take the woman by force if she is here with her war band?* his eyes asked, and Bear knew that all his companions wondered as much. The warriors they traveled with were enough for safety in turbulent lands, not enough to win them the war chief of the Painted People and see them safe home carrying her against her will.

"I shall speak to the lady," Bear said with a white grin. "I shall whelm her with fair words and plain speaking."

His companions laughed, taking his words for a joke. But he meant them. He was the Bear, who had sworn doom to the Legions in Nineve's name when all he had to his hand was a horn-pick and a leather sark. He had come here through words and he would leave here through words, and thus would the matter be.

No king who wishes to hold his throne dares risk being made to look a fool, no matter how far from home he is, or how loyal the escort he bears with him. Even these who were his Riders, who were Lords of the Dance in their own Lodges, would turn upon him the instant he showed himself to be weak, or sick, or mad. For on the Chalk there was no room for any of these three things, and no man would long rule beneath his mother's roof or at his sister's fire who could not outrun the wind, see the dark face of Lady Moon, or sing down the herds by the eloquence of his own tongue.

And Bear thought him well upon what he had learned in the spring, of a woman who could cause

the Painted People to follow her across the heather,
who could bring for them success and wealth in raid-
ing the small red cattle and the swift black pigs, a
woman who could gain them wealth and keep them
from squandering it all to their scathe, as was the
way of raiders. Such a woman was as sharpe a blade
as a sword that did not break, and could she bind
the Painted People to her, to bind the Princes of the
Twelve Tribes were no greater task.

So Bear did not go himself to hear what the White
Shadow would say to him, lest we have to take note
of that which he did not wish to hear. Bear sent
Ancel the Hawk, robed as a messenger, to the camp
beyond the hill to speak with the Sword of the North.
He gave Ancel to tell her that the Great King of the
South, the King who had driven the Legions from
the land beneath the banner of the White Horse Goddess, had come to have speech of her. Ancel was to
say nothing of brides or sisters or swords, or of the
High King's pressing need to marry, only that the
High King would await her at dusk on the crest of
a hill which he and his comrades had passed on their
way here.

This hill was a temple in the old style, with a spiral
path cut into the hill all the way around the hill, so
that one might walk a mile and more before reaching
the top. The path was beaten hard and laid with
shells and stones and bone, so that it made a white
ribbon around the green hill, and at the top where
the hill stretched smooth and flat and green, there
was a Dance, its points marked out with ashers
brought from the hardwood forests across the Swan
Road, and so the Bear had known it for a place of

prophecy, where the oak-priests of the sky-god Thunder would convene to tell the people how the stars would rise, and when the moon would go red or the sun go dark.

Those ghost-choked high places were little used in the South, for the White Horse Goddess had no need of them. She did not mark the wheel of the stars, but the seasons; the oak-priests who had made the high places a mirror of the bowl of night were long gone from howe and tor, trodden beneath the iron sandals of the Legions. The Legions had torn down the markers and built their camps upon the high places, and neither the sky-god nor the Mother of Beasts had stopped them. And now that the Legions were gone, and the high places were free to any, no one remembered what their use had been, nor how to tell anything more than any man might tell by the notches on a stick, that a moon and half a moon came between the Feasts, and that the Great Feasts alternated with the Lesser Feasts like beads on a string. And so the priests of the Hunt Lord counted, and the Lesser Feasts were kept, and the priestesses of his Lady-consort counted, and the Greater Feasts were kept, and the Twelve Tribes kept the Wheel. And no one cared when the moon and sun should change their colors, for those things were in the ordering of the Beast Mother in the Castle of the Silver Wheel, and doubtless she had her own reasons for making them as she would.

So the high places were not in use in these times, though the wandering priests of the White Man often claimed them, saying these were the holy places of their strange mortal god. No one felt it worth the effort to argue with them, wrong though they were, since the tors were of little use as tillage or pasturage.

The Legions had not come to this side of the Wall, however, and so the oak-priest's high places remained unchastened north of the Wall, though Bear and his men had seen no priests or offerings upon them. When he had ridden to the top of the one he proposed as his trysting-place, he had found the marker-stones overgrown, the Dance of white stones overgrown with the passage of seasons, and the pits that held the movable asher filled in with flints and mud. The sky-god was gone from this place as well, and so the Bear did not think he would mind this use of his place. And it was such a place that no armed band could secretly approach, which was the other reason that the Bear had chosen it for his use.

And so at dawn he sent Ancel into the camp of the Sword of the North, who was not Queen here only because the people north of the Wall claimed no lands to be King and Queen over. But the Sword of the North moved as she would, like the wind over the meadows, and pastured where she would, and took what she would, from all the tribes that lived and warred in this land, and so, by all the uses of the South, she was here Queen, and a great troubling to the borders.

And so the Bear set his Hawk in flight, and waited through the day, his Horse and his Hound at his side. He had told neither of them the truth of his dream, nor yet that the dream had become truth, and now he was glad of it, for as they waited in their camp all their talk was of the sword Cale-born, and how the Princes would not dare raise their hand against a sword that could slay a god and set a man's soul to wander.

Ancel the Hawk did not return from the camp of the White Shadow by the time the sun had reached midheaven, nor had he returned by the time the sun began to wester. Soon it would be full dark, and the Bear must leave his warriors in order to reach the place he had said he would be by the time appointed to that meeting, though that his Hawk did not return was a fell omen.

Cei and Cadal both swore they would go beside him, for that if the Sword of the North thought to take him unaware and hold him to ransom, they two by good sword and spear would lesson her that this was an unwise counsel. Yet the Bear would not have it so, for to that meeting upon the high place he swore he would go alone, taking neither Horse nor Hound, bitterly though they cried against it.

But the Bear knew better than they what it was he was about, and to stand in his strength and brandish weapons was in no wise a part of his plan. He did not have the force of arms that would let him stand against the White Shadow and the Painted People, for even did they have no more than slings and bone arrows and polished stone knives, still they were many, and moved like cloud-shadows on moonlit night. He was here beyond the Wall upon his own luck, and by the White Shadow's sufferance and grace now that he had drawn her mind to him, and this being so, the only weapon that he might wield was the harmlessness that he could show her; harmlessness and honesty and true dealing and fair-speaking.

And some of these things were true, and some were less true, but none of them was a lie, for the White Horse Goddess had strictly enjoined the Bear from saying right out a thing he knew not to be true, for the White Horse Goddess was sister to the Ash Goddess who had all the care of runes and memory in her hand, and who had made the solid places of the World out of Truth back in the Morning Time. So those seeking the favor of the Ash Goddess and her sister had to have a care not to undo all the Ash Goddess' careful work by false telling.

So it was that the Bear came to the Castle of Stars beyond the North Wind with no more weapon to his hand than his five strong fingers full with runes.

The Bear had much time upon the high tor to think upon his folly and his flaws. The Starcastle did not make a great height as might be reckoned in the Western Mountains, but high enough it was that the undiverted wind that blew over the top of the howe bit icy through the Bear's thick wool cloak dyed with cochineal and gall, and made his bare knees above the dyed and gilded leather of his boots ache with the chill. The warmth of his horse was some comfort, as it cropped the thick grass of the high place unimpressed by gods or ghosts. The Riders' horses were such beasts as no one elsewhere in all Logres had. Taller than a man they were, with legs longer than a man's legs and the heart and bone to run a day and a night without stopping. The Bear had made certain that all the horses they rode were geldings only, for that the bloodline the Bear had stolen should be stolen again and used against him was a thing not to be borne.

And so he waited, sitting upon the back of a beast so handy he had once jested that its brains had been cut away with its balls. But mild as its nature was, its restless desire to shed his weight and take itself elsewhere to sleep the night out away from the wind only served to mark and mark again how foolish it was that the Bear might discover himself seeming, should the dawn come and find him here on the high place, and the Lady not have made her appearance.

Upon such matters did his mind turn for all the hours that it took for the sun to die away out of the sky, for the spring stars to burn bright against the cold clear sky, and for the golden shield of the moon to inch slowly into midheaven. The creak of leather and the jingle of metal were his only companions, that and the sigh of the wind through the pine trees and the faint, far-off hooting of the night birds. That and his thoughts.

If she did not come tonight, he would look a fool. He would send her a second summons with tomorrow's dawn, but one more night only could he spend in waiting on her, or perhaps, if the White Horse Goddess favored him, two, before he must ride into her camp with all the force he could muster, or have it said from the Wall to the Chalk that the Bear King was one who did not know his own mind, nor yet could seize in the Day World what the Gods had given him in the Night. He held the Princes in just the way that a man led a pig to market, by keeping the animal from seeing that it had any choices. Just so was it with his Princes, the bone and muscle and sinew of Logres. Let them see that there was any choice but to follow him, and bolt they would, like a herd of willful pigs—to be slaughtered just as easily, by the Painted People from the North, by the Northwolves from over the Swan Road, or by the Legions themselves, come again to take back what was theirs. Rumor said that the Legions were called to the walls of the Eternal City in the East and could not leave it, but rumor had lied before.

So he knew already that he must ride, and that such a riding would end badly, for one of them. And Bear found himself wishing the absent lady as well as he would wish himself, that he need neither slay her nor be slain. Perhaps the jewels of the Emperor's Sword would dazzle her enough that she would exchange it freely for the blade of unbreakable iron from which she had taken her own eke-name. But for that to be she must come, for did she not, someone would talk of it, and that gossip would be his death as surely as cold iron between the ribs.

If only she would come. All possibilities would be open then. Anything might happen, did she only answer his summons.

It was a long time till midnight. Time enough for a man to despair, but to hold out, stubbornly, against hope, so that he must not admit defeat until the words were forced from his tongue by the grip of Fate hard and cold about his throat.

And then, when the night was darkest, she came.

The gelding, which had been dozing unhappily, head down and feet set, raised up its head, ears cocked. In an instant the Bear was alert, sliding from its back and dragging its head down, muffling its muzzle against his cloak to keep it from making any sound. And as he strained for silence, he heard the sound that his mount had heard first: the slow beat of horses' hooves against the resonant turf, and the faint singing of a light-bodied war chariot.

Chariots were much used in war, far more so than the greathorse cavalry that was the Bear's own preferred weapon. The horses Logres bred were scarcely larger than ponies, and the weight of a two-man chariot with two horses to draw it was less to either horse than the weight of a mounted man would be upon its back, and so they were fast, and nimble, and terrible upon the field. Against the floor of a chariot a warrior might brace himself to deliver a killing stroke, but the warrior must be brave, and the driver fearless, for neither could wear the strong bronze armor of the man afoot, nor even the studded ring-mail of the Bear King's Riders.

Still the chariot came on, each piece of it making its own special music: the willow-withes of its body creaking and sighing as they moved, the boiled leather of its undercarriage making its cricket-song of strain, the cast bronze of its fittings jingling with the high sweet sounds of falling ice.

And the Bear steeled himself to await it, listening.

It seemed a very long time before the chariot reached the top of the howe, and he saw it beneath the pale light of Lady Moon.

The body of the chariot glistened with fresh paint. The horses that drew it were the small swift beasts of the Highland, and they, too, had been painted and ornamented, their faces white and their legs red, and their bodies marked in signs to turn the spear and ax. Disks of gold were braided into their manes, and beads of amber into their tails, and they carried their heavy heads high and haughty, as though they knew the worth of what they carried.

The driver was small and dark, like all the Painted People—so much Bear could see by the uncaring light of Lady Moon. She crouched in the front of the chariot, making her body low to the ground so that the light and flimsy thing did not tip itself and fly to pieces as it came up the path. Bear could see her hands on the traces; see them mottled with the dark lines and spirals of a skindancer. She wore little that he could see, yet the intricate marks—each the proving of a spell that she could call upon at need—covered her body like a close garment. Her spears stood upright beside her, their leaf-shaped heads pale and glittering in the moonlight as the body of the White Horse Goddess, and so the Bear knew that she bore the fine stone spears of the Painted People, each one wrought with terrible spells and each yet to drink the blood of an enemy.

Behind her, standing proud and upright, stood the woman whom rumors had named Sword of the North, the unbreakable Burning Bright that Bear had come to claim.

She was as bright and merciless as a swordblade, her hair stiffened with lime and clay and swept back and up until it made an egret's haughty plume above her head and down her back, rattling faintly like dry knucklebones being cast as the chariot moved. She was tall and fair, like the Northwolves who had sometime fought in the Legion's pay, and her eyes were merciless ice. She wore a sleeveless tunic of white doeskin that fell halfway down her thighs. It was sewn with plaques of gold-chased bronze, and she glittered like a river. The sides of the chariot were low enough to show him that she also wore the high horsehide sandals that those who had marched with the Legion had worn, and Bear wondered if she had taken them from the body of an unwary soldier who had crossed over the Wall.

The blue rings of one who has been to visit Death were painted around her eyes, and her lips were the bright red of the mushroom-eater. They glistened as blackly as blood in the moonlight. Her arms were heavy with spiraled gold praise-rings, such as one might break off pieces from to reward a harper with, and her hands were heavy with dark-jeweled rings that were for greater gifts. Her hands were clasped about the hilt of a sword that she bore point-downward and naked before her in the chariot, so that its bright pommel-weight rested against her heart.

Surely this was the blade made of magic that had bathed in the blood of the Dead God, the sword that had been forged from the Crown of the Daystar. Its blade was all one long whitefire shimmer in the moonlight and its metal was as smooth as the purling water of the wave. Its crosspiece was wide—long as a man's forearm, and worked with lines of gold so bright they left a pattern behind the closed eyes, and the dazzlement of that sight was so awful that a sane man would look away.

The Bear did not look away. This was such a blade as any man would yearn to wield, a swordbride to

still the tongues of his Princes and make whom he
chose High King thereafter.

The chariot came to a stop a spear's-throw from
where the Bear King stood beside his horse. When
the chariot stopped, the charioteer straightened to her
full height, holding the reins in one hand and reaching for the first of her spears with the other. Bear
could see now the gold collar about her neck, and
the brighter glow of the amber terminals upon it. She
had the skulls of ravens braided in her hair, and by
that he knew two of her names: Mor-Rhiganu, the
Raven Queen, called by the Legions Morgan the Fair.
Her cheeks and chin were scarred in the way that
the skindancer will use to mark those he has chosen
to walk in the nightlands when they are but suckling
babes, and the even black lines upon her face gave
her the look of a badger peering out from cover. She
wore nothing above the waist but her magic, and
stood as though she did not deign to see him, though
her painted fingers twitched upon the haft of the
spear.

Here was a perilous marvel indeed, that such a
mighty sorceress—for one who was not would surely
be struck dead by the power of the marks that she
wore as casually as a mortal man might wear a good
wool tunic—should act as a mere servant to the
woman who rode behind her. If the Sword of the
North could command such power, it was a thing
not to be wondered at that the Painted People followed her, and he would do well to be twice as wary
of her as he had been before, though Bear was as
suspicious as his namesake, and found it as easy to

doubt his friends as his enemies, and to doubt his allies more than either.

There was silence atop the howe, save for the sound of the gelding shaking its harness until the buckles rang, though the chariot ponies stood as still as if they had been carved in the Chalk. The ghosts given form by ancient rites moaned softly as they plucked at the fabric of the Bear's cloak, and the women in the chariot gazed at him with eyes that gleamed as coldly as lynxes'. Bear was hungry for another sight of the sword, and of the woman who carried it.

"Greetings to the White Shadow, Sword of the North," Bear said.

"Greetings to the Earth Man who has taken the city of Legions," the White Shadow returned, and her voice was as cold as the touch and as low as the sound of the blowing wind. "To the Man of Earth who leaves the city of Legions as the he-bear leaves his cave in the spring, greetings. And some might ask, what does the Bear seek in the North? There is honey in the skep, berries in the bush, salmon in the stream in his own lands. A lean guesting would the north-land make to a southern Bear, it is said."

Her words were careful, not asking but telling, and claiming nothing for herself. For a man might be anything here in the dark, and there was no night in the year when the Hunt might not find some unwary traveler and strike his soul from his body with a blow. And so it was all the more prudent that no person abroad in the night should ask any question, lest something answer it, nor yet name themselves as the one who spoke, lest something see them.

"There are other things that a Bear might want," the Bear answered in the same fashion as a prudent man and a mannerly guest. "Things that are found both in shadows and sharpness, some might say. Ought a Bear not hope to seize whatever weapons he can find, one might ask, if he desires peace and plenty for himself and for all who till and reap beneath the shadow of the High Seat? To be a Queen on the Chalk is a great thing, or so some might say."

The White Shadow stepped down from the back of the chariot. The Bear saw her little sorceress turn as if to stop her, the painted hand tightening upon the haft of the polished spear. Then he had no more thought for the dark sorceress, for the bright enchantress approached him.

The blade she carried naked in her hands burned like flame, so that the eyes must choose whether to look upon it or upon the face of its wielder. With an effort, the Bear forced himself to focus upon the wielder and not the weapon. When she stopped, that which her hands held was barely a spear's-length from his horse's head.

"Look well, Earth Man," the White Shadow said mockingly. "For it may be that what the Bear has seen is all that he may take away with him from this place, for all that he speaks of shadows and sharpness. He speaks, too, of Queens, and it may be that he speaks to one who is already Queen in her own place, and will leave with only the sight of his eyes to content him."

"Yet would a Bear take more," the Bear said, and spoke plain and bold in that ghost-haunted place, "Yet would I take more, to your hele and my own.

I have come far in search of you, for you have no like in the world nor yet have I. In such way can we not be matches for one another? For it is in my mind that I would marry, and who I marry shall be mother of the King to come, and so I have sought my match."

"It is said that you did not come in search of a bride, but in search of a blade. Might it not be so that bride and blade both have their match . . . and that you have it beneath your tongue to take the blade and leave the scabbard empty, not to hele but to ill?"

And then he saw that upon her hip she wore a scabbard for the blade she carried, and it was made of gilded pony-skin inlaid with boars' teeth and amber, and surely of such fashioning that there could not be two of them anywhere in the wide world.

And as quick as that, the White Shadow turned where she stood and raised her hand to forbid, and only then did the Bear see that the Raven Queen had raised the spear in her hand, and held it poised to pierce his heart.

Now did the Bear know what power the White Shadow wielded to bind such a powerful magician to her side. The Mor-Rhiganu and she were twinned; heart to heart and arm to arm, as a warrior with his doom or a maid with her lover. And thereby each of them was made greater, and more dangerous than one alone.

And thus it was not one bride that the Bear knew he had come to seek, but two.

"Never," said the Bear with dry-mouthed honesty, "would I take the sword and leave the scabbard empty. A man has to him two hands and two sides, and two women to live beneath his roof is a better thing than one. For I have no mother and no sister, and my hearth is cold and empty." He risked a glance at the Mor-Rhiganu, but the spear had not wavered, and her face was the mask of one who has walked in the nightlands and taken what she would.

"So you say now, but will you say so in a night's time?" the White Shadow said, and spoke now as boldly as he. "Much it has been in my mind to settle the proper gifting of this blade, for as all north of the Wall know, it is free for the taking should the right warrior try. So try then again in a night's time, and again shall I ask you what it is you will give for blade and scabbard both, or go now with that which you may take."

And she thrust the blade down into a cleft between two stones that had been a part of the Dance atop the tor, so that its hilt stood upright like the sign of the Dead God. And before the Bear could quite tell what she was about, she had sprinted back to the chariot and taken the spear from her lover, and the Raven Queen had turned the chariot horses as quick as a merlin could turn in the air, and set them down the spiral path around the dun at the hard gallop.

The Bear thought only for a moment of the sword that she had left undefended in the stone, for as certain as it was that the sun would rise in the morning was the truth that he would never go south of the Wall alive did he think to take the sword without the scabbard. And now that he had seen and spoken with her, it was the wielder that he wanted more. And so, after a moment's hesitation, he vaulted to his horse's back and spurred the gelding after the chariot, to set his will against hers.

The chariot ponies ran swiftly in the moonlight, the gold disks in their manes flashing like fire and the amber beads in their tails glowing like coals. The White Shadow jeered when she saw him, clutching the side of the chariot and shaking the Mor-Rhiganu's spear at him. And even as the Bear set his mount upon the spiral, he saw that he would not catch them, for Fair Morgan had left the path and set the horses to run down the side of the dun so that the Bear's horse could not follow, for did he take their path, he might lose his horse entire, and that was a humiliation he would not endure. So he set the gelding along the path, so that white bone and quartz stone and sea-shell flew up from beneath its hooves.

But when he had reached the bottom of the hill, the chariot was gone into the distance, and all his speed would not overtake it this night. He was confounded and empty-handed, and nothing was there for the Bear to do save to go back to his good companions and think how to tell this story so that no man among them would think that they might do what the Bear could not.

And so he rode into his own camp, where the soldiers waited about the fire, for it was in no man to sleep while the Bear King was gone from them. And he saw Ancel Hawkwing among them also, his arms burdened with good gifts from his guesting among the Painted People, and the Bear knew that Ancel had been honored as a messenger. And at his approach, Cadal the Hound rose up to his feet, crying out that here was a one stealing upon the camp at the dead of night, when no man knew who any man might be.

And the Hawk and the Horse took up burning brands, and their swords in their skill-hands and looked out toward the dark, so that the Bear had one moment to wish that he had brought Cale-Born with him so that all might see and marvel. But he thought him then that it was boy's work to flaunt what he still held hope to gain, and so he held himself from such thoughts and rode forward to where his men might see him.

And so they brought him within the circle of the fire, and plied him with heather-mead of the Painted People's brewing, and with partridge from their hunting, and when the Bear had a full belly and a warm skin he made to tell what he had seen atop the howe.

He told of the Dark Queen and the Bright, of the spirits of fell magic and of the unquiet ghosts, and no less did he tell of the sword Burning Bright whose nature it was to slay both men and gods. He told of how it sang in the night air, of how its sheen was burning water and woven moonlight. But in all the things he told, he did not tell that he had gained Cale-born for his own hand, and he did not speak to anyone of what it was that he hoped from the two Queens.

It was such a tale as might cause any man to laugh, that the High King had gone in search of that which was promised him by the Ash Goddess and had been turned away by unhandsome words, but he was yet who he was, and no man among them was there who dared to laugh, or to say aloud that the Bear had been bested by a woman.

And the Bear did not think that he had, yet even so, that day he thought hard upon the matter, and that day he rode forth at noonday, and learned over all the side of the hill, so that he knew every loose stone and burrow that was to be found upon it. And so it was that he found the well upon the top of the tor, set into the center of the Dance beneath a shaped stone. The water was pure, and cold, and sweet, and the Bear thought much upon what play he might make of this gift.

And that night, as Lady Moon climbed once more into midheaven, the Bear sat waiting. And this time he had painted his face for war, and wore all of his fine things but one: The sword from over sea, whose scabbard was crusted with agates and pearls, he did not wear, for it was laid upon the ground, sword and scabbard both, beside the other.

As for the godmetal sword, it stood where she had left it, struck between two blocks of stone so that it stood up like the sunstones the Western People put up to mark their roads. And the Bear knew that did he put pride before all other things, he could take the sword, just as he could have taken it the night before, and ridden back to his men with such a tale in his mouth as would without any falsehood from him make them arrogant with pride in their High King. A true-tale of how he had taken the sword Cale-born from a faery woman whose body burned like the moon, of how he had wrested it from her and from her demon as well, and how she had be-

stowed a hero's blessing on him, promising him re-
nown and glory in the life to come.

And this would be a good tale, and filling, and
would slake them as they turned and made for home.
And happen it might be that they would even believe
it, for so long as it took the White Shadow to marshal
her painted archers and stalk them through the
heather, killing them all in the way that the Painted
Men killed the wolf and the stag. Then the sword
would be hers once more, along with his bones,
though he would not be here to care. He would be
in the Castle of the Silver Wheel, being reborn of the
White Horse Woman.

But Bear had not sent the Legions home and spoken fair to all his Princes—bitter work that, and fruit-
less as spinning sand into wool—to die here in the
north before he had gotten his full way with them,
and the besting of them for his heir's sake. They who
had followed him for plunder and out of self-interest
and in betrayal were those whom he would see broken to the yoke before he died, so that the child of his
wife might drive a smooth-running team after him.

And so he told it to the White Shadow, when she
came with the Mor-Rhiganu to the top of the howe
to see if the Southern Bear was there again.

This night in her hand she held the small horn-
bow, black and curved like the Hidden Moon, that
could fill a man with arrows as the nettle filled him
with stings, and as quickly. And it gave neither a
good death nor an easy one, for the arrowheads were
not stone, but hollow bone, which had been soaked
in a potion of the Painted People's brewing, so that

the flesh liquified about the wound and made a hurt that never healed.

The Mor-Rhiganu did not like to see him there a second night, and the sword that would render him her lawful prey still untouched where it stood struck through the stone. She scowled darkly, and the animals upon her skin coiled and hissed.

But the Guen-Hwyfar turned to him a face as smooth as a bowl of new cream still warm from the cow, and asked him what gifts there were that might tempt her into the lands of the Southern Bear. And he told her of the tower where he was raised, and of Nineve and Old Snake, whose blood was his blood, and of how he had held it in his mind to free Logres from the Legions, and how it was that this thing was done. And he told her further of the Twelve Lodges of Heaven and the Great Beasts who ruled there, and of the twelve Princes who were each of their Totems to rule men on earth as the Great Beasts ruled the lesser beasts from the stars, and how the Princes and their peoples had followed his banner first in curiosity and then in spite, until at last he had been like the man who rode the North Wind to the castle of the Silver Wheel, who dared not dismount.

"But more than this I would say. I would say that I have no sister to give me an heir, so that my wife's son must be sister's-son to me. And I would say that it is cold in the heather, and that your people are a great trouble to me, so well they are led, and that if a King has no heirs he must have enemies. But rather I would have heirs than enemies."

There was silence when the Bear had finished

speaking. The White Shadow stood tall in white doe-skin, her eyes painted blue and her mouth painted red, and her hair standing out about her like a crest of feathers. She was beautiful and terrible, like Lady Moon and the White Horse Woman. If not for the shadows that moved over her as she breathed, he would not have known that she lived.

"Say to me what you will do, Lady," the Bear urged her, for while he might go empty-handed to his men one night, he did not think he could go empty-handed to them two nights and still be High King in the land.

"It is in my mind that did I give the blade, it would not satisfy you, for you have come for more than that and will not take less," the White Shadow said. "Though you have come for one sword, yet you would have three: blade and sheath and brides to match them."

"You will not!" said the Raven Queen, quick and fierce, so that the White Shadow turned again to face her.

"I will if I choose, and you will with me," she said. "Or would you that I take myself away, and leave you here alone?"

"You will not," said the Mor-Rhiganu, and this time there was pleading in her voice, and the look she turned upon the Bear glittered with her anger.

"I will if I would," the White Shadow said, "but this is a matter I have not thought on. So it is, Southern Bear, that I shall have to leave you yet another night to think upon the matter, fell host that you may call me. So I bid you fare well a second time, High King on the Chalk."

And again the Mor-Rhiganu had the painted ponies turned, and them running cat-quick away through the dark before the Bear yet knew the White Shadow was gone.

Only this time he had scouted the ground aforetime, and hoodwinked his horse's eyes. As quick as they had run he followed, setting the gelding to run and trusting to his own eyes to find the track, and to his knees and hands to guide the beast along it. And so fast did he follow the chariot along its straight track, that he had it before it reached the bottom of the howe. He leaped from his saddle to the ponies' backs, and dragged the team to a halt in a bare instant.

But when he raised his eyes to the chariot, he found that it was empty, and held neither wizard nor warrior. And afar off he heard the hoofstrike of another team, and knew that the Mor-Rhiganu's magic had dazzled him and played him false, and again he did not have what he came for, only fair words that might hold any meaning.

This time the Bear did not return to his men. When the sun rose, he drank water from the spring that lay in the center of the circle of stones, and fasted all the day, gazing upon the sword as it made its cross-shape against the sky. It taunted him by its presence: here, within his grasp, and that for which he had said he had come north of the Wall.

But this was now a truth no longer true. He had come not for the sword, but for the Sword—a truth hidden by lies, in the way of the Weaving Goddess.

He had come for the White Shadow and her sworn-sister, and must somehow gain what he could not take by force or guile, he whose whole life and luck had been the taking by force and guile. Now these two good comrades had deserted him, and he was left naked and handless.

What more was there for him than what he had done? He had spoken her fair promises and wooed her with sweet words. He had given her some of truth and all of dreams, and still she refused him. Force of arms would not serve him, not against cold iron and magic both. He could not think what else there was for him to try.

But he could not yield. It was not in him, once he had set his mind upon a thing, to turn aside from the path that led to its accomplishment. Thus he had sent the Legions out of Logres, though the doing had been a thing of some years. Thus he had bound all the Lodges together, the totems of hawk and hound and horse, of wolf and hare and badger. Thus he had made himself High King over all the tribes, that Logres would have one rule, from the Chalk to the Wall. And it was in his mind that—did he gain his will here—there would be one King even beyond the wall, all the way to the Ice.

So with one thing and another, the Bear could turn neither head nor hand away from this matter, though with his soul he despaired of his victory.

Thus he brooded, light-headed with fasting, as the moon rose upon the third night that he should meet with the Sword of the North. And he saw before him two roads—to win what he sought, or to perish upon this spot—and he knew not of his knowledge which he would find his feet upon when the moon set that night. And so he waited, standing this time at the mouth of the well, and waiting, with a great trepidation in his mouth, for the sound of the chariot's wheels upon the path to the howe.

And so it was that she came.

This time the Mor-Rhiganu led the horses, walking light and cat-footed upon the earth. Her painted cat's eyes glittered as she saw the Bear, and the ravens' skulls shone in her hair. It was plain that she and her sister had been of two councils, and that the skin-dancer had not expected to see him here.

And at this a great heat awoke in the Bear's chest, for he had never turned from a task he had set his hand to, nor turned from the field before his enemy had died, nor turned aside a challenge, a jest, or a pointed world. And he reached out his hand to the sword that stood upright in the earth.

"Here is a strange thing, sister," said the Mor-Rhiganu to the White Shadow. Her voice was low and harsh, like a crow-caw turned to speech. "Here is a southern Bear, come to find summer north of the Wall. All he has found has been a cold welcome, and a hungry one, and yet he has not got him back to his soft southern den. Who is it that has ever seen a bear with so little wisdom?"

He stepped boldly forward and drew forth the sword that had been in the stone, and the sword's weight balanced lightly in his hand, so that the point moved with no more effort than it would take to swish a cat-tail reed through the air.

"Wisdom have I much, little sister, when there is need, yet never have I heard that wisdom is called for to pick sweet berries, no matter how thorny the bush."

The Mor-Rhiganu gasped, to see him brandish the god-sword so carelessly, but the White Shadow laughed, for she, like he, had seen the game board all displayed, and knew that the sword which had slain the god was still in her keeping.

"Yet here is a thorn of unusual sharpness, southern Bear, and such a thorn might prick through the shaggiest of bear-coats." She sprang down from the chariot's floor and strode boldly forward, seizing the sword below the quillons, her callused hand upon the live steel where the blade was not edged, but squared for strength.

Like a man bespelled by nightmare he released it into her grip, not even taking the chance to raise his hand against her when she stood so close. She sprang backward with a cry of triumph, holding the sword above her head so that its blade burned like a beam from Lady Moon in the dark midheaven.

"Now it happens that I will leave you, southern Bear, for you have spoken me as fair as you might and we have forged no bargain. Here stays the sword and here stay I: Go you and your fair knights into the south again, and come no more north of the Wall."

"Which sword would you gain and which would you lose? Look well, Lady, upon that which you hold," the Bear said. He seized then the second sword, which had lain upon the ground in its scabbard of agate and pearl, yet this was not the sword for which the scabbard had been made. And he held them, sword and scabbard together, over the sweet dark water of the deep well, and in the opening of his hand they would both go down to its bottom,

from which no man might free them until the un-
making of the world.

"Do I open my hand, that which you would give
shall indeed be given, but not to man. Would you
be a bride of ghosts, Lady? Think on this thing."

And the White Shadow looked upon the sword in
her hand, and saw its excellence and trueness, and
how the grip was covered in black and white horsehair braided together, and knew that this was not
Cale-born that she had taken from the Bear's hand,
but another sword.

"I will be bride to no thing against my will," she
said in anger, "and what you have taken so is all
you will ever have."

And she stepped up into the chariot, where her
dark wizard-sister already stood, and this time the
chariot did not careen away, but moved stately and
slow as any wagon moved to take a King under hill.

The Bear's horse dipped its head to graze, and in
that moment the Bear saw the ruin of all his hopes.
The war-chariot bore itself away, and so died his
hopes of a high seat in the City of Legions, of a
summer court on the banks of the Cam, of the Tribes
left free in field and forest, their necks unbowed beneath the yoke of the Legions, and the axes of the
Northwolves who came along the Swan Road each
Spring. All these things were gone with that which
he had been unable to gain.

And seeing that, with his beating heart become a
serpent in his breast, he followed in the cart's track
on foot, holding the sword within his hand and crying out: "For my own Name's sake, Lady, do not leave
me who am utterly forlorn and bereft without you!"

And the chariot stopped. The White Shadow regarded him, her one hand clasped upon the false sword. And the Bear seized the other, and pressed it against his heart that she could feel its beating, and said:

"Lady, only stand by me, and I will use you well. But go from me, and it may be that I use the sword I have tricked from you to sever out my heart, for it will be no more use to me, nor I to any man, save that I gain you and all that you are."

"Hear him not," said the Mor-Rhiganu swiftly, but the White Shadow laughed.

"How is it that I shall not hear him, when he has said that thing which long I looked to hear? For I am a sharp edge, and will not go to any who does not know to value me. Yet here is a man who will have me for his right hand and you for his left, and that is a fair speaking, with our children raised as sister's sons beneath his roof. How is it that word shall come of a comelier dowry than this?"

And the Bear saw that the Dark One was still unreconciled to him, but for the love of her sister she would say nothing more. And though the Bear had never turned aside from a thing, equally did he know when victory might be better served in waiting. So fell a besieged city, so came an enemy army to steal away in the night before battle. And so came the Bear to stand here now, with the hand of the Queen of the North in his own hand, her power and her self a sword to his wielding, could he but gain this one last thing.

"Then come, an' you will of your good kindness, that I may make you known to my good companions," the Bear said, "and so that they may be known to your own, that a great feast and ceremony will be settled for our leavetaking."

And he held out to her the sword which he still held, and she drew it from the scabbard and let the scabbard fall, and held out the blade to him in turn. And thus did the Sword of the North put the god-blade into the hands of the Bear King, so that it passed from her hands to his. And she put upon him the harness of gilded pony-skin, and the scabbard inlaid with amber and boars'-teeth that were its furniture, and thereto he set the sword. And then he put the other sword, which was a King's sword also, into her hands, and set the White Shadow upon the back of his own tall warhorse, and so did they go down from the howe for the last time.

And when it was that they three had reached the bottom of the hill, the Mor-Rhiganu leaped down from her place in the wicker chariot, and unharnessed the little northern horses from the cart. And with the lines doubled in her hands she drove them off, so they ran snorting into the night.

"For they will draw no other chariot than this, and this car they will draw no more," said the skin-dancer.

And she broke the ashwood shaft of her spears over her knee so that they splintered, and dashed the polished flint heads of her spears against the rock so that they shattered.

"For I shall bear them against no man's enemies, nor shall any man bear them in his own hand."

And then she took the knife upon her belt and cut through her hair, so that it was shorn close by her ears like a beardless boy's, and the ravens' skulls lay on the earth.

"For I shall not keep the covenants that I swore in elder days, nor shall any man say that I have promised that which I would not do. It is myself only that you will have, son of Earth, and nothing of the powers of Air and Darkness which I have in past times called, yet I warn you now that the powers of Earth and Fire that are left to me are more terrible still than any thought which you might have held in your heart all your days."

"I am so forewarned," the Bear said, taking the last thing of the three which he had come to gain into his hand, "and it is yourself only that I shall take, knowing that the powers which you yet might wield are more despiteful than all the magic you have yet renounced. And in token of this I will call you not Mor-Rhiganu, who weaves the Dark, but Mor-Dhread, the singer."

And so the Bear King made his way into the camp of his own men once more, and took up his Horse, his Hawk, and his Hound. And with them he went among the Painted People and crafted a great song telling of the Sword which the High King had come north to gain. And when they had feasted three days there among the Painted People, the King with Two Shadows turned south again, to return to the River City beside the River Tame to tell his tale to the Princes, who would find their King with strong wives, yet with no sister of the Princes among them.

And so he went south, and in all the battles he was to thereafter fight, the Sword of the North did not break nor bend. And if she has not died, she may yet rule the High King's house there in the City of Legions, for if you have heard the tale in another way, be sure that it is not the tale as it was first told, nor the tale that is still known in the high places and upon the Chalk.

AUTHOR'S AFTERWORD TO "THE SWORD OF THE NORTH"

As students of the Arthurian legends know, the story's original form is far from the homogenized Malory version. In many of the stories, Arthur has a number of wives, most of whom are named Guinevere (or some variant thereof). Sometimes he marries several women in succession, and there's one story-cycle called the False Guinevere, where Arthur's Queen is kidnapped and a changeling set in her place. Eventually, of course, he gets the right Guinevere back.

But it did make me wonder, if, as we know, these tales are all scraps from an older tradition, just what older tradition they were scraps of . . . ?

ABOUT THE EDITORS

Lawrence Schimel is the author of *The Drag Queen of Elfland* and the editor of over twenty other anthologies, including *Tarot Fantastic* (with Martin H. Greenberg); *The Fortune Teller* (with Martin H. Greenberg); *Blood Lines: Vampire Stories from New England* (with Martin H. Greenberg); *Food for Life and Other Dish*; *Things Invisible to See*; *Switch Hitters* (with Carol Queen); and *Two Hearts Desire* (with Michael Lassell), among others. His own writings have appeared in numerous periodicals, including *The Wall Street Journal*, *The Saturday Evening Post*, *The Tampa Tribune*, *Physics Today*, *Isaac Asimov's SF Magazine*, *Marion Zimmer Bradley's Fantasy Magazine*, and *Cricket*, among others, and in over one hundred anthologies, including *The Random House Book of Science Fiction Stories*, *Weird Tales from Shakespeare*, *The Time of the Vampires*, *Return to Avalon*, *Phantoms of the Night*, *Fantastic Alice*, *Excalibur*, *Enchanted Forests*, *The Random House Treasury of Light Verse*, and the *Sword & Sorceress* series, among others. He has translated graphic novels from the Spanish, and his own writings have been published abroad in Dutch, Finnish, German,

Italian, Japanese, Polish, and Spanish translations. He is the publisher and editor of A Midsummer Night's Press, which has produced limited editions of works by Jane Yolen, Nancy Willard, Joe Haldeman, and others. Twenty-six years old, he lives in Manhattan, where he writes and edits full-time.

Martin H. Greenberg is the most prolific anthologist in publishing history, with most of his collections in the science fiction and fantasy genres. He is the winner of the Milford Award for Lifetime Achievement in Science Fiction Editing and was Editor Guest of Honor at the 1992 World Science Fiction Convention. He lives with his wife, daughter, and two cats in Green Bay, Wisconsin.